Altar Music

A Novel by

CHRISTIN LORE WEBER

SCRIBNER

SCRIBNER
1230 Avenue of the Americas
New York, NY 10020

SCRIBNER and design are trademarks of Macmillan Library
Reference USA, Inc., used under license by Simon & Schuster,
the publisher of this work.

Designed by Brooke Koven
Set in Janson
Manufactured in the United States of America

1 3 5 7 9 10 8 6 4 2

Library of Congress Cataloging-in-Publication Data

Weber, Christin Lore.
Altar music: a novel/by Christin Lore Weber.
p. cm.
I. Title.
PS3573.E2165A48   2000
813'.54—dc21   99-39526
CIP

ISBN 0-684-86866-0

For Alyce Lore
Who formed the words

For George Lore
Who focused the silence

For Elizabeth Lore Kensinger
Who listened

Altar Music

Sound moved over the water of Black Sturgeon Lake. Gulls heard. Sound lifted under their wings as air, passed through their hearts and lungs, issued in a cry. Sound moaned in the rocks. Fallen needles of tamarack and fir blanketed the ground, and sound filled them, too. Wind, bees, and the delicate feet of mice scattered the needles. A spider's web became a harp and it sang.

Wild, sound luged through a granite pass the Eagle River carved a thousand thousand years ago and surrounded the bones of deer licked clean by wolves.

Earth opened to sound like a lover. Sound entered every cell, vibrating, setting in motion the circle of the world.

I

Once music touches your soul
you never can be free of it.
It will haunt you
all your life.

SISTER MARY'S MUSIC NOTEBOOKS, 1944

Each morning the road to the inn was littered with carcasses of frogs. Elise crouched on her haunches like Grampa Pearson and examined one of the flattened creatures. Leathery brown, a pancake frog. Not real. Real frogs, green, covered with slime, hid in the tall grass by the old houseboat. If you scuffed along, they jumped and landed with a thud in the shallow water by the reed bed. Some were big as chipmunks. Those could not be caught with hands, only with a pail turned upside down. The small ones could be caught with hands and stored in the pockets of her overalls. She named them and tied little scraps of colored material around their necks. Their feet on her hand were delicate as those of baby birds fallen from the nest.

Elise gazed into the lake from where she sat in a hollow of the giant cottonwood tree that stood in the inn yard. Its branches dipped low, all the way to the water's edge, where twig fingers drew circles on the surface. When she looked up and into the distance, she could see Rainbow Island and Deep Water Gap. Surrounded by leaves, she hid from the sharp voice of her mother. Here she dreamed. She whispered to herself and rocked back and forth while her imagination took her into things. All she had to do was look hard, at the twig, for instance, as it twirled in the water. Suddenly she could feel her fingers becoming wood and the water parting at her touch. She practiced going into the chipmunk that chattered on the branch above her, into the gull that floated over the waves. In dreams she searched for a mother whose voice would be a lullaby, like water crooning to rocks along the shore.

Dreams set her afloat in waters dark and infinite. Infantile dreams expanded to include the shimmering light, human murmuring, the cries of gulls. The child swam in her visions like a fish. Once her mama floated down to her beneath the waters. Mama was not a fish, and underneath the surface, where amber light filtered, her mama could not live. Elise took her mama on her back and swam with her toward shore. But before she reached the sand of Black Rock Beach she awoke, crying "Mama" into the darkness of her bedroom. But the mama must have drowned.

It was in the summer following Elise's fourth birthday that she adopted the cottonwood tree as a mother. It had seven trunks grown together, forming nooks close to the ground into which the child could climb. From these nooks she looked back at Reel 'Em Inn, where she lived with Mama and Gramma and Grampa Pearson because by that time her daddy was fighting a war so that the children in Europe could have bread. The mother tree sheltered her. Even if the Germans and the Japs came across the ocean with bombs, the tree would not fall.

"WHAT's real, Mama?" Her mama, whose grown-up name was Kate, sat by the mangle in the laundry feeding damp sheets through the rollers.

"Hum?"

"Are the frogs real?"

"Of course."

"The thing in the houseboat?"

"What thing?"

"Behind the curtain."

Just then the sheet went around the roller twice and tangled.

"Now look at what you've made me do. How often do I have to tell you not to bother me when I'm mangling?"

"I'm sorry, Mama."

"Go out and play."

If not for the frogs, Elise would have avoided the houseboat. They sang in the long grasses that grew up around the gray wooden boards of its hull. Years ago, before she was born, Grampa Pearson had landed the boat and turned it into a cabin.

"Why don't people stay there anymore?" Elise asked her grandmother.

"It's too old now." Gramma Pearson pulled the clothespins off the sheets and folded them as she took them from the line to be mangled.

"Were people scared to stay there?"

"Scared of what, Peanut?"

"The thing behind the curtain."

"What thing?"

"There's something behind the curtain."

"There's nothing in there, Peanut. Just old jars on the countertop."

"I see something."

"Maybe it's light shining off a jar."

"It's alive."

"It's probably your imagination."

The houseboat sat above the reed bed, its stern sticking out over a rise of land above the water. If Elise stood on the boat stern she could imagine herself a captain of a ship. Inside the cabin were two old beds, a table, and under the window, the counter stacked with dozens of Mason jars. A door separated the space inside the bow of the houseboat from the cabin. The door was locked.

Something lived behind the locked door. Locks couldn't hold it in. One day as Elise was leaving the houseboat and running through the trees toward the inn, she looked back. A face peered out the window.

"Come and see."

Gramma left the laundry basket under the clothesline and walked with her up the gravel road, past the inn toward the houseboat.

"See?"

A face appeared and disappeared.

"My, my." Gramma breathed. "It does look scary, doesn't it, Peanut?"

"Who is it?"

"It's nobody, sweetheart. It's a tear in the curtain and the sunlight on a jar. Just like I said." She took Elise's hand. "I'll show you."

They climbed the wooden steps and Gramma Pearson pulled open the squeaky door. She put her fingers through the ragged Woolworth lace.

"There, Peanut. See?" she said.

When you were inside the houseboat it was a curtain, but when you walked down the path it was a face. It all depended upon how you looked at it. Maybe both were real.

Maybe everything was real.

Maybe what adults called imagination was a real thing you couldn't touch yet.

This thought comforted her until the day her father returned from war. After that, even the song of the frogs gave no comfort. Horrified, she saw them one night as they swarmed across the road; she saw them in the headlights' beam. Her father pulled the car around to the back of the inn, as close as he could get to the wood box and the door of their bedrooms, but Elise couldn't make herself step on the grass. She imagined the scrunching of delicate bones as her foot came down, and she heard in her mind the cry frogs certainly must make as they die.

II

Approach music from the inside,
and enter it with an open heart,
for music is attained
only by surrender.

SISTER MARY'S MUSIC NOTEBOOKS, 1940

Michael Pearson lifted his daughter from her crib each morning that first summer of her life and on into the autumn while the weather held, and he carried her to the dock, where gulls reeled above the fishermen. From Minneapolis, Dubuque, Cedar Rapids, and Omaha they came each year to catch their limit of walleyed pike. Some might even hook a muskie or, if they were exceedingly lucky, one of the almost extinct sturgeon. Michael held his infant daughter up and pointed out the flock of pelicans in the open water beyond Rainbow Island. They could be seen only by the glint of sunlight on their white wings, which, from the distance of the dock, reminded him of fairy dust scattered over the lake. He suspected she was too young to understand or even for her eyes to focus on these things, but who could know, really? He had heard that musicians played Beethoven for newborns to instill a love of music.

It used to be Michael and Kate standing on the dock. Since they were seventeen the lake had been their enchanted place. They walked its beaches picking up flat stones the colors of gull wings. They arranged the stones with diamond willow driftwood, creating designs in the sand. They lay in secluded coves and kissed until the passion rose.

"Gentle," she would say. "Gentle, Michael."

On a moonless summer night after graduation they took one of his father's outboards and motored across the lake to Rainbow Island, where they lay on their backs and gazed through the darkness at the smear of Milky Way. Kate took his hand and pulled him up. They walked to the edge. You could barely see the water. Night voided it. She sang. He thought she was singing to the stars. Something rare in her voice, a breathy quality that made each note ache, moved him deep inside. He reached for her across dark space. He touched her face and it startled him to find tears. He let his hand slide gently down to her breast; never before had she allowed this. Her song ceased and he heard her gasp. She stood still as a deer that merges with the woods. He lowered her onto the warm sand.

Afterward she broke from him and ran. He called her name but didn't find her until dawn.

"We shouldn't have done that." Tears streaked her face.

"I know. I'm sorry."

"I'm afraid."

"Don't be afraid."

He had tried to take her in his arms again.

"No."

"But it's okay."

"No. It was wrong, Michael. Father Murphy says it's a sin."

He spent a lifetime remembering that night her passion flowered and was lost. Even after they were married, a full seven years later, she lay still, stiff even, so that he felt he should instruct her: "You can touch me, Kate darling, here . . . just so . . . and let your hands move this way along my back. You are beautiful, my dearest, so beautiful. I won't hurt you. Rest in my arms, Kate. I'll take care of you."

But her body opened to him with difficulty, and when he entered her she always cried.

She said she felt like an old dead log with a hole in it, and she wished he'd hurry and be done. He knew she didn't speak like that to cause him pain. No woman was as loyal as Kate. In bed at night he bore the devastating words to keep her from turning them upon herself. He blamed the Catholic Church and its celibate priests with their warped counsel and their shriveled cocks.

Despite everything, the child came. Elise Marie. Kate named her after a piano piece she liked and also, she explained, after the pure Virgin. Michael welcomed the part about the music. The Virgin part couldn't be helped, he supposed. Most Catholics had at least one girl named Mary. He hoped the child would soften his wife, but Kate held the infant gingerly, like thin blown glass. She seemed to prefer handing Elise off to someone else, to the grandmothers, Meghan and Dorothy, both of whom were so eager for the feel of a baby in their arms that they didn't appear to notice how busy Kate kept herself with other things.

Instead of the baby, Kate handled the accounts. She saw to it that the cabins sparkled. She maintained the business. She visited old Harry Barber with the gangrenous foot and brought him dinner twice a week. She volunteered to accompany the sing-along at Founders' Rest Home every Wednesday night—simple tunes like "When Irish Eyes Are Smiling" that she played by ear. Eventually she became president of the Ladies' Rosary Society and also directed the church choir. She had no training for it, but her ear for music made her the best that Corpus Christi Church could get.

Michael's own mother, Dorothy, prepared the baby's formula according to the complicated recipe that required scalded milk and temperature regulation of all ingredients or it would curdle like tomato soup made wrong.

"Kate should nurse her," Dorothy told Michael as she filled the sterilized bottles. "Babies are happier when you nurse them. Healthier, too."

"She doesn't believe in it, Mom."

"It was good enough for you!"

"I know. But Kate read an article—"

"Newfangled notions and inventions. Tilly Chapman down on Winter Road would help out. She never went dry after her last one."

Kate told Michael no. No, she wouldn't have another woman nurse her baby. No, she wouldn't do it herself. She had tried. It was impossible for her. The formula would do fine. If Dorothy didn't want to prepare it, Kate would do it herself. She said she thought Dorothy enjoyed the task. Michael said that wasn't the point. Kate said all right, then, let things stay as they are.

Michael never knew, because she couldn't explain, about the warm shock of pleasure when Elise had first taken her nipple, or how the baby's sucking pulled at sensations so deep in her body she knew them only as sin. She would not have her child contaminated. She must keep her daughter safe.

III

Music must be focused
yet free.

SISTER MARY'S MUSIC NOTEBOOKS, 1944

Gramma Meghan said, "There, there." Gramma's green-and-white-checked bib apron smelled of chocolate milk and sugar cookies. She ran her hand down Elise's long dark hair as if she were petting a sleek cat and said, "Now don't you pay that any mind at all. The good Lord doesn't bother himself over a bit of mischief in a child. Seems to me that's why he created small creatures in the first place. Likes the romp and tangle. Kittens all wound up in blue yarn. Makes an awful mess. A mess of laughter, I'd say."

Gramma held Elise and wiped her tears with the soft hanky she kept tucked up her sleeve. Elise gulped her breath. Each exhalation fluttered past the little flaps in her throat. She clamped down on the breath but sobs escaped anyway. Four years old. Too old to cry—that's what her mother said. Crying is for babies.

"So, what would you do with that naughty kitten, darling? Scold? Give it away? Get a different cat, who just sat still all day looking out the window and caring not a whit about chasing yarn?"

"No . . . ," Elise murmured, and the "o" part shook like another sob.

"Of course not." Gramma Meghan smiled, kissed Elise's forehead and each of her eyelids, then the tip of her nose. "You're our sweet little kitten." She put her hand under Elise's chin and tilted her face up so their eyes met. "And we love you so much."

If Gramma Meghan didn't think she was a bad girl, why did Mama get so mad at her? And what would either of them do, Elise wondered but didn't ask, if they found out about the things she'd done with Margaret Henderson?

Gramma Meghan served up stories along with hot chocolate, ice cream in a blue dish, and old photos that she kept in a steamer trunk locked in the storage room of the house with the hollyhocks all alongside. Gramma told stories while she taught Elise to make hollyhock ladies from the flowers. Sometimes they became story-book dolls: Cinderella and the Goose Girl. Sometimes they became real people: Elise's mother, Kate. Someone named Clara Monroe, who had become Sister Thomas Ann. Gramma Meghan and Elise themselves. Gramma set the ladies in their delicate pink-and-white flower skirts in a circle on the table and connected them with a ring of grass.

"Each one must have a strand of her own," her gramma explained as she plucked the long grasses from along the backyard fence. "Then we weave them together, just so, and attach them." She slipped the ends into the weave to create the ring. "So they can dance around it in the moonlight." Gramma Meghan kissed Elise on the tip of her nose. "While you are asleep."

"Why isn't Mama like you?" The sobs had quieted now.

Gramma Meghan cocked her head to one side and looked up as though she could find the answer on the ceiling. "What do you mean, honey?"

"She doesn't like me."

"Doesn't like you?"

"She's mean."

"Maybe she's just trying to teach you right from wrong. That's a mother's job."

"What's a gramma's job?"

"Stories and hugs!"

"Then I only want grammas."

Sobs turned to giggles, but Elise's question about her mama still hung in the air above them like dusky smoke.

"Is my mama unhappy?"

Meghan O'Neil closed her eyes. Something happened beneath her skin that made her face look old.

"She's probably just lonesome for your daddy." She paused for a moment and then brightened. "Or maybe it has something to do with the piano."

"The piano?"

"Yes, dear. Once, before you were born, we owned a piano. Your mother was just a little girl, like you are now, and how she loved playing it."

"She did?"

"You're named after her favorite piano piece, you know."

"I am?"

"My, yes. Goodness. I'm surprised she never told you that."

IV

One sets her fingers on the keys
and plays carefully, without abandon, each note,
listening in the connection between nerve and ivory
for a hidden music of the heart.

SISTER MARY'S MUSIC NOTEBOOKS, 1910

Meghan O'Neil held her breath as the men lowered the piano off
the freight train. What was Willie thinking? Buying a piano. Up and
down the Main Street of Eagle Inlet he'd gone for the past two
weeks, telling the whole world. And why? Neither of them could
play it.

"Katie. My Katie will play it. Just look at those fingers, would
you?" He held the new baby, their firstborn, and let her fingers curl
around his like the tendrils of a morning glory.

"But, Willie, the expense!" A larger house would serve them
better. Or a car. Everyone was talking about that Model T of Henry
Ford's. What with the way things moved so fast these days, she
wouldn't be surprised if Ford started selling them in Sears and
Roebuck.

"No expense is too much for my Katie."

There he was, talking big again. And wasn't it just like a man?
Strutting up and down the platform at the Canadian Northern
depot in his threadbare suit coat and gold watch fob. Looking
around to see which of the town's dandies took time off to witness
his extravagance.

"She'll play in Carnegie Hall, my Katie will."

Probably not. He must try to be realistic. Eagle Inlet was a long
way from New York City. Up in the sticks, right on the Canadian
border, where there wasn't a city for a hundred and fifty miles. Then

you came to Winnipeg. Meghan hankered to go there back in 1905, when she and Willie got married. But here it was, 1910 already. No Winnipeg. And the last of the money going for a piano. Likely Willie would be earning dark money now, just to pay the mortgage.

Eagle Inlet fell under the sway of Winnipeg more than New York, anyhow. It lay so far north that the Great Northern ran more than a hundred miles to the south, chugging its way from Minneapolis to Oregon. When a town had no railroad connecting it to the rest of the country, why, you'd almost have to say it didn't actually belong to the United States. Who could go anywhere from here? What did the Canadians care whether she ever went to Winnipeg? They sent only freight trains. Not even a passenger car.

"This is America!" Willie laughed when she raised her eyebrow over Carnegie Hall. "A person can achieve anything."

What did Willie know about achieving? A grocery clerk at Fouts Grocery can't be called a great achiever. Or maybe he could. Even Julia Lizot left his checkout with a smile on her face. Maybe the ability to brighten someone's day is an achievement as great as being president. Who could tell?

"Bought the piano outright. It's for my Katie girl."

A dreamer he was.

Meghan saw through him the first time he sauntered down Main Street, three years before their wedding at Corpus Christi Church. Even now he could sweep her off her feet with his dreams. And his eyes of such a blue she thought she'd sink in them the way her body sank with his into Black Sturgeon Lake when she was eighteen and he took her out to Split Rock Point. How could she go swimming? she said to him. But he told her that her camisole would do just fine. She let him talk her into it although she was certain the priest would warn against such things. She no longer asked the priest.

And here was Katie. Love child. That's what Willie called her.

The men hoisted the piano onto Shorty Hanson's rig for hauling to her snug house on the hill above the Eagle River rapids. Willie strutted like a peacock. It occurred to her that she'd never seen a peacock. It was a saying, though, and certainly fit him on this day he'd spent their last penny for a piano, which, to tell the truth, wasn't totally useless. Willie had the foresight to choose a Stark player piano. The ad said it practically played itself—ragtime, old-time, even classical favorites. All you had to do was pump.

He'd pump her out a love song. The priest said that a woman had to hold the line on such things, even after marriage. There seemed no end to rules governing what a man and woman could and couldn't do. She tried to follow them to the letter at first. She'd insisted that their bedroom be dark during the conjugal act.

"That's bullshit, Meg."

"But the priest said—"

"What does he know about marriage? He sleeps with his rosary."

"Willie!"

"He doesn't know. The church doesn't know. It's run by celibates, for God's sake."

"Don't take the Lord's name, Willie."

"You're beautiful, Meg. I want to look at you when we make love. I want you to look at me. I know you want it. You do want it, don't you?"

"I can't confess it to him. I wouldn't be able to get the words out."

"We're married!"

"Yes. And marriage isn't lust."

"Lust! You think this is lust?"

"When a body turns to water, Willie, that must be lust, or else there isn't such a thing."

He held her in the dark and she felt his manliness, stiff, against her nightgown. When he came into her she wished that she could see his eyes. She held her body firm but it didn't matter. She dissolved in spite of it.

And here was Katie. A blessing. God smiles on a woman's restraint, the priest said. What did he know of women? And what of dissolving, for that matter? The thing God smiles on is surrender to love's sweet power. Babies teach you that. Being at the mercy of birth teaches a woman that. The strong and tender body of your husband teaches you everything you need to know about God. If she'd learned anything in these five years of marriage it was that dissolving in the act of love has nothing whatever to do with lust. Lust rivets you, makes you hard.

Restraint! Wasn't it funny they never recommended that to men?

"Meet you at the house," Willie was telling Shorty, who flicked the reins and pulled away from the railroad loading dock.

"It's the latest thing," he bragged to Doc Osborn, who'd come to see the show. "Plays itself."

"Amazing."

"It's a stupendous time, this twentieth century."

He took Meghan's arm. "Come on, honeybaby. Let's go make some music!"

Home. It was tiny, to be sure. But it did have a summer kitchen, which helped in the humid times of July, just when the garden started to come in and Meghan put up her green beans. How Willie enjoyed those after the snows fell. He'd pick a jar off the pantry shelf and hold it up to the window so the light passed through it, tinted green.

In winter, when they were glad for the heat, she cooked inside. But you had to be careful of the inside stove, for it overheated the chimney. This summer kitchen was only a shed with a brick floor, but it did the trick. She could can beans and beets from morning to night and the house stayed tolerable.

Meghan set each jar of fresh beans into the big cooker on the woodstove. Careful, girl, she told herself. Later she'd listen for the popping of the lids.

Baby Katie lay in her basket in the shade under the plum tree. Pretty girl. Love child.

"You can play that piano or not, sweetheart. You can do whatever you want."

Of course, it wasn't true. No one could. Life spun you out like spider silk. Who could control it? Pretty soon, there you were, pattern completed, attached between two branches, collecting dew, reflecting the sun.

"You just do it, Katie."

Hopefully it wouldn't be Carnegie Hall she wanted. A woman mustn't want too much. The level of a woman's wants could turn out to be the measure of her disappointment. Why, some women couldn't even get themselves as far as Winnipeg!

Meghan lifted a kettle of beets off the stove and drained the dirt red water onto the ground outside the door. Beet blood. She sat under the tree beside Katie's basket and slipped the beet skins off. Each skinned beet felt like someone's heart in her stained hands. How could she slice them? It was a passing impression, though, and she soon was filling jars and pouring her own secret pickling syrup over the garnet-colored slices.

Willie loved her pickled beets even better than her beans.

"You pamper that man too much." Alice Osborn lifted her eyebrow and her cup simultaneously as seven of the young wives of Eagle Inlet met for tea.

"I enjoy doing it."

"Perhaps, but if you don't train him now, you'll be at his beck and call your entire life."

"I guess I don't mind all that much. I do love the man."

"Still?"

"Absolutely."

"A man can use you up, dear."

"Not Willie."

"Well, we'll see, won't we?"

It wouldn't much matter, now, would it? There were worse things than being used up by love. Perhaps the other wives, including Alice Osborn, kept their bedroom lights turned off.

Meghan set her jars of beans and beets to cool on the table where they would catch the sun.

Katie's fingers itched to make music before her legs could reach the pedals. Willie perched her on his lap and pumped while Katie passed her hands lightly over the keys, which, sucked down by the bellows, sounded by magic. During the day, while Willie worked at Fouts Grocery stocking shelves and carrying bags for the likes of Helga Monroe, Katie climbed onto the piano bench and picked out melodies. By the time she was five years old she could reproduce on the piano any tune he whistled.

"Isn't she darling?" Mrs. Lizot cooed toward Meghan while she sipped her coffee and ate her third sugar cookie. Mrs. Lizot made the rounds of young wives in Eagle Inlet, wearing her mink coat in winter and carrying her ruffled parasol against the sun in summer.

She ate their cakes and cookies and snapped their secrets securely inside her satchel. Or so it seemed. Wasn't it when she reached into that satchel for a handkerchief to dry her eyes over Margie Sundal's latest miscarriage that news of Emily Rosin's black eye, probably from that sullen husband of hers, came popping out? Still and all, the young wives didn't hold back. Mrs. Lizot's gaze conveyed a quality of absolution. And it was good to know that women weren't alone in the things that could happen in what young Father Murphy's sermons deemed the sanctity of marriage.

"You really should get a teacher for her, Meghan." Mrs. Lizot wiped the cookie crumbs from her lips with Meghan's lace-edged tea napkin kept especially for these visits.

"Kathleen's music is inborn. Just listen. Look at those little fingers."

Meghan flushed. "And not quite six years old."

"Martha Kennedy might take her. I'll put in a word, Meghan, if you want."

Although Meghan knew the gossip's name to be Julia, she never would have presumed to address her by anything other than "Mrs. Lizot." The widowed Mrs. Lizot was Julia only to her equals, Julie to no one. Nor would she countenance nicknames in any of the young wives or their children.

"How good of you, Mrs. Lizot. If Willie—"

"Nonsense. Your William loves music. Why on earth would he purchase a piano if he didn't intend that Kathleen learn to play it?"

It was the money, not the intention. But Meghan let that be, thankful for the interruption. Willie wouldn't want their financial affairs spread hither and yon.

Julia Lizot leaned in over the tabletop then and in low tones confided, "Have you heard, dear, about young Clara Monroe? She's left her husband. And her wedding only two weeks past. Poor child."

"Goodness! What happened?"

"Such a tragedy. I hear tell he beat her on their wedding night." Mrs. Lizot put her white-gloved hand to her mouth as she whispered the verb. "Only sixteen." Mrs. Lizot shook her head from side to side. "She locked herself in the bathroom of the Francis Drake Hotel. Poor, dear child. The maid found her the next day." Mrs. Lizot sipped her coffee for dramatic effect. "There'll be an annulment, of course. Not even Father Murphy can object. They didn't consummate their vows."

"No?"

"Helga Monroe told me herself. She and Wallace had Clara checked by a doctor at the county hospital there in the Twin Cities. Did it again, back home here. Our own Doc Osborn."

"And she was . . ."

"A virgin, dear. Pure as the day she was born."

"Poor thing," Meghan O'Neil murmured and resolved to wrap a pretty silk scarf in tissue as a gift for Clara. Most of the wives of Eagle Inlet would do something to help Clara get her mind off her shame. The Eagle Inlet wives would whisk her up in a flurry of attention. They'd love her into forgetfulness of what a man could do. Some men. Not Meghan's man. Not Willie. Poor Clara. Luckily she found out right away while she was still intact. Still whole.

"Sometimes there's no forgetting." Mrs. Lizot sighed as she closed her satchel and carefully lifted the chair under her ample bottom to move away from the table. Katie was playing "Let Me Call You Sweetheart" with one finger, just the melody. "When a girl like Clara's been hurt this way—I'm sure you are aware, my dear—why, she might simply remain a spinster."

"Or a nun. That might be a solution."

"A nun." The women's eyes locked. The romance of this solution, the image of solitary Clara forever veiled, like Guinevere or Héloïse, quickened their hearts and came close to moving both of them to tears. "What a marvelous idea, Meghan dear. A convent for Clara. Why, that could prove to be the very best solution of all."

By the end of the week news of Clara Monroe's dream of taking the veil had spread throughout Eagle Inlet. The dazzle of this news eclipsed Clara's wedding night shame. Clara's wedding became for the wives of Eagle Inlet the first movement of a divine symphony, a tone poem in which her human marriage introduced a theme to be completed only in those sacred vows transforming her into the bride of Christ. Clara's shame took on the glow of sacrifice. Julia Lizot opened her satchel and sighed. She drank coffee and ate cookies with the wives of Eagle Inlet. She brought tears to their eyes, and their hearts grew large.

The morning in 1916 that Clara Monroe entered the Convent of Our Lady of Peace in Bemidji, Meghan walked home from mass. She still tasted the bland, sticky host behind her teeth, where it always lodged. Jesus and Clara. Given to one another. Something in the thought of it made her heart beat faster than it should. Why do you suppose nuns were called brides? They weren't really, now, were they?

The August sun warmed her back. She removed her jacket. Warmth seeped into her anyway. It made little circular motions behind her eyes and in her throat. Her heart beat faster. She slowed her pace. Her heart felt swollen twice its size. She stopped in the middle of the block and leaned against a large elm. Its leaves muted the late summer light.

Maybe there were two kinds of brides, a Clara sort of bride and the normal kind. Brides with bodies to be loved. And maybe, just maybe, God created it that way. The priests got it all mixed up, preaching about restraint the way they did. Just this morning, in fact, Father Murphy held Clara up as an example for the women of the parish. And why? Shamed by a man who was nothing like Willie.

Convents had their place, of course. And nuns. And a purely spiritual love. Surely Jesus would make it up to Clara for what she'd lost. But still, it must be a better thing for a woman to love completely, with her body and her soul. The priest thought differently, but lacking experience, how could he know?

Warmth moved down her body to her belly and burned there. Heavy, heavy. Her legs felt forced apart by a thick, wet heat that ached.

Willie was at work. Meghan removed her hat and the hairpins that held her long auburn hair. She let the wind tangle it as she walked the three more blocks to her house.

At home Meghan stripped the bed and washed its sheets. She ironed them until the cotton was smooth. She plumped the pillows and dowsed them with lilac water. She got out her grandmother's silver candlesticks and the beeswax candles she'd been saving for Christmas, and she arranged them on the dresser along with the last of the roses from her garden.

"How would you like to spend the night with Virginia?" she asked Kate at noon when the girl stopped playing long enough to eat lunch. My, but she was growing up fast.

"Oh, could I?"

"I think it would be nice. She asks you over so often."

"Her mother's always saying I should spend the night."

"If tonight's convenient for her . . ."

"I'll ask Virginia."

"And I'll talk to her mother. We don't want to impose."

"She'll say I should stay. She always says that."

"I'll talk to her."

MEGHAN and Alice Osborn sat by the bay window that overlooked the river. Alice's was a plush existence by Meghan's standards, but her husband was the doctor and entitled to more than a mere grocery clerk. Alice brought tea on a silver tray that she set on a round, claw-footed table.

"One lump, or two?"

"One, please."

Meghan lifted her china cup and Alice used dainty silver tongs to drop a sugar cube into the tea.

"Well, Clara's gone."

Alice offered Meghan a butter cookie.

"Yes. She left this morning after mass."

"I suppose it's for the best."

"It's God's will."

"Well, maybe. I don't know. I'm not Catholic, you know."

"It would have been hard to marry someone else after . . ."

"Yes, no doubt."

"I wonder if she loved him."

"How tragic if she did."

"She'll be better off with the nuns."

"Do you think so?"

"Well, on the other hand, I don't know what I'd do without Willie."

The two women looked at each other. Meghan flushed. Alice smiled and picked up her teacup.

• • •

IT HAD been no trouble at all. Alice said Kate would be no trouble. How good for Virginia, too. Good for both girls. So difficult it must be to have no brothers or sisters. So lonely. Why, Alice often asked Kate to stay. Terrible to let such a large house sit nearly empty. The girls could play in the children's wing. Alice and Francis would hardly know they were there.

And even though Alice said nothing about wives needing time alone with husbands, Meghan sensed a perfect understanding that underscored her every word.

MEGHAN dropped the clothes from her body and stepped into scented bathwater. Delicious and warm, the water swirled around her, exciting her flesh even more. She closed her eyes and thought of Willie, his perfect compact body. The priest warned against sexual fantasy. Sin or not, she allowed her imagination to travel the length of him, seeing every firm muscle, feeling the soft hair of his body against her skin. She moved her hand over her wet breasts, her erect nipples. Perfect breasts. Ripe. He would cover them with his mouth. His tongue would circle the nipples until she groaned, and then he would suck. Oh, the pleasure of it. The tiny bites. The soft, healing tongue.

Steam curled Meghan's hair into little ringlets around her face. She sank into the water. I'm a mermaid, she thought as her hair fanned out, floating. "Willie," she whispered as she caressed her breasts and down the length of her body to the place he would enter her. "Willie, hurry home."

She washed her hair and dried it in the sunshine. She dressed herself in the blue velvet that set off her eyes, and sat on the sofa in her small living room. She watched for the door to open and imagined that he was already touching her.

Poor Clara. How does Christ enter his bride? What kind of intercourse is it? Is it in the mind it happens, or the heart? Certainly not between the legs. Probably the heart. And probably not wet. More like fire. A sword of fire through the heart. Did nuns kneel before the Blessed Sacrament and feel a light from heaven enter them? Did it shimmer and explode in their souls? Did their bodies feel it?

Better to have spiritual intercourse with Christ than to be beat up by the likes of Tom Lenz.

Strange, but the thought of a divine lover ejecting a shimmer of light into the soul of Clara Monroe turned Meghan soft and wet as fresh plum jelly.

SHE LED Willie into the bedroom. She lit the candles. She removed her clothes slowly while he watched, while he kept repeating, "Meghan, Meghan. My beauty. My dearest."

"No. Not yet. Don't move yet. Wait. We have all night."

She danced for him. She let her hair flow over her breasts. A sensuous animal uncoiled within her and she bent and flowed to a music that seemed to rise from her belly.

"Every part of you is beautiful." He reached for her again.

And it was true.

She wound herself around him, continuously moving, dancing her desire, the arousal of her flesh. He touched her breast. She laughed and slid through his hands. She was magical. Quicksilver.

She undid his tie, unbuttoned his shirt. He fumbled to get out of his clothes.

"Wait."

She slid her hands down the front of him to the hardness that strained against his trousers. He groaned. She loosened the buttons and released his hard penis into her hands.

"Meghan! Darling!"

He let his trousers slip from his body. She buried her face in the soft hair above his erection and felt his hardness slip between her breasts.

"Oh, Willie."

He lifted her up and laid her gently on the bed. He kissed her eyes, her nose, her mouth. He ran his tongue down her throat and to the cleavage between her breasts. With his fingers he squeezed her nipples. She shuddered. He took her nipples, one by one, into his mouth and sucked her until she felt tremors run down her body and deep into her vagina. "Oh God!"

"Yes, darling. God."

Her hands were everywhere on him, stroking his back, his buttocks. She reached between his legs and cradled the soft scrotum. Then she closed her hand around his hard penis. Stroking. Stroking.

"Meghan. My God."

The candles burned down and went out. He caressed her thighs.

He put his head between her thighs and drank of her juices. He twirled his tongue over her clitoris until her mind floated away and she was nothing but sensation.

He thrust his penis into her and the shimmering inside her vagina intensified in waves of pleasure.

"I love you."

"I hope it's always like this."

"It always will be."

BETWEEN times they drank brandy from their crystal wedding cup. Three times they loved. Three times he poured his life into her and she absorbed him, his body and his soul. More times than she could count he brought her to the peak of pleasure, to a union so complete she could only cry, "God." This was marriage. This was the conjugal act. Not that furtive and almost futile motion in the dark that would have left her empty and in tears if she hadn't realized that the priests were wrong.

MEGHAN drifted into sleep on the rhythm of her husband's breath. In her mind she saw Clara Monroe, forever veiled, forever pure, pierced by God in a thunderbolt of fire. In her heart she felt the warmth of that flame, and with each heartbeat her soul cried out, "Willie," and it cried out, "God," and they were one name.

In September Meghan found herself pregnant with her second child, and Kate was enrolled with the incomparable Martha Kennedy as a student of piano.

"And what do you plan to do with that?" Meghan held the storm door open while Willie lugged in a case of Canadian Club whiskey and set it down beside the piano.

"Close the door, Meghan. You'll catch your death."

"What's the whiskey for?"

Outside, an April blizzard was kicking up. She prayed the baby wouldn't come early. Poor Doc Osborn. He'd have to trudge through snow up to his hips. Minnesota's perverse weather! By rights, it should be spring.

"Celebration, my lovely! To celebrate my boy."

"Your boy. And what if it's another girl?"

"It'll be a boy. God and me have a deal. He's giving me a boy and I'm putting aside my whiskey money for Katie's piano lessons. This is my last case, Meghan, and I'm not even drinking it. When my boy is born I'm taking it up and down Main Street. Every businessman in Eagle Inlet will drink a toast to my boy. 'My Meghan gave me a son,' I'll say. 'The son of William O'Neil.'"

Such a boy he was himself, with his bright eyes and innocence. She kissed him. "Silly man. But then, you might be right."

"I *am* right." He put the palm of his hand against the moon of her belly and stroked her lightly. "Isn't that so, son? Is your father always right, or not?"

The baby kicked.

"Ha ha! He agrees. Fine boy. Intelligent boy. I think I'll crack open one of those bottles now. Just for practice!"

Children of love, that's what her babies were, whether they were boys or girls. As her body had changed with pregnancy, Willie celebrated the fullness of her breasts, the rounding of her belly, the movements inside her. How could love be sinful? It couldn't be, and that was that. Willie's touch, the way he looked at her, it made her actually like being a woman. Even on Ash Wednesday, with the mark of penitence on their foreheads and the priest's call for abstinence still ringing in their ears, they had mingled fire with water. That's what it was, the love, the sex. Like a bolt of lightning in the lake.

V

At the beginning true music is obscured.
One must listen in the vast space
of silence.

SISTER MARY'S MUSIC NOTEBOOKS, 1917

Willie's boy ripped his way into the world on the eighth day of May in 1917, ruining Meghan's body for the bearing of any future child.

Willie took his wife's misfortune as a lesson in the ways of God with man, that God possesses a divine irony when it comes to making deals; and considering himself properly chastised for his presumption, he flooded the Almighty with profuse gratitude for sparing Meghan's life. "God dealt lightly with my sin," he told the priest. And since it was a feast day commemorating an apparition of Saint Michael the Archangel, and because Willie believed in signs and wonders, he named his boy Michael—*Who is like God.*

Meghan, for her part, refused to wallow in self-pity over her torn womb and the bleeding that weakened her almost to death before it miraculously ceased. She held baby Michael to her breast and thanked God for preserving her life to care for her children. She held tight to her rosary and prayed to accept the justice of God, whose truths far surpass what a woman can know. She rested her lips against the baby's downy head. She breathed his sweetness.

She admitted that she had been wrong. God is God. Sex is sex. Willie is Willie. Marriage is a service of the heart, unselfish and unremitting. Motherhood is a woman's salvation. Or virginity. But that was Clara's path. Either way you looked at it, God had corrected Meghan's mistake regarding sex. For her unrestrained passion and sinful fantasies, God had exacted sexual abstinence for the remainder of her life. The priest insisted that the church's law was clear. If there could be no possibility of conception, the conjugal act became a flagrant excess of fleshly desire, unworthy of a good Catholic woman.

Real married women, it now seemed quite obvious, must hold to the ends of ropes pulled in opposite directions. One end pulled you toward your man, to give in to his desire. The other pulled you to restrain him. Never would Meghan speak of those nights when she made herself refuse Willie's touch, when she lay so still she could barely hear her heart. For men are the weaker of the sexes when it comes to such things. Although he knew the rules, and although he had repented of their former sin, his desire for her could overwhelm him. She listened to his muffled groans as he gave himself relief. And finally Willie honored her, if you could call that honor. He gave in. Left her alone on her side of the bed. Mumbled, "Good night, dear," and never touched her while she lay there burning and not knowing what to do.

Until she died she would be unable to share with any other woman how she touched herself in that ruined spot between her legs, making the fire rise in her loins and her eyes fill with tears. With her other hand she fingered her rosary beads and begged the Mother who was also a virgin to pray for her now and at the hour of her death.

Father Murphy alone knew. She could hear him breathing in the dark confessional, on the other side of the purple velvet curtain permeated with the stench of sin. She breathed into herself the sickeningly sweet, nervous sweat of every Catholic body in Eagle Inlet. The priest had heard all their secrets. The lies, the fornication, muffled desires that could make your stomach clench, hatred and betrayal like a screw turned inside your heart. She added her pain to the mess. Her sin. *"Ego te absólvo,"* said the priest, and she ought to have left the confessional freed from burdens. But there was no believing it. She continued and would continue to conjure the afternoon of her original sin, when Willie had been God in her and Michael was conceived. Each week she would slide the velvet curtain aside and kneel in the closet of sin, breathing sin in and out. Breathing all sin as one sin hanging in the folds of velvet like the thick smoke of hell.

Meghan O'Neil entered this hell and prayed for absolution. She whispered her shame to the priest, who was, after all, a man who asked for details, who wanted a description of her touch, how long a time, whether there had been climax, fantasy, and the nature of the fantasy if there had been such a thing. Soon his breathing entered her sin and became part of it, because she knew, on those nights of fire, what he would ask. His questions led her on to further and further shame and increased the intensity of pleasure and pain that were inseparable. The breath of the priest and the fire in her loins also were inseparable, and when, on Sunday morning, that same priest laid the sacred host on her tongue and touched her wet lips with his consecrated fingers, the fire rose again. If the parishioners of Corpus Christi Church in Eagle Inlet mentioned Meghan O'Neil's flushed cheeks as she returned from the communion railing each Sunday morning, at least they couldn't know it was as a result of sacrilege. And when she began to attend daily mass, and as she entered the confessional before mass several times a week, the old women of the town gossiped of her virtue and devotion.

At the last minute before they left home, Meghan grabbed the box of photographs off the kitchen table. She'd been sorting them. The new ones of Michael. The sepia-toned pictures of her parents at the homestead in Ontario, just after they came over to escape the famine. Her wedding picture. The recent ones, the snapshots of the children taken with their own camera. How easily it could be done. She would show them to Sister Thomas Ann to pass the time. The nun would like to see how things had changed in the three years she'd been gone. Mrs. Lizot's gray hair. The addition to the school.

The road to Bemidji cut west from Eagle Inlet toward Baudette, before it finally turned south. It passed through pine forest, acres of which had been burned the year Kate was born. Nine years ago already. Fire had leveled Baudette, unlucky enough to be sitting in the way of the prevailing winds. Charred tree stumps stuck up here and there around the town alongside newly built stores and houses. Meghan always stopped for breakfast at the little café on Baudette's Main Street when she went to visit Clara Monroe, who wasn't Clara anymore. The nuns had renamed her Sister Thomas Ann.

"Come on, Katie. I'm famished."

Even with a car you couldn't go fast on gravel roads. Willie made her promise. "Take it easy. Promise me." She always did. This was the reason the trip took two days. But it was good to get away from time to time. Her absence purged Willie of a sullenness he'd acquired like a case of gout. A day or two of taking care of Michael, though, cured him. Then he wanted her back, sex or no sex.

KATE wanted pancakes and Meghan ordered soft-boiled eggs with toast and orange marmalade.

"It's nice to be just the two of us, don't you think?" Kate said with her mouth full of pancakes.

"Don't talk with your mouth full, Katie." Nine years old. You never knew how she'd be, child or adult. Hard to balance being both her mother and her friend. "And wipe that syrup off. Wait. Here, let me." Meghan dipped her own napkin in her ice water and dabbed at the edges of her daughter's mouth. "There. That's better."

The child took another bite, slurped the syrup, and dabbed at her own mouth.

"Do you like coming with me to see Sister Thomas Ann?"

"I love it."

No wonder. The nuns made such a fuss over her, letting her play the chapel organ, bake cookies, build sand castles by the lake, pick string beans in their enormous garden. It must be like having scores of aunts all vying for her affection. Just so they didn't lure her to join them. Though why Meghan dreaded that, she couldn't imagine. Marriage certainly turned out to be no bed of roses.

She had begun visiting Sister Thomas Ann last fall. Of course, she couldn't make the trip during winter, so this was the first in a long while. She resolved to go every month from now until the snows came back again. Except for Willie's sullenness, she wasn't sure why she went. She offered herself a lot of reasons. Time with Kate. Charity for the nun, who ought to have visitors from her own hometown. The convent itself, so peaceful. So—clean. When she closed the door of her private guest room with its single bed, its hand-braided rug, the desk and chair, utterly simple, she always sighed. It felt as though she'd been holding her breath ever since Michael was born, but at the convent she could breathe.

Kate had cleaned her plate.

"We'll just use their ladies' room and be on our way." They still had a hundred miles to drive.

⟶

Willie lit the inside stove to warm a bit of Meghan's potato soup before he went to bed. So good it tasted, made with onions and celery and the special herbs she grew in the backyard. She had a way with foods, his Meghan. She could fix a shoulder of venison like no other woman in town. You had to cut off all the tallow and soak it in salt water overnight, then roast it slow out in the summer kitchen, where the stove could be left on for the time it took. She stuffed the crook of the shoulder with wild rice the Indians brought down from Kenora in gunnysacks. He bought a ten-pound sack each year, and even then it didn't last till the next harvest.

He ladled the steaming soup into a bowl and left the remainder on the stove to keep warm. Strange how he felt more of a hunger when she was gone away to that convent. Why she insisted on visiting Clara Monroe, he'd never understand. Back when the nun lived in Eagle Inlet, Meghan barely knew her.

Michael cried. Willie put his spoon down on the table and left the kitchen to check on the boy. Must be a stomachache. Maybe the beginning of a spring cold. Maybe only a bad dream. He lifted Michael from his crib and rocked him for a while, then lay down beside him on the big bed.

What does a person sing to stop a child's crying? He'd heard Meghan hum but never paid much attention. Oh well, it couldn't make that much difference. "Just a song at twilight," he began, "when the lights are low." Michael's sobs began to subside. Willie continued with "In the Sweet By and By" and "I'll Take You Home Again, Kathleen," because it reminded him of his daughter. Then he hummed quietly for a while until his humming drifted into the heavy breath of sleep.

THE potato soup congealed on the bottom of the pan and scorched, then crisped and blackened. Creosote in the chimney turned red-hot. A wind came up around midnight and fanned it into flame. Poisonous fumes backed up through the stove into the house, and the sleeping man and his son breathed them in. Flames leapt from the chimney into the dark sky, sending up chunks of burning ash. The roof caught. The boy cried out once but Willie didn't hear.

⌒

Birds awakened Meghan before the knock on her door. Kate still slept beside her in the small bed. She'd come in during the night and snuggled up. A nightmare or something. Now Meghan watched her breathing and she blessed the Lord who bestowed such miracles.

Clara stood in the doorway, dressed not in her religious habit but in a black bathrobe and white cotton night veil. Meghan would see the image of her a thousand times as the years unfurled. She would hear her thoughts. What's wrong? She would know there must be something wrong or Clara would be dressed. Her face would be framed in white linen. The beads on her long rosary would be clicking together as she walked.

"There's a telegram." The nun held out the sulfur-colored envelope.

"Willie?"

"I don't know."

"Not Michael?"

"I don't know, Meghan."

How could one open such a thing?

"Open it."

She did it in a dream. In a dream she saw the words. Her mind refused them. She didn't feel a thing but cold. She couldn't breathe. She was underwater, freezing in the swift currents of the Eagle River as a forest burned over her head.

"Meghan?"

"Dead." It was all that she could say.

IN THIS manner the pictures were saved. Her treasures. The fragments that remained of her life. It must have been by the mercy of God that she had taken them with her to Bemidji to show to Clara Monroe, because they survived the fire. As did her silk wedding dress. It was at the cleaners along with some clothes that didn't mean a thing to her. She packed away the pictures with the wedding dress after that night. The night the chimney caught fire and Meghan's house burned and the piano was lost. The night that Willie died and baby Michael with him.

❦

She had said nothing to Kate the whole long drive back home from the convent. Her hands grasped the steering wheel, the knuckles white as though the skin had evaporated from them and left only bone. She held her breath. If she breathed, both she and her daughter might turn to ash and blow away.

Hell had risen up and consumed her house. They rounded the corner. Nothing but smoldering ash and stink. The guts of hell where once her house had been. She took breath in through her teeth.

"Don't walk on it," she told the girl.

It was too hot.

"Where are they?" The child's voice trembled like a bird's.

"What do you mean?"

"Daddy. Michael."

"Dead."

"I know, but where?"

"The mortuary."

"I want to see them."

"We can't."

"Why?"

"We never can see them again."

She stood at the edge of hell until her body reeked with the stench of it and her tongue tasted oily soot.

When it cooled she came there in the afternoons and sifted through the ashes for something she might be able to remember. She found no bones. She looked for bones, Michael's bones, bones of a baby, holy relics, but all the bones had been collected and locked in coffins, buried. Father Murphy called upon the angels to take the bones to heaven.

"*In paradísum dedúcant te Angeli,*" the choir sang, and she cried.

She found globs of glass and twisted bits of metal so transformed that she could not imagine what they'd been.

She should have been at home. Had she stayed home they would have stayed alive.

On such fragile choice our futures rest.

She would have been the one to heat the soup on the old wood stove.

She would have seen to it that the fire was out.

Or if the fire hadn't been put out, she slept so light she would have wakened at the first crackling of flame.

Instead, she went to Bemidji and they died.

⸺

The wives of Eagle Inlet, summoned under the watchful eye of Julia Lizot, gathered the pieces that remained of Meghan O'Neil's life and began the task of stitching them together. Was there money? No. Poor William O'Neil, young as he was, saved nothing for the future. Had he wanted to, he could not, for every penny he earned as assistant manager of Fouts Grocery went for food and clothes and to pay the mortgage on what was now a pile of cinders. And Meghan, or the widow O'Neil as she soon would be called, had few prospects for remarriage. What man would take on a ruined woman with a daughter? It was unfair, to be sure, but it was the way of the world. Father Murphy reminded the women often, quoting scripture, that it was futile for them to kick against the goad.

"Maybe Nick Fouts could give her Willie's job," Betty Thompson offered.

"He'll want a man," Marge Bates discouraged. Nick and Sarah Fouts played bridge with her and Mitchell Wednesday nights at the Moose Lodge. Nick ogled every woman there and said things like "Ain't that a juicy piece" in his gravelly voice. Once, Nick put his hand on the back of Marge's neck just where wisps of fine hair escaped from the intricate knot, and he laughed low in his throat as the devil might laugh. Meghan O'Neil couldn't get that hard up for money.

Alice Osborn, who'd felt Nick Fouts's hand cup her right buttock just last Saturday as she bent over the apple barrel to pick the firmest fruit for her Sunday pie, concurred. The grocery wouldn't be a fit place for Meghan O'Neil. Besides, there was the question of a house.

It was in this manner that Meghan O'Neil and her daughter, Kate, came to live in the small cottage behind Corpus Christi

Church. Once, it had housed the priest. That was in the early days of the parish, when the church building itself was new and the parish house not yet built. Angus McDougal, one of the settlers of Eagle Inlet, sold his one-bedroom cottage to the Corpus Christi congregation when he left town to live with his son in Winnipeg. Father Murphy sometimes used it for guests. Mostly it stood empty.

Mrs. Lizot approached the priest.

"Father"—she weighted her voice—"you are aware, I'm sure, of the plight of Meghan O'Neil and her daughter, Kate."

"I am, Mrs. Lizot, that I am."

"The parish ladies have been good to you, Father."

"Fine ladies, all of them."

"We've cooked and cleaned, washed your clothes."

"It's been a blessing."

"Yes."

Julia Lizot looked the priest straight in the eyes and waited. She saw his brow furrow as he tried to decipher her meaning.

"Are the ladies needing something, then?"

"We're proposing a bit of a change."

So MEGHAN began keeping house for the priest in return for room and board in the cottage plus a small bit of cash.

The wives of Eagle Inlet observed Meghan's face, flushed with sanctity, as she returned from the communion railing on Sunday mornings and they felt satisfied they had saved the widow O'Neil from shame.

KATE O'Neil grew to womanhood in the shadow of the church, sheltered by her mother in Hollyhock Cottage, which was what they took to calling their home once Meghan had planted the flowers. In place of piano, Kate practiced the commandments. Her mind hovered over them, sensing their nuances as her fingers had once felt magic in the air-activated keys of Willie's Stark player piano. In place of that real father, Kate now had the priest, who was called "Father" although he had no actual children.

Meghan's widowhood moved the reverend mother of Our Lady of Peace Convent to permit Sister Thomas Ann to correspond with her. Letters of a charitable and consoling nature, letters of counsel on the part of the nun. Letters, which certainly could be considered an expression of the convent's apostolic mission. Meghan, who knew nothing of apostolic missions, poured out most of the secrets of her heart.

Once a month Meghan and Kate made the trip to Bemidji. They ate dinner in the guest dining room with Sister Thomas Ann and spent the afternoon in the parlor or walking the wooded paths outside the cloister gardens along the north shore of Lake Bemidji. Sometimes Meghan cried. The nun held the widow's hands in her own and told her that the ways of God are not our ways. The women sent Kate off to the water's edge, where she skipped flat stones off the surface as many as four and sometimes five times before they sank to the bottom. But she heard. She heard the nun tell her mother they were sisters in the way of sacrifice. She heard the nun say virginity could be regained. She heard the nun tell her mother God had chosen both of them as brides, one to remain in the world, the other to be sheltered from the world. But both were the beloved of God. She said the priest was, for Meghan, the emissary of God. His hands were the hands of Christ. The nun said Meghan needn't worry, Father Murphy would lift both her and Kate as he lifted the sacred host in his consecrated hands, and the women, like the bread, would be filled with Christ.

Kate looked hard at the beautiful face of Clara Monroe framed by white linen and emphasized by her black veil, and she thought of all that God could take away. Husbands, fathers, brothers, music even. God could take your life if he wanted. God could take anything. What could a woman do but endure, be faithful, and hope to be spared some small thing she loved, something perhaps God didn't want?

After each visit, Meghan returned to Hollyhock Cottage and to the hands of the priest touching her wet lips as he placed the sacred host on her tongue. She returned to the eyes of the priest searching her heart. To the ears of the priest hearing her secrets every morning in the velvet-curtained confessional. To the voice of the priest asking for details, lingering over details, knowing who she was, calling her by name in the intimate darkness, inviting greater imagination in the creation of those secrets she could tell only to him.

VI

Anchor every energy
in your desire for music.

SISTER MARY'S MUSIC NOTEBOOKS, 1927

"He's watching you again," Virginia whispered during study hall in the big library at Eagle Inlet High.

"Shhh."

"No, I mean it. He is."

Kate pressed her pencil hard into her math paper. She felt an uncontrollable need to go to the toilet. Don't look, she silently ordered herself. Don't.

Michael Pearson, like anything a woman loved, could be taken away. The first time Kate saw him, in 1924, just after his parents bought the land by the lake, she felt a warning. Be careful! His eyes were too blue, his manner too gentle. She didn't speak to him for a year. If he came down Main Street toward her, she suddenly remembered something her mother wanted her to tell the owner of whatever store she was nearest and disappeared inside.

Sometimes Michael Pearson didn't come to school, because he had work to do at home. Reel 'Em Inn, one of a string of resorts lining the southwest shore of Black Sturgeon Lake, was a grouping of ten log cabins plus a lodge with a lake stone fireplace, a bar, and a tackle shop, and living quarters for the Pearsons. It advertised as "cozy." If the guests wanted restaurant meals or a guided fishing trip in a launch, they went to Ma Bauer's place at Split Rock Point.

• • •

VIRGINIA drove her dad's yellow Packard convertible out along the lake road. Kate's newly bobbed hair fluffed in the wind.

"We'll just drive past, that's all."

"It's too obvious."

"Don't be a ninny, Kate. He's crazy about you."

"We could say we're on our way to Black Rock Beach."

"We could invite him along and go skinny-dipping."

"Virginia!"

"Well, we could."

The relationship had taken on more complex dimensions that May, just before the junior prom, when both Kate and Michael attended a party at Virginia's house. It was the perfect opportunity, she told Kate. Her parents would be in Minneapolis at a medical convention. And Kate needn't worry about her precious virginity. There would be safety in numbers.

Dr. Francis Osborn kept a supply of Canadian liquor and Alice bought every new dance recording, all of which was available to Virginia's friends on that spring night in 1927. The Charleston, the fox trot, the waltz. Boys and girls paired up for dancing and then for moonlight walks along the river.

"You look beautiful," Michael told Kate when he asked her to dance.

She had worn a royal blue silk dress Virginia found among her mother's cast-off finery. "She'll never miss it," she'd encouraged when Kate tried it on the afternoon before the party.

He pressed his hand against the small of her back. Such thin silk. He gathered her body into his and danced her into the music.

"You avoid me."

"I do?"

"Yes. Why?"

"Maybe it's your imagination."

"It isn't."

"Does it matter?"

"It matters a lot."

Later they sat on the grassy bank watching the moon make a path across the river. He held her hand.

"Why does it matter?" she asked him.

"Because I'm going to marry you someday," he said.

The priest told Kate that Michael was a fine boy but there could be problems with his Lutheranism. Father Murphy sat with Kate in the church basement, where they spoke face-to-face about sexual abstinence. He placed his hand over hers across the table, looked into her eyes, and told her she was strong, a strong, courageous girl whom he trusted to do the right thing. He described all the mortal sins in detail. He told her a boy might try to thrust his tongue into her mouth and how she must resist. French kissing it was called. It was a foretaste of sexual intercourse, with the man's tongue imitating what his penis wanted to do. A boy's penis had a mind of its own. He said she had a flower between her legs, a rose, like a mystical rose, that would drop its petals only in the sanctity of marriage when she was deflowered by her husband for the purpose of making a baby. No one must touch this rose, not Michael, not even herself. It was sacred. It belonged to God and to her husband. He said her rose would sometimes throb at night and she must take great care not to bring her hands to rest there or the devil would enter through her fingertips with the burning fires of hell and the burning would spread upward to her brain and drive her insane. But if, and Father Murphy squeezed Kate's hands, in her feminine frailty she touched her rose, even by mistake when she was bathing, perhaps, or in her sleep while dreaming so that it wakened her, she should come to him before mass the next morning. She should tell him every detail of her act, every feeling, every fantasy, every movement of her flesh, and he would absolve her of this female sin and take away the fire. Father Murphy loved her. She was his child in God.

Kate went from the priest and his rigid laws to the boy and to his gentle touch. She tasted sweet heaven on Michael's lips. She kept the tension taut between the law and love. She kept her rose intact all through her senior year at school. Her whispered confessions revealed only minor weakness such as any girl might have, and behind his confessional curtain Father Murphy smiled and admonished her.

Finally, one spring night when she was alone with Michael on Rainbow Island, the will containing her dissolved. Her mystic rose melted, every petal turned to rain and fell from her. Michael whispered of love, and her body became a storm of rain that flowed away from her. Afterward, she knew that she could never reveal this complete loss of herself to anyone. She recovered what she could and began to arrange it into a semblance of the girl she once had been and never could purely be again.

Kate spent Sundays with her mother, at Hollyhock Cottage, in town.

"Why not marry the boy?" Meghan questioned her after mass. Truth be told, it did give Meghan a start to think of having another Michael in the family, as if the Lord played tricks; or maybe life just circled round and round, laying in your lap the very things you loved and lost. Not exactly what you had before, just different enough to make you wonder, but like enough to wring your heart. Consequently, she mentioned it offhand, not wanting to cause undue influence on Kate or the Lord. Even so, at every mention of a wedding, something closed over her daughter's face.

"Not yet."

"Is it the Depression?"

It wasn't the Depression. Stock markets and bank closings hadn't deprived her of a job, and she had no savings to lose. Since the fire Kate had never not been poor. The Depression changed nothing.

It was the devil.

"I'm just not ready yet, Mama."

The hollyhocks dipped in the summer breeze. Meghan and Kate sat on the wicker rockers under the poplar tree. They drank lemonade with a minimum of sugar. The folks from the eleven o'clock high mass were just coming out of church into the sunlight. Father Brian Murphy, still wearing his green chasuble and his long white alb, extended his hands to each of them. The sun glistened off his balding pink head. Up and down he dipped in the sun like one of the hollyhocks.

"Do you miss playing the piano, honey?"

"What?" The word "piano" knocked her out of her reverie.

"The piano, do you miss it?" Meghan hadn't spoken of the piano since the fire. "You used to love it so. I can't help but wonder if you don't feel cheated, and I wouldn't blame you if you did. Martha Kennedy, you know, said you might have been very good, might have made piano playing your career. And I was thinking, if you really missed the piano, that could be why you haven't married Michael."

Meghan's roundabout reasoning lassoed Kate's mind and pulled tight. She attempted to slip from what might be a trap.

"I don't even think of the piano anymore," she said, and the words on her tongue felt honest. "And besides, I don't see the connection between the piano and getting married."

"Well, good, then. I just wondered." Meghan poured herself more lemonade. "I just worry about my girl."

But Michael did remind Kate of music. When they sat together by the lake and he traced the contours of her cheeks with his finger and touched her lips as if to smooth them before a kiss, she still rang like the treble of Beethoven's "Für Elise." His touch continued to vibrate through her entire body. Michael played her like keys.

How could Kate explain to her mother that more than eight years after meeting the man who was more than music to her, she could not yet allow herself to marry him? He had asked. She had said she couldn't now; not yet.

Not until the vibrations stopped and she was redeemed from her sin. Kate practiced the commandments and she prayed for composure. In the confessional Father Brian gave her composure as penance. Be still, he said, still as the breath of God. God is not in the whirlwind. Still yourself, my dear daughter. Practice composure. He had no idea how far from his understanding she had fallen.

Still, Kate tried. She wrapped her hands in a scarf to control them during the night when she awoke from dreams of Michael. Michael lying with her on the beach of Rainbow Island in Black Sturgeon Lake. Michael touching and melting the petals of her forbidden rose. Michael slipping the pure white strap of her brassiere off her shoulder. Michael cupping her large, full breast in his hands and taking her throbbing nipple into his mouth. Michael opening her flesh and entering her with the firm wet sweetness of life and death. Forbidden dreams. Forbidden acts. The vibrations of her flesh bore witness to her lost virginity. Kate thickened herself against the sin. She deadened her memory whenever she could. She rested her hopes in Sister Thomas Ann's promise to her mother. Virginity can be regained. She fingered her rosary and placed her trust in the Virgin Mary.

Kate waited and she prayed. At last, when she was twenty-five, the dreams ceased. Her body and her mind were still. She was thick enough.

Kate O'Neil married Michael Pearson in 1935. But it took until 1939 to conceive her daughter, and by then Kate had schooled herself in a virtue so strong that she felt nothing where her mystic rose once had flowered. Nothing. Nothing at all.

VII

Let there be no separation
between the player and the music played.
As the piano is an extension of your body,
the music is your soul.

SISTER MARY'S MUSIC NOTEBOOKS, 1940

A scent of incense clung to the heavy purple draperies of Corpus
Christi Church. Not a clean smell. Thickly sweet, burned around
the edges, and sufficiently imposing to bring on fainting spells in
some of the ladies. Men had been known to faint, too, but Brian
Murphy wasn't thinking this as he gathered what he needed for the
baptism of Kate's baby. The basin on its stand. Salt. Chrism. Holy
water. A beeswax candle. His book of rituals.

He moved deftly from sacristy to sanctuary, through the purple
curtains, in the white clapboard church that was, even now, filling up
with Kate's and Michael's friends and families. He saw Meghan gen-
uflect and go into the first pew. The Lutherans lingered in the
vestibule, talking, laughing, a regular welcoming committee. Well,
better there than right in church like they did at Our Saviour
Lutheran. They'd lost all sense of awe, the Lutherans had. Given up
mystery for fellowship. Well, what could one expect of people who'd
put the Word into the vernacular, made God commonplace? He
crossed himself and whispered a prayer of thanks for the true church
and his vocation within it.

Sunlight filtered through the windows, a cheap-quality stained
glass in amber, blue, and rose, with images of Jesus and the saints.
He rang the brass bell that hung by the entry to the sanctuary and
took his place in the circle of gold light that streamed through the
heart of Jesus onto the polished oak floor.

• • •

When Brian Murphy poured the baptismal waters over the head of tiny Elise Marie Pearson, saving her soul from perdition and claiming her for the kingdom of God, he wept for joy. It was as Patrick Ryan, the seminary rector, had told him all those years ago when Brian approached him with doubts that he could spend his life without a wife and family of his own.

"Do you think, then, Brian, that you're more generous than our Lord?"

Well, no. He couldn't think that, could he now?

"Did you give up your father and your mother?"

He did do that.

"And a wife and children of your own?"

Those he'd never have.

"A generous lad."

Well . . .

"I say the same to all you boys, and what I say is, don't you go believing you're the first who ever had these thoughts. I tell all you boys that God will not be outdone in generosity. Do you hear that, lad?"

He heard. But he never felt it like he did today.

He imagined Clara Monroe felt the same as she held the child over the makeshift font. Meghan and Kate did well to ask the nun to be godmother, although it was highly irregular. If both Kate and Michael died, Clara could hardly raise Elise in the convent. Antiquated notion, to be sure. Still, if something were to happen, it would be a shame for the child to go over to the Lutherans.

He poured carefully, pronouncing the sacred words, noticing as he did so the slender white hands of the nun under the child's head. She'd been just a girl—sixteen is the age his mind conjured—back when he married her to Tom Lenz. Such a fragile thing. In those days he considered fragility in a woman synonymous with beauty. Poor girl had been married less than a week when the duty of examining her injuries fell to him along with Doc Osborn. Clara's parents sought an annulment, and along with Doc's testimony that Clara's virginity remained intact, the priest decided to include in the official documentation his own account of the beating. That day Brian Murphy came as close as he ever would to wanting to kill another man.

Clara lay under a white sheet in Doc Osborn's examining room.

Her long blonde hair had been washed since the incident on her wedding night and looked to the young priest like a saint's halo. Her right eye was swollen shut and the dark purple of the bruise extended down her cheek. A laceration in her upper lip swelled it twice its size.

"Father!" she sobbed when she saw him.

"What happened, Clara? Why?"

The priest placed his hand on her head, on the soft blonde hair.

"I don't know. He . . . he . . ." Clara looked at the priest through tears as if pleading not to be required to continue.

"Go on, my child," he encouraged.

"He couldn't . . . He'd been drinking, Father, and in bed he couldn't . . . He said I was a whore!"

It was all the information she could manage.

"If you'll allow us to examine your injuries, now, Clara," Dr. Osborn intoned. She closed her uninjured eye as he removed the sheet from her shoulder and left breast.

"Her husband broke three of her ribs here on this side."

The doctor touched the spots lightly but Clara winced anyway. The priest, who had never before seen a woman's breast, stood transfixed. Blue veins laced milky skin stretched taut over a fullness, the sight of which struck like a blow in the priest's own chest and moved like lightning immediately to his loins. Guilt rose from his stomach into his throat with a taste of acid. Bruises covered her torso, welling up from deep in the muscle.

"She may have internal injuries we don't yet know about. We need to watch her carefully."

"One man did all this?" The priest struggled with a confusion of horror and lust.

"Tom's a strong kid, Father. He could have killed her easily."

The doctor covered Clara's torso with the sheet and turned to face the priest.

"He made a mess of her back; there's blood in her urine. Kidneys are injured. I think they'll heal, though, in time."

"But she's intact?" he questioned the doctor again.

"Amazingly, yes, she's a virgin all right. He didn't touch her there."

"He must be insane."

"Yes, I suspect he is."

The priest gazed at Clara's tear-stained face and said he was sorry, immensely sorry, as if he could make up somehow for the cruelty. He told her he'd take care of it, take care of everything. There would be no problem with the church's law at all. From that moment Tom was no longer her husband. He had no longer any claim to her, no control; she was free.

Brian Murphy gave Clara Monroe his blessing and returned to Corpus Christi Church, where he knelt before the altar and sobbed until his chest ached and his eyes, which had seen such things that day, burned from the salt of his tears.

IF anything, Clara was more beautiful now than then. Brian Murphy noticed, as he often noticed about nuns, that the religious habit had a way of making women appear ageless. Face and hands were, after all, the extent of what a person could see, unless one were a connoisseur. The flowing garb revealed as much as it concealed the erotic subtleties of a female body, if a man used his imagination. A nun was a work of art; you had to take the time, stand back a bit, contemplate. And because nuns were also the safest of all women, Brian Murphy took whatever liberties he could with his eyes. Clara Monroe at forty retained the well-formed breasts, the small waist, the curving back, and flaring hips of the girl he had examined on the doctor's table. He imagined, as he placed the salt of wisdom on Elise Marie Pearson's tongue, how white Clara's body must be now that she had covered it from the sun and from the gaze of men for almost twenty-five years.

It seemed a peculiar irony to him, however, that Clara had been given Tom's name after all, despite what the man had done and regardless of the annulment. Surely the nuns were aware. The only sense the priest could make of it was that the Thomas of the gospels grappled with faith as Clara must be required to do each day. Who could know how God may have joined those two in spirit as well as name? She, like Christ, might be the sacrifice exacted for the man's salvation. And perhaps it worked in Tom's case, since he had married again three years later to a plain, somewhat stupid girl, a Congregationalist with whom he had three sons.

•   •   •

As IT turned out, women were the stronger of the sexes. Clara taught him that, and Meghan also, the widow O'Neil, who despite the sensuality she had never overcome, was, in her devotion to him and to the church, a model Christian woman. If the truth could be told, Brian Murphy thought of Meghan O'Neil as a kind of wife. Her knowledge of him was intimate. She washed his sheets and knew about the shameful emissions. Yet she never treated him as other than he was, the priest of God. She knew of his tempers, of his black Irish moods when he disappeared into his study and wouldn't eat. When he thickened the air with pipe smoke, the perfume of his blend mixing with the rancid wet stench of its leftover tar in the ashtray, she never complained. She cleaned it up. She emptied the mess from ashtrays on the desk, beside the easy chair, on the bed stand. Always, Meghan cleaned up his mess. Always, she remained kind. Always, virtuous. Who shall find a virtuous wife? Brian Murphy felt blessed. God will not be outdone in generosity.

He took care with her. He listened to her sins and forgave them. He touched only her hands and her lips. Her hands for comfort, her lips for something beyond his ability to describe.

MEGHAN, on this baptism day, the feast of the Annunciation of Mary, looked young in her lavender dress and little hat. A grandmother she was, despite her auburn hair. And Brian Murphy a grandfather of sorts. A pure love the two of them had enjoyed all these years. A love based on sacrifice and renunciation. She'd had her struggles with feminine frailty, but the struggles gave her strength and more compassion than women who'd made themselves too rigid to feel those movements of human nature that were, paradoxically, God-given and sinful, a source of grace even as they tormented the soul.

"Receive this white garment." Brian lifted the end of his priestly stole and placed it on Elise Marie Pearson. The fringe hung over the long fingers of the nun. His consecrated hands followed the fringe down and brushed against those fingers as they passed. He continued the prayer, "Never let it become stained, so that when you stand before the judgment seat of our Lord Jesus Christ, you may have life everlasting."

He looked up into Meghan's eyes, over at Kate standing with her hand in Michael's, at the veiled head and downcast eyes of Sister Thomas Ann, and finally at the infant, Elise Marie, who would grow. And he knew, in a depth of himself to which even his soul did not reach, that of all God's creations, nothing was as strong, as complicated, as sinful, as glorious, as frustrating, or as beautiful as woman.

"Go in peace," he said to those assembled, including the Lutherans, "and God be with you."

VIII

The heart breaks; body reaches its limit.
You are dissolved, becoming like air and the vibration of air,
a silence making space for sound.

SISTER MARY'S MUSIC NOTEBOOKS, 1941

Michael rushed into the living room because Elise was screaming bloody murder. The radio blared behind the screams.

Kate was kissing her downy hairline, crooning, "Hush, hush, it's all right," but it was not all right.

"What happened?" Michael had scooped both of them into his arms and was holding them firm. All of it unfolded like one continuous motion of a dance, a choreography of terror. The motion repeated itself outside the house, where wind keened around corners and under the eaves, pelting the living room windows with sleet.

"The Japs bombed Pearl Harbor. We're at war."

Elise's breath came in short burps of sound, but she'd stopped screaming.

"I'll have to go, you know."

Kate didn't know. She stood in Michael's arms, holding their baby, not thinking about the possibility of Michael's leaving them. She thought instead of Minnesota's winter light. She thought how most every day from November through February passed in twilight, a slanted light, casting shadows even at noon upon the snow. Blinding days did come, of course, from time to time. Days when it was so cold no clouds formed. Then the light slanted off the snow crystals to pierce your eyes like a million fiery swords. Glare ice.

There couldn't be a war. Michael couldn't go to war. She needed him.

"You're too old, Michael. Young men fight wars. Eighteen. Nineteen."

"Boys. They need men over there." He stared out the window as though he could see right through the sleet all the way to the fields of battle.

Kate watched the morning light fall from the sky in gray-white frozen mists like wings. The whole sky was a bird or an angel, caught, trapped, beating its wings against her entire world.

Michael the Archangel, defend us in battle . . . but not her Michael. Not now. Not ever.

"That goddamned Hitler in Germany, and now this!"

"Don't swear, Michael."

"It's a time for swearing if ever there was one, Kate. The world's on its way to hell!"

She knew there would be no stopping him.

⌒

Edward R. Murrow reported news from the front. Kate accompanied Meghan to daily mass and kept Michael's picture tucked in her prayer book, where it marked the invocation to the archangel. During mass Elise opened and closed the clasp on Kate's handbag. She dumped the contents on the pew between the two women and positioned the coin purse and the rosary and the embroidered hanky like characters on a stage. She whispered the lines for each of them, lost in her own drama, as Father Murphy also appeared lost in the sacramental drama he enacted on the altar.

Kate stared at the photograph of her husband, so stern in his uniform, so unlike the real Michael, her Michael. He had gone to hell. Italy. He hadn't said it in so many words, but it must be Italy they were headed for. If you put Murrow's reports together with plain common sense, there wasn't any other conclusion to draw.

Elise shook her finger at the tiny doll Kate had tucked into her handbag that morning as a surprise for the child. "A speery comes," she was telling the doll, "and says two and two is oh."

Kate chuckled. *Et cum spíritu tuo.* Children constantly tried to make sense of the Latin prayers. *Te rogámus, audi nos* had sounded to her own little-girl ears like "They go round your soggy nose." Like Kleenex. Even now it was difficult to keep the dripping nose image out of her mind during the solemn litany of the saints.

Other images as well. Images of war. Images of Michael blown to bits.

From Pearl Harbor day until he left, she rehearsed a scene of bravery. She memorized her lines in bed at night while she listened to him breathe. She collected each breath like a treasure, storing them up to use later, one breath at a time, one each night that she would sleep alone. She became a miser, not wanting to fall asleep for fear of missing the sound of his breathing, the warm wetness of breath at the base of her neck. There would be ample time for sleep while he was gone.

How could they send them off so fast? One week back in Eagle Inlet after he enlisted, one mere week for listening to him breathe, a sound that she might never hear again.

Dorothy and Charles took the baby that day.

"We'll just stay here at the house till you get back, dear." Dorothy gave Kate a hug and then she stood a long time with Michael until Charles put his own arm around her and pulled her slowly away like you'd pull tape off a window after you painted the sill. Careful. You wouldn't want to chip the finish.

"You give those Japs a run for their money," Charles told Michael as he clapped him on the back.

"It might be the Krauts, you know, Dad. I don't know which front I'll be on."

"Well, we're not actually in that war yet."

"But the German's have declared, so we will be. We all know that. Eventually we'll get our crack at Hitler."

"Just do your duty, son, and come home. You've got a family here that needs you."

Kate put the baby in Dorothy's arms and took Michael's hand. Good-bye, and then good-bye, back and forth among the four of them. Good-bye. Be safe. Come home. Drive carefully.

"If the roads are slick, Kate, you stop at Kelliher or Blackduck. Don't drive home alone if there's ice," Dorothy called out the front door as Kate and Michael made their way through the snow to the car that was already running, getting warm, on the street in front of the house.

Michael drove the hundred thirty miles to Bemidji, where he'd catch the bus to the training camp. Kate watched his hands on the wheel. His long fingers. She felt how he had touched her just last night and how her flesh fought against her mind for release. But if she let go to him now, if she felt the pressure of his body on hers, felt the gentleness, felt it all as love, then she would cry and never stop. If, as he entered her body, she let him in completely, let him into her every cell to linger there like sound along the pathways of her mind, and if after she had opened herself to him that completely, he was killed in this war, she would not survive it. The sound of him in her would become a fury. She knew it. It would tear her apart, and what, if anything, she might gather up and piece together afterward would be deaf and blind and dumb.

She watched his hands and remembered just how calm she made herself, like porcelain under his fingers. Cool.

"Love me, Kate," he'd pleaded. "I'm going to war. Why can't you love me?"

"I do love you, Michael." But he couldn't know how much.

Winter light filtered through the windows of the car. They reached Baudette and then turned south to drive the forty miles of bog to Waskish. Wind dusted the road with fine moving clouds of dry snow. People had been known to see visions on this road, drive off into the ditch, wait there an hour before another car came along. She counted the telephone poles. There was an emergency phone at every mile.

He could have waited until after Christmas to enlist. But he didn't. She looked at him again, this time at his face. God, but he was handsome! Beautiful, actually, but you didn't say that to a man. Surely it couldn't hurt to take his face into the cells of her mind, imprint upon herself that part of him more spiritual than his touch. The look of him, the way his eyes blessed her every day. How she would miss that. How could she live without that blessing?

He smelled like the warm sands of Rainbow Island. She wanted to move close to him as if they were still teenagers and breathe him in. She turned on the car radio instead.

"I think it's time for *Ma Perkins*, and then there's *Our Gal Sunday*."

"I don't know what you see in those stories."

"They pass the time."

"I suppose."

Now, why did she go and say that? She didn't want time to pass. Stop time. That's what she'd prefer. Stop time right here, right on the outskirts of Waskish. Live in the car until the war's over and everyone's safe again. If a person could only get stopped in time, put under a spell, like Sleeping Beauty, until every danger passed and Michael's kiss wakened her to a new world at peace.

In Bemidji they ate lunch at the bus depot cafeteria. Michael talked of practical things, the will he made, Elise's education. Kate's mind slid over his words like they were greased. The cafeteria smelled like old smoke, burned coffee, and an unwashed grill. Her sandwich had a long black hair in it. The tines of her fork needed to be straightened and she used the knife blade, focusing all her attention there.

He left so fast. They called his bus and he grabbed his bag and her hand. In front of the bus he crushed her to him. He said he loved her. She couldn't breathe. She opened her eyes wide to keep away tears. He let her go and disappeared into the bus.

She couldn't watch him leave. She turned, she heard the sound her heel made as snow crunched against ice, and she walked away.

"DÓMINE, *non sum dignus,*" the priest was saying now as he held the white host up before the scattering of people at daily mass. Lord, I am not worthy that you should come under my roof; say but the word and my soul will be healed. Kate bent her head, and as was prescribed by the ritual, she struck her breast three times.

I am not worthy, Lord, but bring Michael home. Stop this ugly war and bring him home to me.

⟿

Sister Thomas Ann visited Gramma Meghan at Hollyhock Cottage. Elise and her mama stayed in town after mass on Sunday and Elise paged through the small Peter Rabbit books while the women talked.

"We must accept God's will in this, Meghan." The nun leaned

toward Elise's grandmother, who was holding tight to her embroidery hoop and jabbing the needle through the cloth. Each jab made a popping sound as the tight weave resisted. Elise looked away. She concentrated on Mr. McGregor with his pitchfork and poor Peter scampering to escape.

"But, Sister, people are so insecure these days," Kate inserted after a quick glance at Meghan. "We've lost so much already. There are four gold-star mothers right here in Eagle Inlet. I don't think that on top of it all we should have to lose our priest."

"It's difficult, I know, especially for you and Meghan. Father Murphy must seem like a member of the family." The nun's placid gray eyes held Kate's in a look meant to instill realism. "Of course, Meghan could go along with him."

"Oh?" It was Kate. Abrupt. Sharp.

"There are priests who take their housekeeper with them when they move."

"Leave Eagle Inlet?" Meghan leaned down to her sewing basket and picked up a muslin towel. She spread it on her lap, placed the hoop with her embroidery on top, and wrapped it before she tucked the whole package away. "Leave my Willie's grave? And little Michael's? Never! And that's that!"

She reached down to the child-size wicker rocking chair, where Elise sat with the Peter Rabbit book, and placed her hand on the child's head. "We'll get another priest for our church, isn't that right, Elise?"

Elise put her arms around her Gramma Meghan's neck and kissed her because of the tears in her eyes.

"WHY was Gramma crying?" Elise asked her mama on the way back to the inn. They were eating cherries from a brown paper sack and spitting the stones from the fruit's center out the windows of the car.

"Father Murphy has to go away and Gramma will miss him." Mama spit a cherry stone.

"Will Father Murphy fight the war so children in Europe can have bread?" It seemed a peculiar thing that fathers did, this fighting for bread. Dying even. Margaret Henderson's father died so children in Europe could have bread, and now Margaret didn't have a daddy. "Is he going to die?"

"No, darling." Mama laughed. It was the first time that afternoon. "Father Murphy isn't going to the war, just to another parish. He's too old for wars, and priests don't fight wars anyway."

"But Gramma's sad. He should stay with her."

"He can't, Elise. Father must obey the bishop, and the bishop must do what's best for Mother Church."

"Who's Mother Church?" Elise would have liked to talk with her, tell her about Gramma Meghan's tears. But just then her mama looked away from the road and over at Elise's hands, which were stained red with the juice of cherries. She swerved the car as she reached toward the child.

"Keep those off your dress!"

Her voice was a knife that cuts to the place where tears are stored.

After her mama spit on a hanky and wiped the cherry juice from her hands and dried her tears, they watched a mother duck lead her ducklings across the road to the ditch on the other side. One little one lagged behind and Elise forgot she'd asked a question that her mother never answered.

In the evening after supper, when Elise went to sit in her tree, she heard a sound like pudding bubbling on the stove, and when she got closer she saw that the mother tree was boiling with birds. It was a war of birds. They were not singing. They were crying out warnings. The birds fought over seeds, pecking at the tree and at one another until some of them were red as the juice of cherries and they fell. Then as the child stood, horrified, the boiling ceased and the birds rose into the twilight sky like a swarm of prehistoric winged reptiles, forming a black cloud that shifted as it moved out over the lake and disappeared.

The tree stood silent, but the child ran from it. Her heart was a stone in her throat and she couldn't cry out.

⁓

Michael Pearson stepped off the train in the Saint Paul Union Depot. His wife and daughter stood hand in hand on the platform, and it was all he could do to keep from turning around before they saw him. He had come back from war minus the nerves that held up the left side of his face. His eyelid and mouth drooped, fleshy cups collecting tears and spit. An angry red line ran from above his eye, behind his left ear, and along his jawline to the center of his chin. Elise took one look and screamed. She buried her head in the front of her mother's paisley print dress, between Kate's legs, and clung. The child's reaction was nothing less than what Michael felt in his own heart, and he experienced a kind of gratitude toward his daughter for her genuine horror.

Even his outward appearance was no match for the slaughterhouse in his mind, a swirl of blood, greasy smoke, indescribable sounds, bodies turned inside out. Arms, legs, heads, exploding into a dank sky. He'd landed at Anzio and made the thrust through the Alban Hills toward Monte Cassino. He lived while every other man in his company was lost.

Was lost. He would never, to the end of his life, be able to say those words without a sense of betrayal, because he lived. Because what happened to them was unutterable compared to simply being lost. Oh, to be lost. The rich unknowing it implied. For them to be lost, merely lost. The relief, the purity, of it.

Their blood and brains had slickened the rock under his hands as he climbed on their deaths up the holy mountain of Saint Benedict toward the monastery defense of Kesselring's Gustav Line. Sergeant Jim Olsen opened his mouth to yell an order and took a bullet straight through it and out the top of his head. Ralph "Bulldog" Johnson charged into enemy fire like he couldn't die, and burst apart, a spray of blood and bone. The others. The others. Dead. Not lost. The stones of Italy awash with American blood. Birds scavenging the bones.

He had awakened in a hospital in Rome with half a face, a daughter back in Minnesota, and a wife who didn't deserve this. Better for Kate if he had died. Better for them all.

EVERY night Michael was overseas, Kate had clutched her rosary. She made herself pray each Hail Mary perfectly, leaving nothing out, refusing sleep until all fifty-nine beads, the crucifix, and the tiny silver medal that connected the circle had been held and prayed upon. She dreaded Tuesdays and Fridays, when tradition dictated that she pray the sorrowful mysteries. Mary's own son died and there seemed to have been nothing she could do to stop it. Maybe now, in heaven, Mary held more influence.

"Remember," Kate whispered before the first sorrowful mystery, "remember how it felt. Remember the blood and the tears. Remember the agony of holding him there at the foot of the cross. Then look at me. I'm not strong. I know there are thousands of women losing husbands and sons, but they must be stronger than I am. I couldn't survive. So bring him back. No matter what, please bring Michael back."

WHEN she saw him climbing down off the train on that chill morning in November, she finally understood that God cannot do everything, and she felt pity for the Creator whose world had spun so far off its course. It surprised her that she had no need to assign blame for the ravaged face that turned to her like a question unasked. She only wished she were able to open herself wide and take all the wounded to her heart, including God, who must be so sad about the broken things.

THE CHILD retained no memory of the father who had carried her every morning to the lake to watch the sun rise and the fishermen lower themselves from the long wooden dock into their boats. She clung to her mother's cotton dress and willed the man with the crooked mouth and loose eye to disappear. Her mother kept repeating in a voice that was low and at the edge of breaking that she must not be afraid.

"Daddy's just hurt, darling. You know about being hurt. Remember when you fell and hurt your leg?"

Her mama murmured that Daddy loved her. He loved the children in Europe, and it was for them and so they could have bread. Look how brave. Brave enough to go to war. Don't be afraid. Not of this brave, brave man who loved her and had been hurt trying to protect her and all the children.

Finally her mother bent down to her and whispered in her ear. "Please, darling. Please." And she was crying.

Elise let go of her mother's dress and turned her head toward what she would later always think of as the two faces of her father.

"Get my good side," he would say years later when cameras came out; and he'd laugh.

That day of his return from war she looked up from her mother's dress and saw a man with a face split in two. She saw an eye that always wept. She saw exactly how this man looked at her and recognized in his divided face something she could understand.

The father's eyes drew her. She would remember years from that day how she entered into him. She would be reading an ancient text, discerning in the words a primal movement of her soul, *"wakened with the drawing of this love and the voice of this calling."* She would lift her hand to her face.

She went now toward the man with the divided face and he bent to receive her touch. The child's small fingers traced the jagged path of the scar. She explored the flaccid eye, the turned-down lip. He smiled and the other side of his face leapt to life. She laughed. He lifted her up into his arms.

WHEN the ice went out of the lake that first spring after he came home, Michael Pearson strapped Elise's small body into a life jacket, lowered her from the dock into one of the fishing boats, and the two of them started off toward Gull Rock. The rock, paste white with bird droppings, was the first of the granite islands outside Deep Water Gap, where the river emptied into the big lake. Above the rock, white-and-soft-gray gulls wheeled and dipped, crying out, *klee-euw*. Here they laid eggs, tended hatchlings.

"Only if we find a baby gull that's an orphan," Michael explained to Elise as he cut the engine, "because we wouldn't want to take a baby from its mother."

She agreed but found herself imagining a mother gull on a fisherman's hook. She'd seen that once. The fisherman cast his line with its minnow wiggling at the end of the hook, and while it was still in the air a gull swooped down and swallowed it, hook and all. The gull tried to fly but the line stopped its flight; and startled, the bird fell, threshing and squawking, into the water. What could the fisherman do? He cut the line. The gull rose from the lake, the white feathers on its throat stained red.

Suddenly she could taste the blood.

"Let's go home, Daddy," she said in a desperate attempt to redeem her desires. "I don't really want a baby gull."

But Michael had already spotted a small brown chick isolated from the other birds.

"Look, Elise!" He pointed and maneuvered the boat close to the rock. She reached out and closed her hands around the soft feathers.

"This chick's mother must have died." He smiled with one side of his mouth and frowned with the other as she lifted the tiny bird into the boat and settled it onto her lap. "You can be its mother now."

She named the gull Cleo because it was the name each mother gull cried out, and she fed it dead minnows from the tank. It followed her everywhere, waddling along behind.

"Just look at that!" Her daddy laughed. "Would you look at that!"

He built a chicken-wire pen behind the icehouse.

"Why, Daddy? Cleo won't run away or fly. She can't fly yet."

"It's to protect her, Peanut, not to imprison her."

Her first thought on waking was the bird. Sunlight streaked through the curtains and she was up, pulling on her shirt and overalls, running to the pen, to Cleo. And the bird greeted her with squawks and the flapping of downy wings.

"There's a monster in the houseboat," she told the bird as she fed it that morning's dead minnows from a pail. She sat inside the fence on the grass. Afterward she'd take Cleo for a walk. "But don't you worry. I'll protect you."

Later in the summer, when Cleo made attempts to fly, Elise felt in her own heart a longing for wings. And sometimes at night as she drifted off to sleep, she saw Cleo's real mother behind her eyelids in what was almost a dream. She flew alone like a white-and-gray ghost above the lake, calling for something lost that she could never find. The mother gull's throat had turned red with calling.

IX

One day you will be convinced that music is impossible;
your fingers will defy you.
On that day especially
you must play.

SISTER MARY'S MUSIC NOTEBOOKS, 1947

Nothing relieved the longing, neither good nor evil. Elise gave her favorite necklace to Norma Swanson, who had nothing pretty ever. But goodness merely catapulted her into a mania of giving. Her doll with the porcelain head. Her collection of silver dollars—forty of them. Crazed with generosity, she might, like Saint Martin of Tours, have given the clothes off her back, had her mother not found out and retrieved the possessions. One by one the other mothers clucked the air in through their back teeth and shook their heads in sympathy. Where do children get these ideas? Maybe it's the times, this modern world. Must have been the war, the bomb. Terrifying. They're made to hide under their desks, you know. Makes them frightened, insecure. Such complicated times.

God, who gives birds wings, must be the source of such desire. Didn't the priest pray, "I will take the wings of the dawn and fly to the farthest corners of the earth"? But people had no wings. Reason mattered little to the child, and the wings of dawn and of the bird and of her own desire became for her one impulse toward flight. Just as strong, though, was her longing to be tethered, held firmly to earth. If Elise broke a commandment or two, then God might see that she was not a bird and free her to be a child like other children. But lies couldn't do it, or disobedience. Not even spreading her legs for Margaret Henderson, who explored the delicate pink folds that quivered in her fingers like a living clam from Black Sturgeon Lake, not even that could bind her spirit.

It was a secret that instinct required be hidden, because Elise's longing didn't stop with flight. It cried out. It rang, *klee-euw*. It was a tone vibrating on the air, pulsing in the wind. It reached all the way to God. It became a love of air and sky, a love detaching her from earth. It became a love for something maybe birds could reach when their wings were strong enough. It became a love for God. And Elise realized that she didn't love God as her mama loved him, a way of loving that made you want to keep the commandments. Elise loved God like Saint Rose of Lima loved him. Saint Rose, who made a coffin her bed, who fasted on bread and water, who wore a hair shirt under her long white habit. Saint Rose, whose ecstatic longing lifted her, singing, into the clear sky.

Longing sounded a tone in the mind of the child as though she were a broken flute that could be played only by someone with an unending supply of breath. It was a tone she heard even in her sleep. God tormented Elise with a longing that perched like a shining bird on the child's heart, that spread its wings and dug in its claws as it sang.

~

Church was like fairy tales, only real. Next Sunday, when Elise made her First Holy Communion, she would become God's bride. Sister said so. Like the little mermaid who would receive an immortal soul when the prince married her, Elise would become a part of God. She wondered if she would shine. The saints in heaven shine like the sun at noon.

The white satin dress Mama sewed was at home hanging in her closet. Mama made Elise stand on the table and turn round and round, slower than the big hand on a clock, while she pinned the hem. Everything must be white: dress, shoes, long stockings, even her underwear. The best of all was the veil. It was Gramma Meghan's wedding veil and hung all the way to the hem of the white dress. Gramma promised a crown of flowers, lilies of the valley that grew under the ferns on the north side of Hollyhock Cottage.

• • •

GOD gives children whatever they pray for on their First Communion day. It was a lot like the three-wishes tales. If you got three wishes from an enchanted creature you must be wise about what you asked or you could bring misfortune down upon yourself and your family. Prayer might work the same way. Sister Thomas Ann had said just that morning that God takes seriously the prayers of children.

"Take great care in what you ask." Sister Thomas Ann had reached her hand around behind her neck under her veil and lifted the material up and down in a fanning motion. Jack Tobin squirmed on the wooden slats of his folding chair. A fly buzzed around Barbara Thompson's head. Several of the children nodded sleepily in the damp June heat of the choir loft.

Hot, hot, hot. But Sister Thomas Ann must be hotter in that long dress and veil. She came every June from Bemidji to teach the first communicants their catechism. Already last year, when Elise was six, Sister let her be in class even though she hadn't even started regular school. Now she was a whole year ahead and could receive her First Communion early, with the second graders. Mama said that in big cities Catholic children went to schools that belonged to the church. But a school like that would be silly in Eagle Inlet. Elise would be the only Catholic in her grade.

"Great care," the nun emphasized. "The innocence of children moves the heart of God. On your First Communion day your souls will be as white as they were at your baptism, and God will be unable to resist your purity. He will answer your prayer. He may not answer immediately; God does not work magic, children. But God will answer."

Elise had raised her hand.

"Elise?"

"Is God real, Sister?"

"Perfectly real."

"As real as I am?"

"More real than you or me or anyone."

BEFORE you could receive First Communion you had to tell your sins to the priest. Every sin took something real away from you, until you finally became just a big empty hole with no light in it. Pretty

soon you were so dark you couldn't see a thing. Only a priest in confession could bring back the light and make you real again.

FIRST Confession was scheduled for one-thirty in the afternoon.
That morning, before the prayer to Jesus, Elise's stomach crawled as
if it had hatched worms. She felt certain that none of the other children would have sins as terrible as hers. Stealing. Lying. Playing
naughty games. Father Quinn wouldn't know who she was because
of the darkness of the confessional and the cloth draped over the
window he would open between them. Sister Thomas Ann had
practiced the ritual with each child. When the child before you came
out through the velvet curtain that hung in place of a door, you went
into the tiny room and knelt on the hard wood. Or if you were too
short, like Margie Newstrom, you could stand. You were to wait for
the sound of the shutter in front of the window as it slid open. That
sound meant Father was ready for you to begin.

How could people remember it all? Elise's prayer book had four
pages of sins that children might commit. It was like a multiple
choice test in school. You looked at each sin and figured out if you'd
done it and how many times. Who could remember how many times
they lied or disobeyed? She made up a number—five times if the sin
was something she did seldom, ten if the sin was a habit. Sister said
it would be a good idea to repeat over and over in your mind exactly
what you wanted to say to Father once you were in the confessional
and his ear was pressed up against the window and you were whispering into it. Often the people who wanted to go to confession
formed long lines outside, and as you stood there waiting you could
memorize your sins.

Then there was the formula. Every afternoon, sitting in long
rows in the front pews of the church, the first communicants had
recited the confession formula until they could say it in their sleep.
"Bless me, Father, for I have sinned. This is my First Confession. My
sins are . . ." Then you told your sins, the bad ones first. When you
were finished you had to say the hard part of the formula. The words
seemed twisted around one another and difficult to understand. "I
am sorry for these and for all the sins of my past life, especially
for . . ." Then you were supposed to mention the most terrible sin
you'd ever done, something that was the devil's snare and that would

surely land you in hell for all eternity if you didn't get God's special help. Naughty games again. That had to be the worst of anything.

AFTER she let Margaret Henderson touch her private parts, Elise had prayed to see the Blessed Virgin. Being a regular kid was one thing; eternal darkness and damnation was something else altogether, and Elise knew instinctively when she felt Margaret's fingers between her legs that she'd gone too far.

"Don't touch yourself down there," Mama had warned during her bath, but she hadn't said anything about Margaret Henderson. If Elise's own touch felt sweet, Margaret's was pure honey. Margaret's touch was a thing you'd like to last forever.

"I don't think we're supposed to do this," she'd told Margaret as she lay spread-eagle on Margaret's mother's big bed. Margaret's mother worked in glassware at Anderson's Department Store on Main Street so she never was home after school.

Margaret had lifted a white silk scarf from her mother's dresser drawer and was draping it over Elise's naked body. When she pulled it slowly, slowly over that bare skin, Elise shivered.

"I know," Margaret said. "Now you do it to me."

Elise's stomach fluttered. Fair's fair, though, and Margaret hadn't yet been touched.

"Go round in a circle on my butt."

"What? That's nasty."

"No. It tickles. Here, I'll show you; turn over on your tummy."

Round and round went Margaret's finger in that very private place until Elise began to drift, hypnotic, her mind lifting away, her body pure sensation.

After that it had to be Margaret's turn. All the private places on Margaret's body, Elise explored. She traced each crevice, examined every opening. She saw places that on her own body she couldn't see. Margaret smelled like the woods by the lake after a rain. She told Elise exactly what to do.

At home that night Elise knelt in front of the statue of the Blessed Virgin and prayed the whole rosary.

"Please, holy Mary, don't let God send me to hell. Please come and tell me God's not mad at me. Come to me like you came to Saint Bernadette."

But Mary didn't come.

"Come on. Let's go to my mom's bedroom," Margaret insisted every time Elise stayed in town after school.

"Let's play with your dolls."

"No, we can play dolls anytime. Let's play doctor."

"Why do you call it 'doctor'?"

"Because the doctor can order you to take your clothes off and you have to do it."

"DID you have fun at Margaret's?" Elise's mother always asked.

"Yes."

"What did you play?"

"Dolls. Margaret has baby dolls you can wash."

ELISE promised herself that after her First Confession she would never play doctor again. If Margaret said they couldn't be friends, well then, she just wouldn't like her anymore. It was bad enough to have to tell Father Quinn that she'd put herself in danger of eternal darkness and damnation by playing naughty games. That's how she'd determined to put it to him: "Bless me, Father, for I have sinned. I played naughty games that my mama told me not to." Her mother, of course, knew nothing of such games. Her mother had no idea that children could think up such things. Still, it seemed the best way to tell the priest. Maybe he'd let it go at that and forgive her, turning her as pure as on the day of her baptism so that on her First Communion day the Blessed Virgin finally would appear to her and tell her that God understood. The Blessed Virgin would say everything was all right and God loved Elise as much as he ever did and now she could be his bride.

During the noon hour before her First Confession, Elise walked down the aisle of the empty church, past the small statue of the Infant Jesus of Prague, which the Ladies' Rosary Society dressed like a doll in silk and gold. She knelt at the communion railing directly in front of the altar. Even if she wasn't yet as pure as on the day of her baptism, she was a child. God might listen to her prayers based simply on that fact, blindfolding himself to Margaret Henderson's games.

"Please, Jesus," she prayed, "let me be a saint. Make me your bride. Fix my daddy's face. Make my mama happier. And don't let me play doctor ever again."

The purple velvet curtains draped behind the altar gave every-thing the look of palaces and kings. Jesus lived in the golden taber-nacle in the center, and Elise directed her prayer straight through the closed door. Dust floated in muted rays from the top panes of the stained glass windows, and Elise imagined each particle was an angel small enough to dance on the head of a pin. A touch more delicious than any Margaret Henderson's finger ever produced set-tled in her heart, and although neither Jesus nor Mary appeared in the light, Elise felt certain that she had been heard.

At that moment Elise knew she was like Bernadette, who saw the Virgin, and like Rose of Lima, who suffered the torments of the flesh. For this suffering Jesus loved her like a bride and took her to his heart.

MAYBE she didn't believe God really took her sins away. Maybe that feeling of holiness, when she had been certain that God heard her prayer, was called into question by Father Quinn's reaction to her confession of naughty games. Her stomach turned over and blocked her throat when she tried to say the words for what she and Mar-garet Henderson had done. The priest had scolded her. It was a whisper of a scolding, to be sure, but it deafened her to the merciful voice of God.

"Come, children." Recess followed First Confession, and Sister Thomas Ann motioned to her First Communion class of seven-year-olds, who scrambled to sit as close to her as possible, on the cir-cle of her skirt if they could. She twirled. Her skirt billowed around her like an upside-down black tulip. She whirled and whirled, laugh-ing, and then settled like a ballerina onto the fresh spring grass in the churchyard.

Elise peered out from behind the lilac bush that grew next to the new priest's door. Purple flower cones brushed, cool as her mama's hand, against her face. From her hiding place she could see all the way over to Gramma Meghan's hollyhocks. She couldn't twirl with Sister Thomas Ann and the other children. It was out of the ques-tion. They weren't really angels that she had seen in the beams of light, Elise told herself; they were dust. And the Blessed Virgin doesn't appear to naughty girls.

"Here's the way you do it, Peanut," Michael instructed his daughter as he positioned her hands just right on the casting rod. She'd been morose lately, probably lonesome for that bird of hers.

"I'll spend a bit more time with her, Kate." And then it was Kate who suggested the fishing. Elise could fish from the dock if she knew how to cast out toward the reed bed. Toward it, not into it. The girl would need some skill to position the cast, and just the right rod and reel. He had the perfect equipment in the tackle shop. A light rod, short enough for her to manage.

He'd found her in that tree, staring out at the circling gulls.

You'd save your children from the pain of this world if you could, he'd thought as he approached her. How much could she understand? The bird was dead. Nothing could be done. She'd forget. Children forget; that's the mercy of it, because who could live otherwise? You'd go insane, wouldn't you? You'd never take another step. You'd be shot down, just like that, right where you stood.

Michael reached up for her and she let him lift her from the tree. It wasn't him she blamed, then. He accepted this realization as a gift, as the miracle it surely was.

She took his hand and walked along beside, two steps to every one of his. She smelled like rain in a cistern and was tan as a berry. His mother always told him that when he was a boy. My Michael, tan as a berry. He thought it silly of her. Chokecherries, blueberries, gooseberries, none of them are tan. Acorns are tan. Tan as an acorn is what it ought to be.

ON THE dock they were alone. Maybe Kate watched from the window above her desk in the lodge office. Maybe she was too busy for that. Guests of Reel 'Em Inn had taken their gear and rented boats out on the lake hours before. Now the midday sun glistened in rainbows of gasoline on the surface of the water and water bugs drew their lazy circles.

"You can fish any time of day, Peanut, but fish bite more in early morning or late afternoon."

"Breakfast and supper."

"Right. The fish have schedules, too. But people don't always fish just to catch something."

"Why?"

"Well, my little Peanut, people fish to become quiet inside. You'll see. There's a current in the water that pulls on the line a little and you can feel it through the rod in your hands. It's a kind of rocking. Peaceful."

"Do they ever go to sleep?"

He laughed. "Sometimes they do, my little nut, sometimes they actually do."

He checked the position of her hands. Perfect.

"Now, put your thumb there, on the string where it's wound on the reel. There. That's it. And now you bring your rod back over your shoulder, straight, and up, and back . . ."

All of her concentration went to the action of the rod in her hands. The sun made her hair glisten and intensified the rainwater smell of her.

"Now! Snap the rod forward with your wrist, and as it goes just past the vertical position, take your thumb off the line and let it feed out."

She tried it. The hook plopped into the water and the line tangled.

"What happened?"

He helped her with the snarled line. "It's okay, Peanut. It's called a backlash. You have to keep just the slightest pressure as the line feeds out or you get this backlash. You'll get the feel for it."

His temptation was to do it for her, but he had to let her try it on her own. Someday she'd be grateful. Someday she'd understand. All of this—what happened with the bird, and now the fishing—in all of it he meant only to teach her how to live. And right now she needed to get a feel for the snap of the pole, for the precise instant of release.

X

Repetition is never exact.
Develop nuance, subtle shading—
Soul.

SISTER MARY'S MUSIC NOTEBOOKS, 1950

Michael bought Osborn's grand piano for Kate as a gift to celebrate her fortieth birthday and provide for her the opportunity to start up exactly where she left off when Willie O'Neil died in the fire, taking the Stark player piano and Kate's musical aspirations down to ashes and dust.

"Oh, Michael," she moaned when she walked into the tiny living room of their new house in town.

"We'll build on," Michael had promised as they stood in the kitchen that day, two years before, he so proud at having the one hundred dollars to put down on those four rooms, not counting the bathroom with the claw-foot tub too small for his body to fit.

The piano filled half the living room, leaving space only for the sofa, the Philco radio from Reel 'Em Inn, Meghan's lamp with a mauve tasseled shade, and Michael's overstuffed chair.

"Michael . . . I'm too old."

"Nonsense, Kate. You're forty years old. And you're born to the piano; you play all the time at the Founders' Home, at church . . ."

"For others."

"And now for yourself." Half of Michael's face smiled.

"It's too late, dear. What can I play? 'Old Folks at Home.' I'd want Chopin, the sonatas, and Liszt; oh, Michael, I'd want to play Liszt and I'd never be able to produce what I hear in my head." She held out what looked to him like perfectly good hands, long fingers, slender, strong. "My fingers, they're too old. It would take seven hours a day, and even then I'd probably not measure up." She ran her hand over the gleaming wood. "The pain of mediocrity would be too much."

"I wanted you happy, Kate."

"But I'm already happy."

THE first time Elise touched the piano keys she felt a bond, as though each key were a magnet drawing her, or as if her fingers, incomplete before, had found a wholeness, an unanticipated life. The weight of fingers on ivory keys, the press of mind, and the resulting tone opened an avenue in her formerly undiscovered, its gates locked tight, gates that had waited only for the magic of fingers on keys to tap them like the magician's wand.

She pressed a black key near the center of the keyboard and followed that with a white one high in the treble range. It rang in her. It was a glass bell. It was rain in one of Gramma Pearson's cut-glass goblets. She struck the clear high note with more force. The air vibrated around her. She vibrated, and the pleasure of it surpassed Margaret Henderson's touch and equaled the sheer gasp of delight she had felt when she was alone in the velvet-hung sanctuary of Corpus Christi Church and God had made himself a shimmering around and within her and called her his bride.

Elise Marie Pearson knew herself that day to be pure sound. She ranged, endless, through what she could know of the universe. And in later years, playing Mozart, playing Liszt, playing Schumann, Schubert, Beethoven, Chopin, Strauss, Bach, Brahms, she would remember that first day and her discovery that all music is a variation on the one divine tone at the core of being.

THE incomparable Martha Kennedy was long dead and the only piano teacher in Eagle Inlet was Emma Bergstrom, who, Kate said confidentially, of course, didn't have the talent of a titmouse. They would make the trip once a month to Bemidji—Elise, Kate, and Meghan—where the women could visit with Sister Thomas Ann and Elise could receive instruction in piano from no less than Sister Mary of the Holy Cross. She used to be Imogene von Bingen, who at nineteen had played in Carnegie Hall. If Sister Mary had not been called by God to a life of prayer and good works, she would be in New York, Paris, London, and Munich, dazzling those whose talent in life is the appreciation of genius. She would not be giving lessons to children like Elise Marie Pearson.

The nun blew into the room, a storm of energy, her veil streaming behind her, the white of her linens outlining a sharply featured face and intense eyes so dark they seemed all pupil. She reminded Elise of the bust of Beethoven in the music room at school, hair electric, eyes like thunderbolts.

"So. Show me what you can do."

Elise sat at the Steinway and Sons concert grand she later would discover had been donated to the nuns by Imogene von Bingen's parents after they lost all hope that she would return to them and to the concert stage. Her convent vocation defied understanding. They merely acquiesced and sent the piano to preserve some fragment of the life for which their daughter had prepared since she was three years old. She had sacrificed a normal childhood and adolescence to seven hours of practice every day. She had studied in Europe with the great teachers, with Wanda Landowska and Artur Schnabel, and later, at the Juilliard School of Music. How she ended up in Bemidji, a nun hidden away on the shores of some insignificant lake among Minnesota's ten thousand, must be one of the major wonders of God's work in a woman's soul.

Elise played her core note. She held it until the ringing ceased. She played it again, softly. Her heart fluttered in her throat. Again she played the note, this time with her third finger, and she held it down, feeling its pulse, hearing the complex relationship of the three strings sounding, vibrating off one another. Then she lifted her hand like a bird from a branch of the mother tree, her arm floating up, curved like the bird's wing.

"You say you are ten years old?"

"Yes, Sister."

"This is what you can play?"

"Yes."

"It is good. You have done well. Already you make beautiful music; already you understand the essence, the soul, of the one note. Now we lift that note a third, like this. Someday you will study Mozart."

THE nun worked with the child's body, teaching her how to sit, how to strengthen the muscles in her back, in her arms, in her fingers and hands. She taught her to hold her elbows out from her body while playing, not in tight against her ribs as people do when they are frightened, to protect their hearts.

"What you learn in the beginning is what you will do onstage when the lights dim over a filled hall and all is hushed as you place your fingers on the keys. Never merely exercise. Always play for beauty. Play the simplest note beautifully. You sense this. You have always sensed this. If you merely exercise, you will revert to exercise when you are onstage. Play every note as though it is the only note. Beauty, Elise, only beauty. Always."

Now the child awoke at night to the cry of music in her mind, dreams of pure sound, sound never to be reproduced on any earthly instrument, the sound of stars colliding, ringing in the sky. She dreamed she heard Chopin played by rain and Beethoven by the vol-cano's roar. Always the piano held the sound together. Always the piano brought together earth and sky, animal cries with the grinding of stone upon stone in the pounding of waves. Always the hammer from the deep innards of the piano hit strings wound taut within Elise's mind, resounded in her heart, made her skin burn until she awoke on fire with delight or in tears at the impossibility of this composition, this music of the gods.

Her small fingers struggled to produce some echo of her dreams. After school each night she ran home to her piano. She played scales and listened for the echo. She learned the études of the masters, the simple ones first, then the more advanced. She strengthened her fingers to control the tone, over and over repeat-ing movements, fingers over thumb, thumb propelling the hand gracefully, simply, powerfully, until every cell of every muscle in hand and arm contained the memory of that movement. In this compulsion toward beautiful sound, Elise lost all desire for Margaret Henderson's touch, the sweetness of which was nothing compared to music. Or perhaps that sweetness had been absorbed, along with Black Sturgeon Lake, the mother tree, the flying gulls, the wildflowers in the woods, even her awful longing for God, into an all-consuming beauty of sound. One note, expanding. The beginning and end of everything.

Only then did Elise receive the vision that, as a child, she had desired with all her heart. She was twelve years old. It was long since the time that she had learned to play Beethoven's "Für Elise," after which she had been named. Her fingers, in fact, were full of music, as full as her mind. And in her heart she carried the image of her teacher, Sister Mary of the Holy Cross, whom she considered a second mother, the one who gave her an expression for her soul.

It was April. Little patches of snow lingered along the north side of trees in the convent yard, close to Lake Bemidji, on which the ice looked black and honeycombed. The paper birch had produced buds golden and near to bursting out green. A red leaf from last fall lay trapped alongside a rock in a clear pool of water just off shore.

Kate and Meghan hadn't finished their monthly visit with Sister Thomas Ann when Sister Mary suggested that Elise go outside to think about what she told her about Juilliard. It seemed that Elise had the talent to become a concert pianist, a true artist, maybe even, someday, a composer. She ought to be in New York, at least by the time she was ready for high school. Eagle Inlet could not nurture her. Such talent required an artistic environment, required teachers, not just one day a month of teaching but teaching every day of every month all year. Music must be lived. Sister said she knew Elise realized that. Arrangements could be made. There was a scholarship, money reserved from Imogene von Bingen's inheritance, money that hadn't come to the nuns when her parents died, money for a musician to take Imogene's place if Sister Mary ever were to discover such a one. That one was Elise.

"You have a great talent. You can develop that talent, but it will mean leaving your home. It will mean constant work, eight hours a day of practice. It will steal your girlhood. It is something you must want with every fiber of your mind and heart or you will fail."

Elise's mind stretched out over the expanse of Lake Bemidji and left her body feeling weightless. Something kept her from choosing. She asked herself if she felt too young to leave home. No one she had ever known had left home before they were at least sixteen. But the question raised no fear. Was it Daddy? Mama? Was it Black Sturgeon Lake? Again, no fear. Strange to feel no fear. Until the music, fear had accompanied Elise constantly. Fear of the houseboat thing, of demons, of the empty spaces, of sin and hell and the darkness just before sleep. Now every space resounded with that one tone from which all music spins in eternal circles of sound. She found no reason to say no to Sister Mary, and yet she continued to hold back.

Just then she was aware of someone coming down the path from the direction of the convent. She looked up over her shoulder to see a woman and a man walking toward her. The woman wore a long white dress and a blue shawl. Her black hair hung loose and lifted on the breeze as she walked. The man was younger and wore a brown wool robe like that of Saint Francis in the El Greco painting that hung in Sister Thomas Ann's office. Both of them smiled.

Elise stood to meet them.

"My child," the woman said.

The man held out his hands. Elise's heart began to burn.

"Are you real?" she whispered.

"I love you," the man said to her. "Follow me."

Elise knelt in front of him and bent to kiss the hem of his brown wool robe, but when she reached for it her fingers touched nothing. She looked up. The path was empty. Last year's leaves made a hollow sound as the breeze scattered them across the stones, and from the convent tower came the deep tone of a bell calling the nuns to prayer.

⌒

At their yearly retreat the priests' housekeepers slept in narrow beds set two feet apart in a large dormitory. Each bed had white curtains drawn around it at night for privacy. For three days the women, fifty of them from around the diocese, met to pray and hear sermons that stressed virtues of service and sexual restraint. Meghan lay awake listening to the snores and sometimes the weeping of other women who guarded the secrets of their priests even at the risk of their own souls. In all the years she attended the retreat no housekeeper ever shared with her a story of love for the priest in her charge. Surely she couldn't be the only one with such love or the retreat masters wouldn't harp on it so. Womanly virtues. Patience. Restraint. Discretion. Chastity, chastity, chastity. Meghan turned on her side in the narrow bed and reached under the pillow for her rosary. The feel of the tiny bead between her thumb and forefinger steadied her. "Blessed are you among women," she whispered to the one who almost got herself stoned to death for the decision to take that blessing on.

AFTER the bishop transferred Brian Murphy out of Corpus Christi Parish to assume the duties of chaplain at Saint Vincent's Nursing Home in Crookston, Meghan couldn't keep food down for two weeks. She lost twenty pounds.

"It's like that influenza bug that missed me in nineteen nineteen finally hit," she told Kate when she could finally stomach chicken noodle soup. The Ladies' Rosary Society kept the new priest fed, kept the beds made and the dishes washed.

Brian might as well be dead like Willie, she told herself, and myself once again a widow. But no one else could know the extent of it. No one could be told. Not Kate. Certainly not Sister Thomas Ann, who seemed to have an intuition about the bond between Meghan O'Neil and Brian Murphy. But no matter what secrets Meghan confided in the nun, she seemed unable to grasp the extent of it. She couldn't have imagined in a million years the sweetness, the tenderness, of those times alone after dinner when he would invite Meghan to sit with him in the parlor, when he read poetry aloud to her or played his albums of the London Philharmonic in concert.

"Meghan" was all he said when he took her hands in his and gazed into her eyes. Willie hadn't been able to do that without wanting her in his bed the next minute. Willie never had the patience with sexual tension that a priest must develop. Brian Murphy gazed sometimes for thirty minutes and she could feel the tension build, but he never lowered it to sex. He allowed his gaze to melt her heart.

HE READ aloud the love poems of W. B. Yeats. "Listen, Meghan," he said, and his eyes shone with a glow of fire smoldering in the wood's dense core. She'd felt deliciously captured in his huge wing-backed chair. Brian had paced up and down in front of her, holding the book in his right hand like an actor auditioning at the Abbey Theatre.

> When you are old and grey and full of sleep,
> And nodding by the fire, take down this book,
> And slowly read, and dream of the soft look
> Your eyes had once, and of their shadows deep;
>
> How many loved your moments of glad grace,
> And loved your beauty with love false or true,
> But one man loved the pilgrim soul in you,
> And loved the sorrows of your changing face;
>
> And bending down beside the glowing bars,
> Murmur, a little sadly, how Love fled
> And paced upon the mountains overhead
> And hid his face amid a crowd of stars.

And so she did, often in these days, years after Brian Murphy had left her and the young John Quinn come to take his place, a place that never could be taken. Meghan often lifted from her shelf the very book of Yeats given to her by Brian the day of his departure for Saint Vincent's and read the poem, remembering.

And Meghan never told a soul about the night that Brian Murphy married her.

It was the winter of 1938. Meghan had stayed late at the rectory listening to Brian's new recording of Mozart's *Requiem*, fifteen large black disks, both sides. When the last note faded and the phonograph needle scratched against the burgundy-and-gold label, Brian rose from his chair, and as he walked to the machine he said, "You know how dear you are to me, don't you, Meghan?"

She stilled herself so profoundly she could feel the tiny pricks of the chair's upholstery on her arms.

"I've considered this long and hard. And, well, it seems to me we're more married to each other than most couples in this parish."

She stared at him. What was he saying?

"A promise between us, why, it wouldn't change a thing, except to give the heart relief."

She went that night to Hollyhock Cottage and lifted her creamy satin wedding dress from the trunk where she'd placed it, wrapped in tissue, after Willie died. She carried it back across the snowy path to Corpus Christi Rectory. All the lights in the neighborhood were out. Brian waited for her in the little winter chapel off the living room while she dressed herself in satin and secured the lace veil on her head. Then they stood together before the Blessed Sacrament, reserved in the small gold tabernacle on the chapel altar, and made their promises.

"I will love you," the priest said to her, "and will be the faithful offerer of so pure a gift. I will honor you always, so that, though our bodies can never be joined on earth, our souls will be one in heaven. This I promise as I take you, tonight, to be spouse of my soul."

"And I will love you," Meghan said, her heart pounding, "and serve you, and be faithful. I will honor you and, God willing, I will meet you in heaven." And she added, "Amen," because this act seemed more a prayer than an actual marriage vow.

He didn't kiss her. He took her hand and led her to his bedroom. Clothed in white satin, she lay beside him through the night and awoke at dawn still enfolded in his arms.

WHEN God closes a door, he opens a window. That was the old wisdom, anyway. It certainly seemed true in Meghan's case. God took Willie and gave her Brian. Then God took Brian and gave her John Quinn, who, it seemed, was a double gift because he was the age baby Michael would have been had he lived. Now she had both spouse and son because although Brian had moved, he continued to write to Meghan and she did see him once a year in his apartment at the nursing home. They kept their correspondence in locked file boxes with *To Whom It May Concern* notes affixed to the top, instructing that the contents, strictly private, be burned in the event of their deaths.

From her conversations with friends in Eagle Inlet who had lived out their lives with husbands of thirty, forty, even fifty years, Meghan judged herself to be most blessed. Brian Murphy's correspondence never lost its poetry, and his expressions of love tended to refine themselves over the years into a rare and warm beauty. It was the women whose husbands sat with them at the dinner table but rarely spoke who really were alone. Meghan could unfold last week's letter and allow its words to embrace her mind and heart. This uncommon spouse of hers was more faithful than the more common husbands of other women for whom passion had diminished as youth slipped away.

John Quinn, as was quite proper to Meghan's mind, treated her like a mother. He asked her advice about parish matters and how he ought to approach various individuals. She spoiled him as she might have spoiled Michael, had he lived. She pampered him as she never could pamper Brian for fear her passion might overcome her. But this priest was a boy, or just newly a man, and enjoyed her doting over him. He relished her cookies and her home-baked breads. He noticed the new doilies she crocheted and the afghan of granny squares she made for the end of his bed to warm his feet on cold Minnesota winter nights. He asked if he could call her Mom O'Neil, just between the two of them, of course, and she felt herself blush like a girl.

"We've both been blessed," Meghan confided to the Mother of God the following day as she sat on the garden bench at the retreat house by the Lourdes grotto. Her rosary lay idle on her lap. The lilacs were blooming late this year. The air was heavy with sweetness.

Meghan sensed that the Holy Mother's heart beat in exactly the same rhythm as her own. Life comes back, doesn't it? No matter what is lost. No matter what is taken.

⁓

At first he came while she slept. He walked through the child's dreams on rose-colored paths the likes of which she had never seen in her waking life. He walked up mountains like he must have wings. He surrounded her like wind, a gentle whirl of almost sound. He motioned to her, "Come." It was not a word so much as a swell of water off Black Rock Beach. It rose from nothing, like rain from the calm of a summer afternoon. She followed him.

He took her into caves where lepers sat keening. He kissed them, and faces reappeared where at first there had been shadows. Fingers blossomed from fleshy stumps and on them delicate shells of pearl. She followed him where children danced in circles and church bells laughed in the morning air. He showed her everything. Wars and shattered hearts. Women in an ecstasy of love. She witnessed the first strokes of color on an artist's white canvas and felt in her chest the first tones of a new song as if she were strings on which invisible fingers played.

She went with him to secluded places. She walked where no paths were, among the wildflowers, into the woods. They sat on moss under a tamarack tree. His thoughts passed directly into her mind from his. His thoughts penetrated her as light into the depth of Black Sturgeon Lake. He called her "beloved." He called her "my bride."

He showed her all that she would leave behind. She saw her babies cradled in her arms, felt their heartbeats against her own, smelled their milky warmth. "Whoever is not willing to leave her land, her mother and father, her husband and children, and come to me, is not worthy of me." So that was how it was. She looked into his eyes. "Will you be with me always?" she seemed to ask.

"I am with you always, even unto the end of the world." And again he did not speak in words but as a hawk cries in the early dawn over a ripening field of wheat.

These might be dreams but she felt them, nonetheless, to be real. At times, when he left her like mists inhaled off the lake's surface at midmorning, she thought she had not slept at all. She opened her eyes. "He was just here," she whispered to herself. "I could have reached out. I could have touched him."

She began to attend mass each morning. She thought she could go from the sanctuary of her dream to the dream of the sacrament. She believed she could take him into her body, infuse her cells with his flesh. She matched the priest's Latin to the English translation in her missal. "I will go unto the altar of God," he prayed and she prayed. The priest ascended three steps to the altar. Three steps to heaven, where the angels carried the prayers like incense to the throne of God. She placed herself in their hands. She felt lifted up.

A question haunted her, one she dared not ask. Can people fall in love with God?

After a while she sensed him everywhere. She didn't see him. It never was that clear. Not since that first time, on the convent path.

But he left traces of himself in everyone and everything. He played hide-and-seek with her. He summoned her with the cry of gulls.

She remained a child doing all that children do. She learned to apply lipstick. She played with dolls. She rode her bicycle to the edge of town. She learned which boys could be trusted. She sat on the rocks where the Eagle River turned to white water that obliterated her thoughts with its roar. She practiced her piano. Music became the language she spoke back to God.

The convent was God's home in this world. The priests taught this truth. The convent was God's keyhole, a magical place from which, once you entered there, you could be transported anywhere in heaven or on earth. It was a constant dream of walking down a path with God. If God cried, "Come," it was to the convent you must go.

XI

The music
will reveal you to yourself.

SISTER MARY'S MUSIC NOTEBOOKS, 1953

Kate banged the cupboard door. She was alone, what did it matter? Who could hear? Elise didn't eat a thing for breakfast. Fresh strawberries, toast just the way she liked it. Turned up her adolescent nose. And this one wanted to enter the convent! Not a chance. And no way Kate would let her go. No siree! Thirteen years old she'd been this March! Good heavens. Taking a child away from her mother at thirteen. Just a baby.

And what was this nonsense about Jesus and Mary? Imagination. That was all it was. If Jesus and Mary appeared they'd tell her to practice her piano. Jesus was no fool. And Mary was a mother herself. Thirteen!

Kate dumped the strawberries out of the dish into the garbage can under the sink. A flicker of thought: You could have put them in the fridge. But she wanted to murder them. Same with the toast. She opened the back door and threw it to the birds. A flock of crows swooped on it as though they knew her secrets and had been waiting.

Hell with the nuns, a voice in her head screamed. God damn them all to bloody hell! She gasped. Elise's glass of milk slipped from her hand onto the linoleum and shattered. Kate stood in a mess of milk and glass. Milk soaked through the soles of her bedroom slippers. She lifted her hands to her head and pressed her fists against her temples. "I didn't mean it," she sobbed just in case anyone was listening.

"GIRLS outgrow it," Meghan assured her. Every Catholic girl thinks she wants to enter a convent. Girls are romantic creatures, and what could be more romantic than the cloister, than being a bride of Christ, for heaven's sake? Girls are mesmerized by the long dress, the flowing veil; they think every day will be their wedding day. "Don't worry, honey. Pretty soon she'll notice the boys. You won't be hearing talk about the convent then."

Besides all this there was the piano. One of these days Elise would notice that Imogene von Bingen was accompanying the sisters while they sang "Holy God, We Praise Thy Name," not performing Chopin's Sonata no. 3 in B Minor at Carnegie Hall.

Best that Kate have a word or two with Sister Thomas Ann when they visited in May. *Mother* Thomas Ann. The nuns had made her their mistress of novices, put the young ones in her charge.

"SHE insists that God is calling her, Mother Thomas Ann."

"That may be, Kate."

The three women sat on formal, high-backed chairs in the convent parlor. The room smelled of wax with just a faint edge of incense. The incense penetrated everything, especially the clothes of the nun. Sweet and mildly sickening, it unsettled Kate's stomach like slightly turned milk.

"But she's only thirteen."

"God has been known to call even younger girls than your Elise."

"How can we be sure? You don't know her imagination, Mother."

The nun smiled. "It really isn't for us to decide, now, is it, Kate? If this desire is not of God it will pass long before the time comes for Elise to seek out a religious community. She needs to be at least fifteen."

"Please don't take offense, Mother Thomas Ann, but if all this is just her imagination, I'd as soon she got herself under control as quickly as possible. I don't want her hurt."

"Hurt?"

"What if she gives up her music?"

"What if she does?"

"But she can't be happy without her music, Mother."

"Can you know that, Kate?"

Kate made her face impassive in order not to reveal the shadow she felt passing over her heart.

After a few moments, Mother Thomas Ann spoke quietly. "You could test her."

"Test her?"

"Yes. You could see if she has the strength of character necessary for convent life. Also, Elise's willingness to undergo such a test would give you a fairly accurate indication of the strength of her resolve."

"How do I do this?"

MOTHER Thomas Ann outlined a strict regime intended either to prepare Elise for convent life or to discourage her from the pursuit of her desires. Mass at seven-thirty every morning and no sleeping late on weekends. A daily schedule that would include precise and unchangeable times for study, chores, piano practice, and recreation alone or with friends. No boyfriends. Perfect obedience to her parents and teachers. No reading of romance novels. Only movies rated A-1 by the Legion of Decency, and among them no romance movies. As daily penance there would be no snacks between meals and she would require herself to drink the first water that came from the tap, lukewarm.

The nun assured Kate that if Elise agreed to these conditions and devoted herself to practicing them for a year, then the girl probably did have a religious vocation. Most likely, though, Elise would immediately reject the test and return to the task of growing up like any other girl her age.

⌒

"Today, I play for you," Sister Mary placed her hand over Elise's, which had just collapsed on the piano keys. "You sit over there." She motioned to the antique walnut bench set at an angle to her piano, from which Elise would have the best view of the nun's fingers.

"Key signature tells you of the music's soul. We will spend the hour with A minor, with Mozart, Brahms, Rachmaninoff, and Chopin, and you will feel how A minor winds an intricate path through human sorrow."

The nun rummaged through her collection of musical scores until she found the ones she wanted.

"Do not let yourself be fooled by the absence of sharps and flats into thinking that this music is written in the key of C. Appearances deceive, *Liebling*. When sorrow is immense, the way through it is simple but not easy. It is as if the composer's sorrow prevented him from raising his fingers to the black keys. He needed the stability of the white keys, the closeness they have to one another, the nearness to his body. And yet he requires himself with each note, each phrase, to move through the sorrow. It is what must be done, child. If we are not willing to move through the sorrow, beauty will be lost, art will be lost, soul will be lost. There is no other way. So it is. A minor."

Elise watched Sister Mary's fingers. She noticed the way the tips, over the years, had been shaped to her art, grown outward slightly, flat and padded where they touched the keys. Her own fingers, still soft and pointed at the tips, had not yet grown pads. She wondered if they would.

"Now, Mozart's Rondo in A Minor, KV511."

Sister Mary opened the music and scanned the notes. "That boy"—she smiled and shook her head—"that poor boy."

"Mozart?"

"Yes, *Liebling*. A boy with an ancient soul. He finished the Rondo in Vienna on March eleventh, in seventeen eighty-seven, the same year his father died. It was a time of much death for him. Friends died. Young men. All of them young. Mozart also was young, not just to meet up with death at every turn but to write such things, to feel what must be felt."

The tiny muscles in Sister Mary's face accompanied the music her fingers produced. Her head tossed back and forth in what seemed an agonized movement. Her whole body became the music, was one thing with the piano. Then Elise lost track of the piano, of the nun's body, of the room, of all of it as being separate from what she herself was. For an hour the composers, Sister Mary, the music, and Elise were one movement through sorrow.

"Thank you, Sister," Elise whispered when the music stopped.

"Now you have A minor." The nun took her hands and looked at her as if she knew the secret that Elise had decided to keep from everyone. "You will feel better now."

LAST week, when her mother had explained the convent preparation plan, Elise felt a pain in her stomach as though she had eaten something disgusting. She tried to swallow and couldn't. Her mother asked her what she thought. Could she agree to those things? But Elise only stared at her. She searched her mind for something to say and found nothing. She turned and walked out of the house, paying no attention to her mother, who was calling her name. She walked the seven blocks to Corpus Christi Church, thinking she was actually on her way there, to sit in the velvet-draped calm under the red sanctuary lamp, but she walked right past. She ended up by the water, where the inlet opens toward Black Sturgeon Lake, where swallows build nests in the clay banks.

How easily a person's world could fray, like a braid undone.

She sat in a nest of lake grass and picked the long stems one by one. Gramma Meghan used to make rings of grass. Almost unconsciously Elise began to select grasses for Mama, Gramma Meghan, Gramma and Grampa Pearson, and, of course, Daddy. Sister Mary ought to be included, and Jesus, and last of all herself. She braided them and joined them in a ring, careful to secure each end, and then she sat staring out over the water until the sun set.

"WHERE were you?" her father wanted to know.

She glanced at the kitchen table. Her plate of food looked pasty. A thick puddle of grease surrounded her pork chop.

"Oh, around."

"Around? That's no answer, Elise. What were you doing?"

"I don't know."

"We waited for you. Supper got cold. We worried, Elise." Such statements of fact were her mother's way of inquiring.

Elise kept silent.

"Answer me."

"What did you ask?"

"Where were you?"

"I told you, just around."

"Well, you'll have to eat cold food."

"I'm not hungry." Her stomach felt full of rocks.

THERE were things that could be told and things that couldn't. Until she figured out which was which, it would be better to keep quiet. She had told her mother about the vision of Mary and Jesus on the convent path. She told her last April, the night after it happened, when Kate came to sit on the bed before Elise went to sleep, observing the ritual developed years before when the mother still read the daughter fairy tales at bedtime. Once the child had learned to read for herself, they spent this time sharing secrets of the day.

"It must have been people visiting one of the nuns," her mother had attempted to explain.

"No, Mama, because they disappeared when I knelt down."

"Then it was your imagination."

"No, because he talked to me. They were real."

"Remember the monster in the houseboat?"

"But Jesus and Mary were real, and Jesus wants me to be his bride. Mama, I want to enter the convent in Bemidji."

"That's lovely, dear. Perhaps someday."

"No, I want to go as soon as they will have me—in my freshman year."

"That seems awfully young. We'll talk more about this later."

But the next time they spoke it was a year later, after all her dreams, after she knew without a doubt. And then her mother spoke only about convent preparation rules. A trick. A trick to turn her away from what Jesus wanted.

THAT evening on the bank of the inlet at sunset, Elise had felt the fraying of her mother from the weave of her life. Sister Mary made a better mother. The tree, even, was preferable to Kate Pearson. She gathered herself in, wrapping her hopes in silence, braiding her loves into a ring so frail she would, during the next five years, almost forget she hoped for or loved anything at all. Were it not for the piano, she herself might have disappeared altogether.

WHEN she was fourteen, Elise learned Chopin's Waltz in A Minor and Sister Mary told Kate that the family really needed to consider sending the child to New York to study with Klaus Vonderhorne.

She would arrange it; she knew him personally. He needed to hear such interpretation as this in one so young; such longing, such a fine restraint, yet a dance.

When Elise played Chopin she felt her soul in her fingertips. She played the Impromptu no. 3 in G-flat Major and the music transformed her into a spirit woman. The ghost of a nun from past times possessed her. Teresa of Avila, perhaps Claire, maybe even the vivid Héloïse. Any one of them contained the music like a flame is contained on a candlewick. The music took her to the convent in her mind. In music's spell Elise lived her dream of God. But she wouldn't go to New York.

Elise's decision made little sense to anyone.

"It would be selfish of us to hold you back from such an opportunity." Her mother's face had smiled. Her mother's eyes had glistened. Her father's face looked calm; one side almost matched the other, except for the tears that always collected in the cup of flesh under his left eye.

Elise did understand that she could go. She could leave Eagle Inlet. She could study Chopin and Mozart and Beethoven. She could eventually play in Carnegie Hall.

"I want to stay here and study with Sister Mary."

"But, darling." Her mother looked suddenly stricken. "This is the chance of a lifetime! Sister Mary is wonderful, to be sure, but Klaus Vonderhorne! It's what we've always dreamed of. Don't waste this, Elise."

"It's your dream."

"It's your talent. Don't waste your talent, Elise."

"I'm not wasting anything."

"You are too young to understand."

"When I was thirteen you said I was too young to go to the convent, and now, just one year later, you want me to go to New York. Did I grow up overnight, or what?"

"This is different."

"It's not."

Her mother turned and walked out of the room.

Elise didn't look at her father. His eyes would shatter her heart.

Michael watched Elise from behind his newspaper. She hadn't said much to either him or Kate in the months that had elapsed since the standoff over the convent versus Juilliard. At least she was home. What a mystery she was; he could hardly believe she came from him. Maybe every adolescent girl is like this and you don't notice it all that much until you have one of your own. At this moment she seemed unaware he occupied the same room with her, engrossed as she was in examining Christmas ornaments, lifting them one by one from the cardboard box he'd brought in from the garage and set in the middle of the living room floor.

He tried to remember when she'd begun to change toward him. He preferred to think the distance he felt from her hadn't begun until the argument between her and her mother. He'd attempted to stay out of that. Of course, he'd wanted her home, right here where he could watch her, protect her. But he feared an increase of the distance that, if he was going to be honest, began opening between Elise and him years ago. Elise began to lean out from him, and he couldn't fathom when exactly it started or why. It must have been a breath of difference, that first leaning away, subtle as the breeze from a bird's wing on a quiet summer day. Afterward you can't say for sure such a thing has happened. Or, even if you could say, you can't believe it could matter.

It might have been when the three of them started visiting the convent. Dorothy asked him then why he was allowing that additional Catholic influence, as if there were a thing he could do to stop it. There must be other piano teachers, she had insisted. But, of course, there weren't. In Winnipeg, maybe. In Fargo or Grand Forks. None of them as close as Bemidji, and no teacher with the genius of that nun. Anyway, if the convent was the key, he had to take the blame. He'd brought the piano into the house in the first place.

You never know what's going to come of what you do.

He put his newspaper down on his lap and looked at her full on. She'd gathered her long black hair up into a ponytail that swished over her shoulder every time she reached deep into the box. These women of his sure loved Christmas! Meghan, Kate, Elise, all of them. This year he ought to buy Chanel No. 5 for Elise, too. His own father gave it as a gift each year to his mother, and he'd taken up the tradition as soon as he returned from the war, giving it on Christmas Eve to both Kate and Meghan. Now Elise was becoming a woman. Fifteen next spring. It was time he added her to the list. He'd give it to her along with the necklace he'd found at Emerson's Jewelry. The necklace was silver, a bird, all wingspan, reminiscent of the crescent moon and of that pet gull of hers.

Likely it was nothing, this distance he felt. Probably girls just had to do this as they grew up.

This year he'd cut their balsam fir from the stand out by Black Rock Beach. It was one he'd eyed for a few years, waiting for it to develop to exactly the right size. Always before, Elise came with him. Not this time. He'd asked her like usual, but she had other things to do. He didn't ask her what other things. He just went out alone. He trudged knee deep in snow, through the paper birches on the hill, down into the gully where the firs grew. Snowflakes drifted. He thought how she would love it. The silence. The breathless winter. One side of his face received the snow's kiss. The other side felt nothing. The other side stayed always cold. Dead. He'd never gotten used to that numbness.

Perhaps that was it. Perhaps Elise had come, with age, to see him again as he really was.

"Daddy?"

So she did know he was in the same room!

"Yes, Peanut?"

"Will you help me put up the mistletoe?"

"Sure. You want it in the usual place?"

"Right in the doorway so people can't help but walk under it."

"And what people might those be?"

"You know, you and Mama and me and—"

"I suppose you'll be inviting all your boyfriends in."

"Daddy!"

"Well, Peanut, we could invite your friends for caroling. You could play the piano and your mama could serve Tom and Jerrys, without the rum and brandy, of course, and that way the ol' mistletoe could get a good workout."

"But there aren't any boys I want to kiss."

"No?"

"You know I want to go to the convent, Daddy."

So she had decided to invite him into this world of hers after all. It was a foreign place with a language he could never hope to learn.

"That's a hard one for me, Peanut." He fingered the mistletoe. It was last year's, dry and brittle, preserved in a cellophane bag and tied with a red ribbon. "Really, Elise, I'm afraid I don't understand why you want to do this. All this Catholic stuff, you know; it can get pretty strange for me."

She looked away from him, down at the box of ornaments.

"I just need to, that's all."

How could a man like him engender a daughter like her?

"Daddy?"

"Yes, Peanut?"

"Daddy, why did you go to war?"

So it was his face after all. He knew how her school friends glanced at him. She would be noticing that, now that she was an adolescent. Maybe she was embarrassed, even ashamed of having a father who was scarred.

"What do you mean?"

"Mama used to tell me you went to war so that the children in Europe could have bread. I imagined you like Santa Claus with a bag full of bread, and all the soldiers had those bags. Up and down the roads you went, putting warm rolls into the hands of children who ran out to meet you."

"It wasn't like that."

"I know."

"You've studied the war in school?"

"No. I knew the minute you came home."

"My face?"

"Yes."

She reached her hand toward him and touched his ruined cheek just as she had done when he first arrived at Union Depot.

"I love you even more than if you looked like every other dad."

He never told her why he went to war and she didn't explain what drew her to the convent. Perhaps, he reasoned, neither of them knew.

THAT night in bed he moved close to Kate and took her in his arms.

"Michael?"

"I'm so sorry, Kate. I didn't understand."

"Understand what?"

"I thought you couldn't want me this way."

Was she breathing? All he could hear was his heartbeat.

"Kate?"

"It was my fault."

"No, Kate. I leaned away."

"I always want you, Michael, even when I'm distant. But it's hard for me. I don't know how to show you. I haven't known since . . . well, since we were children. Maybe then, for a moment, I knew how."

Could she be remembering the night on Rainbow Island when they made love for the first time and she ran away? Now she reached to him and touched his face.

"They wounded you."

"Yes."

"I'm wounded, too."

He kissed her then and tasted her tears. Her tears fell on his ruined face like rain on shriveled ground, and he could almost feel them fall.

XII

You can train your fingers to produce each nuance.

You can form your mind according to the intricacies of the score,

but to bring forth the music itself,

there is nothing you can do.

SISTER MARY'S MUSIC NOTEBOOKS, 1956

"I ordered it from Schmitt's. Can I learn to play it?"

Sister Mary of the Holy Cross watched as Elise reached into her music bag and pulled out a blue-covered copy of the Rondo in A Minor.

"Ah, the Verlag *Urtext*. Well done, *Liebling*."

The girl had been campaigning to learn the composition since the day she first heard it, three years ago. True, she was maturing, both as an artist and a young woman, but even at fifteen she had no idea what such a piece would require of her. Sister Mary opened the cover and smoothed the first page of music with her hand before setting it on the piano.

"It isn't too difficult. I've already learned much harder."

"You think so, do you?"

"You don't agree?"

"Mozart's simplicity is deceptive, Elise. You probably already sat down at home and sight-read it; am I right?"

"Yes. But I know that's not anywhere near enough."

"You do have the technical competence, true. But you are right, it's not anywhere near enough."

"What will it take, Sister?"

That she could ask the question stood as proof that she wasn't ready.

"Years, *Liebling*."

"What?"

"It is because life is needed, *Liebling*. Life. Life is what turns us, lifts us up, takes and gives all in one sweeping movement. The fingers can only reproduce what the soul has become. Five years, perhaps. More likely ten. Maybe your entire life. Can you give that much?"

"I'll give whatever it takes."

The girl had no idea. None. How like an adolescent. Well, Mozart may have felt much the same way before death entered his life as the dominant theme. Perhaps one ought to begin such music when still a child or one might not begin at all.

"Very well, then. It is A minor, of course, and begins on E. What does that tell you?"

"The fifth."

"Yes. This is why you are drawn to it. Can you imagine why?"

Elise let herself hear the progression of notes, let herself feel as she always felt when listening to this piece. An aching. A longing so intense she had no words to communicate it.

"The fifth is incomplete; it needs resolution."

"Exactly. It is a longing for home, for the center point, the open stability, where the movement is anchored. And in this composition what is that point?"

Of course. No wonder she loved it.

"It's A. My core note."

"Aha! There. You see?"

Sister Mary sat beside Elise on the piano bench. She played a few measures.

"Listen to the boy, *Liebling*. Just listen. It is a confession. It is intimate. It is light and frolics like the child he still is, but underneath is the inevitable, the footstep of grief. Such an irony life has."

"What you expect is never what happens."

"Exactly. And yet the entire composition is an extension of what you hear in the first phrase. Each time through the musical theme, the sigh is extended. Finally, you say, this will be the end. But the resolution does not come. Grief is tightened like a screw. Time and time again the sigh extends and reaches on, all the way to the end. And even then, even when the final note has died away, you know that with just a subtle turn it will begin once more."

Sister Mary went back to the beginning and played the first turn.

"The way you treat this first turn, *Liebling*, tells the tale. You have either lived the music or you have not. Attention to detail in life is the measure of your willingness to live fully. If you are just trying to get to the end, to the final note, you will overlook the elegance, the slight lingering on the E before it is resolved in the A. And you will have missed the very thing that could have turned your heart."

She rose from the piano, bowed deeply from the waist, and smiled at her family, who, with Sister Mary, were sitting in the front row of the concert hall for her sophomore recital. This March she had turned sixteen. Her fifteenth year had passed with no mention of entering the convent. Perhaps they all assumed her convent desires had dissolved, but what really happened to those desires, she could not articulate in words. They went into the music, just like everything went into the music, but not to be obliterated. Music intensified desire.

The other girls, girls like Margaret Henderson, measured their desires by the boys they dated. Now and then Elise wondered if she could be like them, like Margaret, lying on the soft grass with a boy, murmuring secrets in the backseat of the car. In April, Margaret started dating Jeremy Walker. Jeremy, with his large hazel eyes and the eyelashes Mama said God ought to have given to a girl if there were any justice in this world.

A week after the recital Margaret visited her at the inn. The summer tourist season had begun, and bleached white sheets from the cabins flapped in the wind like giant snow geese wings. Elise stuck a wooden clothespin down over the folded corner of cloth and fed what remained of the sheet through her fingers, pinning it three more times along its length to the clothesline. Margaret leaned against a birch tree. She picked the long grass that grew next to the trunk, extracting the sweet white core from its sheath, then twirling it in her mouth, between her teeth, before she bit it off.

"He kissed me, Elise. Finally." Margaret traced the grass's delicate tassel down the curve of her neck toward the rise of her young breasts.

Elise felt her heart quicken. "What was it like?"

"Sweet."

"But what was it really like?"

"Like he took my breath."

Elise pictured a silver moth fluttering over her own lips.

Margaret continued to trace the contour of her breast with the feather of grass. "Next I'm going to get him to touch my breasts. Maybe even kiss me there."

"Margaret!"

"No, really. That's as far as I'll go, though. I heard Bonnie Jackson lets boys go all the way."

The moth fluttered down Elise's body and she shivered.

"That's a sin, Margaret."

"It's all a sin, Elise. One big delicious sin!"

DELICIOUS or not, sin didn't attract her. She was attracted by desire. She had noticed Jeremy's eyes, of course. Who hadn't? She had imagined this boy or that one holding her as if she were a fragile bird's wing. She had never forgotten Margaret's touch, and sometimes at night while drifting off to sleep, she could feel those fingers reaching up between her legs and could imagine that a boy was doing this to her. Then her heart beat violently and her body throbbed. Such things must be told to Father Quinn in confession. The telling flushed her cheeks with shame despite the priest's gentle voice and his assurances that a girl's imagination sometimes cannot be controlled. God understands the efforts we must make at sublimation. These are temptations, not sin, and she was a strong girl and would not act on them.

The priest gave her a copy of *The Tidings Brought to Mary*. "What man understands a woman?" says Mara of her husband. Then Elise read the words of Violaine, the leper who had sacrificed everything for the love of God. "Happy is she who can be known, heart and soul, who can give herself utterly."

Margaret could have Jeremy or any other boy. Elise had God. She would be the bride of Christ and marry the divine bridegroom every day of her life, in every prayer she said and in every note played by her fingers on the keys.

Christ would be the silver moth upon her lips. Christ, who

entered her like the first soft light of morning. Christ, whose voice washed like waves on Black Rock Beach. Christ, shelter of the mother tree. Christ, in whose heart her own heart beat. Christ, who knew her thoughts. Christ, who cradled every desire she'd ever had as though it were his own child. "I will come to you," she prayed each night, no matter what erupted in her poor human body. "I will be yours."

ELISE practiced the rondo. In every turn, her fingers making the intricate transition from the E of desire to the A where desire came to rest, she could feel the draining from her heart of something both necessary and impossible.

ONE year later Elise played that rondo in her recital, stringing each note against the previous one like a pearl precisely larger, a perfectly graded sphere of tone. She spiraled through the aching refrain, each time initiated by a different sequence, each refrain a drink of some liquor that seeped farther along neural paths to deeper and more secret sources of desire. Loss, she felt, was endless. Her left hand picked up the haunting, then her right hand again, pianissimo, almost not a sound at all, the final chord an intake of breath, and silence.

⁓

"You have matured, *Liebling*." Sister Mary kissed Elise lightly on both cheeks and poised herself to contain the emotion that now filled her whenever Elise performed. For the sake of this talent, nothing must be allowed to come between teacher and student, particularly not emotion. The passion for music could too easily be misdirected toward the musician, creating the illusion of love. Such was the danger in which they worked. The responsibility belonged to her, as teacher, to focus the passion and keep it pure.

"You are pleased with the rondo?"

"I am pleased, yes. And you, *Liebling*, are you pleased also?"

Elise leaned against the back of the chair in Sister Mary's studio and closed her eyes. "I think so."

"You think so? You aren't sure?"

"I'm not sure of anything anymore, Sister. My life feels all blurry. I listen to myself play and don't know what's good and what isn't."

Such a confusing time adolescence could be. It was during her own adolescence that Sister Mary relied so heavily upon her music notebooks, a practice she had continued right to the present day. In them she recorded what she learned of the process of music, its mystery, its similarity to her other passions. Over the years her entries seemed to have become a metaphor for life. Now it occurred to her that what she had written to help herself might be of some solace to Elise as well.

"Let me show you something, *Liebling*."

The pages in the oldest notebook had yellowed and the ink had faded to a dusky brown. She was so young, not even ten, and the words must have been those of her teacher, as they were far too sophisticated for a child. The later words, the aphorisms, questions, even bits of wisdom, all were her own.

She watched Elise turn the pages with such care. She saw the girl's eyes fill with tears. She heard her catch her breath.

"Oh, Sister. This is so like myself."

"We meet in the music, *Liebling*."

"Why do we have to give so much?"

"It is the nature of our passion. It is the requirement of life itself. There is no other way."

"It's so hard!"

"It rends the heart and transforms the soul. But you are already doing it, Elise. You have played the rondo."

Sister Mary looked down at her hands. Could it be that her own talent and every skill and wisdom she'd acquired over all the years had brought her to this moment, to this focus on one girl? Could God be so prodigal with his blessings? She nearly laughed aloud. All the gifts she thought were hers, God meant for her to pass them on. She looked up at Elise and smiled. In giving her gifts away to this girl, she'd received the greatest gift of all.

XIII

When mind is still,
poised like a bird at the edge of flight,
the music will be air
and you will become the music.

SISTER MARY'S MUSIC NOTEBOOKS, 1958

Who could have believed the end would come so quickly? Years of recitals and of crescent moons floating over the lake like wings carried her forward in her life while seeming to circle back, each time, to the place she had begun. Now she was graduated from high school and about to begin again, inside a different circle, a circle strange and new.

She opened the black steamer trunk and arranged her music on top of her convent trousseau. Such a strange assortment. Black cotton stockings, men's white linen handkerchiefs, old-fashioned petticoats and pantaloons, enormous white granny nightgowns in flannel and seersucker. Gramma Pearson had wrapped a silver place setting from her wedding sterling. "You should have something old, something treasured. Like a bride." Another package contained bedding with the Reel 'Em Inn emblem embroidered in forest green. All would go with her, convent necessities cushioning Chopin, Beethoven, Schubert, Schumann, Bach, Brahms, Liszt, Strauss, and lastly Mozart.

This is the last time I will sleep in this bed, Elise thought as she settled her head back onto the pillow. It was the thought that had accompanied everything for over a month. This is the last time I'll see the lake in the moonlight, or wear a swimming suit. It's the last time I'll eat supper with my parents in this house, the last time I will listen to rock 'n' roll, or see a movie. She slipped her fingers from bead to bead of Brian Murphy's pearl rosary, but she couldn't fall asleep.

She felt as if she were trying to get to the other side of some-thing. She was like one of the frogs with delicate bones who couldn't resist crossing the road between the woods and the lake all those years ago when she was a child and wept to see them in the head-lights of her father's car. It was just past midnight. She slipped out of bed, dressed, and tiptoed out of the house.

Air off the lake silkened the night. She took her father's car and drove through the darkness to Black Rock Beach. Here the wind blew stronger, riling the waters, dashing waves against the stones. She left the car and walked in the complete darkness toward the sound. Even in daylight the lake's other shore could not be seen, but now, in a night without a moon, the waters seemed to come toward her out of an infinity the source of which she could never reach. She could hear no music in this sound. She sat down in the lake grass at the water's edge and sifted the sand through her fingers. Her hand closed around a stone, rounded and smoothed by the waves since ancient times. She felt its solid weight in her palm, and for a reason she could not articulate, this calmed her heart. She sat there, saying good-bye, until the first glint of morning delineated the foam on the lake's surface, and when she turned to leave, the spray from the waves couldn't be distinguished from her tears.

Elise lifted her teacup. It was the bone china one Gramma Meghan had given her, the one with the delicate rose pattern brought from Ireland. Gramma let her use it for their tea parties, and then gave it to her as a birthday gift when she was thirteen. This is the last time I will drink from this cup, she thought, involuntarily, and was sud-denly light-headed. Her fingers let go of the cup and it crashed into her breakfast strawberries, splashing tea all over the buttered toast, and breaking in two.

"Oh!" she cried as bitterness rose into her throat. She pushed back from the table to run into the bathroom, where her stomach turned and she vomited bile. Then she cried.

Kate stood in the bathroom door, her face pale, her pink chenille bathrobe hanging crooked, her hair not combed yet. Elise wanted to crawl inside her mother, become a comma in her womb. Kate reached out and Elise collapsed against her.

"It's not too late," Kate murmured. "You don't have to go."

She caressed her daughter's long hair.

"But I do. I can't help it."

A wild thing took her; it ran around inside her head, bumping into walls; it spread its wings; it soared, crashed into a ceiling, fell, rose, and crashed again.

"I have to go."

She tore herself from her mother's arms and ran out the door.

The night after senior music competitions, when her mother still was gleaming with pride over the superior rating, Elise finally told her parents that Mother Thomas Ann had accepted her request to enter the Sisters of Our Lady of Peace.

"You're sure?"

"Yes, Mama."

"Then I suppose you have to do it."

No argument. Her father said nothing.

But this wasn't as she had imagined her entrance day. She had expected to feel joy like the sweet breath of Christ. At the very least God could show some satisfaction with her sacrifice. So, where was he? Saint Thérèse of the Child Jesus hadn't felt this way. She found peace on her entrance day.

Downtown, Elise took Main Street to Sam's barbershop. The thing in her head was screaming, Cut your hair, cut it, cut it, cut it. She sat in line on one of the straight-backed wooden chairs. Also waiting were old Wallace Monroe, who must be nearing a hundred years, along with his basset hound sleeping at his feet, and nine-year-old Timmy Johnson, who fidgeted.

"Mornin', Meghan," Wallace croaked.

"I'm Elise." She smiled.

"You thinkin' to cut that lovely hair?" His thick eyebrows scowled.

"I'm on my way to the convent." As if that explained it.

"Shame. My Clara, nuns got her, too. Damn shame."

Sam brushed the hair off the collar of Elmer Olsen and flicked the large grayish cape in the air, scattering little nests of hair and dust across the rough wooden floor.

"Your turn, Wallace," Sam announced as Elmer regarded himself in the mirror and reached in his hip pocket for his wallet.

Wallace hobbled to the chair. The basset opened one eye and closed it again. Timmy's foot wiggled, making the floorboards creak. Sam's radio blared "The Great Pretender."

"Sorry, but I'm in a bit of a hurry," Elise mumbled, and escaped out the door.

At noon she would leave Eagle Inlet to enter the convent. She'd packed her trunk. The two thousand dollars in war bonds, her dowry, was tucked into her purse to be given to Mother Thomas Ann that afternoon. She'd signed the papers. The Sisters of Our Lady of Peace had accepted her request to become one of them. There was no turning back. Why, she was practically a nun already.

Elise walked home. The nuns could cut her hair when the time came.

HER father loaded the steamer trunk into the back of Gramma Dorothy's station wagon that had REEL 'EM INN written in square black letters on each door. Everyone was coming to Bemidji for the entrance ceremony, a caravan, Grampa and Gramma Pearson in the station wagon, and Michael, Kate, Gramma Meghan, and Elise behind them in the '52 Olds. One hundred thirty miles, the end of the earth.

"Are you feeling better, dear?" Kate searched the eyes of her daughter.

Elise smiled. Her heart was a stone in her throat, but the rushing in her head had ceased.

"Good. Go get ready, then."

THE empty space under her bedroom window where the steamer trunk had stood for six weeks reminded Elise of the hole left by an extracted tooth. She shook her head to clear it. In her closet hung the red Mexican dancing dress with white lace ruffles that she'd worn to the farewell party at the Moose Lodge the previous Saturday night. Boys had lined up to dance with her, twirling her to Elvis's "Hound Dog," whipping the skirt a wide circle around her body. At the end everyone sang "Auld Lang Syne."

She took the dress off its hanger and slipped it over her head.

She stood in the center of the room and looked at everything. She stamped each image indelibly upon her mind. Her music awards, framed and hanging all over one wall. The wicker rocking chair, in which she had been rocked to sleep, read to, comforted after nightmares. At the last minute she picked up the stone from Black Rock Beach and slipped it into her rosary pouch alongside the black nun's beads that replaced Brian Murphy's pearl ones.

Outside, the family waited.

"Darling"—her mother raised an eyebrow—"isn't that dress a little . . ."

"Oh, leave the girl alone." Gramma Meghan laughed and gathered Elise into her arms. "No sense plucking the feathers till you kill the chicken, right, sweetheart?" And then whispered, "I'm so proud of you, honey, so proud."

Later she would remember snapshots of the day, the way she laid her silver gull-wing necklace in her father's hand and said, "Keep this for me." He nodded, his face solemn on both sides. She would remember touching the ruined side, which had turned leathery over the years, and then standing on tiptoe to kiss his fallen cheek. God hadn't fixed this face, despite her First Communion prayer.

She would see her mother's bra strap hanging out from under her dress as they climbed the stairs to the chapel. "Fix your strap," she had whispered just before Mother Thomas Ann whisked her away to the front pew to sit with the other postulants. After the ceremony the families had been ushered out.

Fix your strap! What difference did it make? A bra strap hanging. So what? Had she known then that when the ceremony was over her family would be gone, she might have said I love you. She might have said good-bye.

XIV

Play the music
from the chamber of your heart, in which is protected
a secret and different self.

SISTER MARY'S MUSIC NOTEBOOKS, 1958

Mother Thomas Ann rose that morning to the sound of the bell. She bound her breasts in muslin sewn with a curved French seam. She bound her head in linen bleached white as altar cloths. It was the rule. She draped white cotton and thick black wool over her body, once golden as lake grass and ripe grain, paled now as marble in the convent wall. Upon her head she pinned two veils, the long one to hide those eyes still yearning to see the world. She pulled her cincture tight around her waist.

Since the baptism of her goddaughter, Mother Thomas Ann had prepared herself. Eighteen years of prayer, restraint, refinement of affections, readied her for this day on which her motherhood would be fulfilled. Finally Elise would come to her, would find her rightful home.

Five years ago, when Kate first told her of the child's intentions to enter the Convent of Our Lady of Peace, she held her tongue. Naturally she wanted to say yes. But a deeper instinct reined her in. The girl was only thirteen. She might have developed resentments later, wondering what she had missed. Eighteen was the perfect age, two years older than she herself had been when she first submitted her will to the rule, her soul to the gospels, and her life to her sisters. Her heart was a different matter. Every day she bound her heart as she bound her breasts.

She had no mirror in her room, nor would she have gazed into it had there been one. She assembled her clothing perfectly, needing no reflection, and she had no desire to look into her own eyes. She saw herself in the eyes of her sisters, and they saw her as their mother in God, the mistress of their souls. As novice mistress she had initiated many of them into the mysteries of religious life. Spiritual motherhood wasn't enough for her but she had learned long ago that nothing ever could be enough.

Elise would be different. Her eyes would see a mother whole and entire.

She dressed without looking on the fine line of scar tissue etched across her belly where the doctors had opened her up and removed her womb. It never had been right anyway, and once menopause began it bled and bled until Reverend Mother Esther told her she was white as her linens and had to get it taken care of. Strange how it affected her, having it gone. She wasn't using it, so what good was it anyway? All it gave her right from the beginning was trouble. Cramps that put her into bed each month. Years of cramping up around something never to be there. Thirty years, until that day she stood up to chant the hours and bled all over the chapel floor. Clots thick as a fish slithered out warm and dead. The singing stopped. Sister Josepha led her out and down the hallway to the infirmary. Wherever she walked she left a trail of blood.

It was Tom all over again.

Or maybe not. Maybe this time it was God taking her womanhood for good and all.

When the doctors hollowed her out, the love of her sisters flowed freely into that emptiness. The sisters held her hands, they read to her, prayed with her, sang to her. Her first night home from the hospital Sister Josepha climbed in bed with her, because she was afraid that if she went to sleep her breath would catch on death like a thorn in her heart.

"You won't die," the infirmarian said.

"How can you know?"

"I will hold you. If you stop breathing I will feel it and give you CPR. I won't sleep. I'll watch."

All night long the nun's fingers rested lightly on Mother Thomas Ann's pulse.

Such love loosened the bonds from time to time and Clara Monroe's heart beat freely.

Strange, nonetheless, how the absence of her womb affected her. I'll never be able to have children, a small voice whined from a dark cave in her mind. Well, of course not! Vowed to celibacy, now too old, what did she expect? And still the whining that wouldn't listen to reason.

She knelt and kissed the floor beside her bed. "I kiss the earth on which you walked, my Lord, and I offer myself to you again this day humbly and completely." For years her tongue curled on these words. Her mind seized, refusing to cross into what it considered a lie. Now, looking back, she believed her offering to have been the most true of anything in her, even more true than her marriage vows to Tom Lenz, which she thought had formed the contours of her soul.

Now she knew that over time the rule can shape even the most deformed soul until it becomes a vessel for the bridegroom. The hands of the sisters can heal any pain. What in the beginning had been Sister Thomas Ann's incarceration became over the years her perfect security. All she sacrificed to God would be returned to her one hundredfold. She knew herself to be ready.

Mother Thomas Ann rose from her knees and walked quickly and deliberately to the chapel for morning prayer.

XV

Elise knelt in the chapel at eight-thirty in the evening, obediently examining her conscience before retiring to the postulants' dorm, where she would learn convent rituals for going to bed. In the silence of Our Lady of Peace chapel, where it smelled of incense and wool and the bodies of women, she knelt motionless, staring at the crucifix above the altar.

After her childhood meeting with the Lord and Lady, Elise had expected to see the holy pair again at any moment, standing among the hollyhocks at Gramma Meghan's cottage or walking along the beach of Black Sturgeon Lake. She had awakened deep in the night thinking she saw the Lady in her wicker rocking chair, but it was only an accumulation of neglected clothes. She had prayed to be visited by the Lord after she told her family of her convent plans. She needed to be certain, she said into the empty air by the wild roses in the backyard of her parents' little house in town. The air didn't change. In the house across the alley the Smiths' baby cried. That was all.

Even though she could make her eyes perform tricks with the tabernacle in Corpus Christi Church on dim winter afternoons after school when she stopped for her daily visit to the Blessed Sacrament, nothing of an extraordinary spiritual nature had happened to her. She had attended daily mass, prayed her rosary, confessed her sins every Saturday night, and, except for her musical talent and what the Lutherans called her religious eccentricities, had become a normal adolescent.

Now she squinted at the convent crucifix. Nothing.

MOTHER Thomas Ann clapped her hands once. Out of the corner of her eye, Elise saw the seven novices, who sat just behind the new group of five postulants, rise on cue. Sister Mary William, the novitiate equivalent of an army drill sergeant, bustled to the front pews and ushered the postulants out. They walked two by two, except for Amy Anderson, who was shortest and genuflected alone, then led the procession of nuns like a flower girl at a wedding.

Elise glanced at the pew by the stained-glass window of the assumption of Mary where, that afternoon, she had expected to see her family. The pew was empty now as it had been five hours before. Acid rose onto her tongue as it had then. She swallowed and lowered her eyes. The nuns must have their reasons, but it felt unfair, even cruel. She imagined her parents and grandparents sitting in their cars, stunned, unable to drive away, expecting that any moment one of the nuns would become aware of the mistake. She would hurry out the front doors of the convent, waving them back, expressing embarrassment. Certainly the parents could say good-bye. Of all things! Of course, no girl must give herself forever to the Lord without saying a proper good-bye to the very people who brought her into the world in the first place. But no one came. Elise remembered hearing the old muffler on the station wagon as her family drove away.

No one asked why the parents left so soon. No one told the postulants a reason for what Elise would always think of as the first mistake the nuns made in her behalf. That afternoon the five new members of the Sisters of Our Lady of Peace had been led from the chapel to the community room, where all the nuns welcomed them with smiles and hugs.

"Your presence here is God's blessing on the faith of your dear grandmother. Never forget that. We do not choose this life for ourselves. It is a gift." Mother Thomas Ann folded Elise within her long serge sleeves and pulled her close. Her cheek felt cool and dry.

"I will remember, Mother, and I also remember that your

prayers, as my godmother, may have moved the Lord to bring me to this community." It just came out that way. How odd. Her stylized voice reminded her of Jennifer Jones in *The Song of Bernadette*. She blushed. Mother Thomas Ann's face could not be read.

Sister Mary of the Holy Cross, who had been seated alone by the community room window, stood when Elise approached her.

"Well, then, here you are." Sister Mary lifted a dark eyebrow. "It is what you wanted, yes?"

"Oh yes, Sister."

"Then I pray you will be given courage, *Liebling*."

"Courage?"

"The love of God, Elise, there is no end to it, and no end to what that love can ask. You think today that you have given all. Today you gave but a sliver, an atom. So, courage, child. Courage."

Elise's heart moved toward this woman who, because of the music, knew her soul.

"But I'm not alone, Sister. You are here."

"Perhaps. Perhaps not."

"What do you mean?"

"Every nun is alone, *Liebling*."

ELISE's mind still reeled with the events of the day as she stood by her white-curtained bed in the postulants' dorm. While Sister Mary William prayed aloud, Elise and the other new postulants removed their unfamiliar black gabardine dresses with the white starched collars and the black wool veils that fastened tightly over their ears and under their hair in back. Elise's ears already showed a rash from the scratchy material.

The nun was explaining how to use the large seersucker nightgown as a modesty tent.

"We protect ourselves and others from temptations of the flesh." She slipped the gown over her head and in several deft motions underneath its folds, she produced first her white undershirt and then her bra, petticoat, pantaloons, girdle, and black cotton stockings. "Nothing to it, Sisters." She grinned.

Now Elise tried the stunt on her own. It wasn't as easy as it looked. A pile of undergarments collected on the floor. She stepped over them, inserted her arms into the sleeves of the gigantic nightgown, and bent to gather the garments onto her bed for folding. The cotton stockings already bagged at the knees. They smelled from perspiration. Eighty-five degrees during the day and all that wool, it was no wonder. Amy Anderson, wearing a black robe over her nightgown, walked past Elise's bed carrying her stockings to one of the three sinks at the end of the dorm. Why hadn't she thought of that?

AMY Anderson from Duluth, whose father owned a lumber business. She wore black Girl Scout shoes, size four.

Suzanne Behr from Pelican Lake, who said she found the will of God for her in the soft clay along the lake's shore.

Sarah Beauchamp, fifteen years old, from the reservation at Red Lake.

Imelda Jendro, a farm girl from Stearns County. Twenty-three years old.

And Elise.

They, all of them, washed their black cotton stockings. They hung them over their towels on the antique oak commodes beside their narrow beds. They didn't talk. Sister Mary William continued to murmur, without feeling, prayers of unknown origin. Then it was silent.

Elise knelt beside her bed to perform her own familiar ritual, those prayers taught by her mother, recited together. Prayers to ward off the fears sometimes brought on by darkness. She sank into the prayer as though into her own bed, exhausted and relieved, home again. She closed her eyes.

"What are you doing, Sister?" Sister Mary William tapped her on her shoulder.

"Saying my prayers, Sister."

"That's not necessary. We said our night prayers."

"It's all right, Sister. I want to."

"From now on, Sister, you will say the prayers of a Sister of Our Lady of Peace. Now, get off your knees and into bed."

ELISE lay on her back listening to the other girls' breathing. The nun snored. Next to her Amy Anderson whimpered. She blew her nose. Down the line of beds, someone got up and shuffled toward where Amy slept.

"What's wrong?" A whisper. Probably Suzanne.

"My mom and dad. I miss them."

"It's the devil."

"What?"

"The devil. The devil would do anything to get us out of here. The devil uses whatever is available to weaken us. He's using your love of your mom and dad."

"But I miss them."

"Don't pay any attention to him. Pray. Say the Hail Mary."

"I did. It doesn't help."

"I'll pray for you."

The shuffling again. A few more sniffles and silence.

Elise reached to the top of the commode, where she had set the little rosary pouch. She opened it and found the stone from Black Rock Beach. She closed her hand around the stone and fell asleep.

XVI

Music once heard
cannot be suppressed.
Earth itself will sing.

Sister Mary's Music Notebooks, 1945

"Devils. Whores of Babylon!" Suzanne's father whisked her up in his arms as they passed the two nuns. She was five, almost six, and the family had come to town for school clothes.

"What are they doing here?" her mother whispered. "I didn't remember they could come out—on the streets, I mean."

"Oh, they come out."

He made them sound like the roaring lions. Preacher Isaac warned about the lions. Roaming the earth. Devouring anybody, even children. Children who lie; children who steal; children who disobey; children who speak when not spoken to; children who look down when they are expected to look up; children who blush and who stutter when asked to say the blessing; children who do acts so terrible they cannot be mentioned.

Suzanne wrapped her arms around her father and clung, her face nestled into the curve of his neck just above the shoulder bone, where the scratchy whiskers stopped and the smooth skin began, smelling of rain. He was like the smooth mud at the bottom of Pelican Lake when she waded in and sank and it oozed up through her toes. You could draw with it. You could bring it up by fistfuls, smear it on rocks, create shapes of birds and horses. The mud by the dock was gray, but in the reed bed where the suckers lived it was black as licorice, and at the end of the point it was a shade like eggshells. You could collect it, mix it, make the bird pictures look so real it seemed they might fly off the stones into the sky. One way or the other they disappeared. Sun dried them, turned them to dust. Rain washed them back into the lake. It didn't matter. God made lots of mud.

The whores of Babylon wore black and white. She watched them flow away from her along the sidewalk. They wore soft veils that caught the summer breeze. She'd heard of silk. Her mother owned nothing made of silk. Maybe the whores' veils were silk. Preacher Isaac's voice went low and his eyes narrowed to slits in his face when he talked about women who wore silk and who painted their faces to lure good men to hell. The whores hadn't painted their faces, so maybe their veils weren't silk. The whores looked at their black shoes as they walked. They kept their hands in their sleeves as if it were the middle of winter and they had no mittens. But it wasn't winter; it was dog days. Pelican Lake was fit for only dogs. Humans couldn't go swimming. Green slime smeared the surface like finger paint. Little girls could get sick on green slime even if it did look pretty on your skin. Suzanne painted herself just last week with every color of mud and with the dog days slime. But her mother said she was not a water sprite at all but just a dirty little girl who needed to take a bath immediately before all kinds of germs crawled out of the green and down her nose and throat and made her sick unto death.

Probably the whores didn't have legs, just feet attached some-how to the bottom of their skirts. They didn't move in the jerky way of people with legs. And if they didn't have legs, then they couldn't go to the bathroom, because where would it come out? So they must be the devil just as Daddy said. But their faces weren't red as fire and they didn't have horns or tails, unless those clothes covered all of that. Their faces looked calm, even pretty.

Suzanne's mother was pretty and it was her bane. A bane is like a birthmark. It's where the devil touches you and claims you for his own. The devil's bane. It means you are the devil's child and only the sweet grace of Jesus can save you. Preacher Isaac brought Suzanne's mother to the front of the Church of Holy Jesus and the Freedom of God on her birthday, the day she curled her shining red hair.

"Isabelle," he boomed like God's thunder, "how many of the good men of this church are lusting after you in their hearts? Repent of your vanity, woman, you Jezebel."

On the way home she cried. And after that she pulled her hair back and wound it tight enough to trap all the lust and save the men from sick hearts. Daddy said it was the right thing. "Issie," he said, "it's just the heretic way you were brought up. But now you're God's holy daughter and my woman. You're not for the eyes of other men."

Suzanne drew a picture of hair and eyes like a peacock's fan, and when her mother asked her what it was, she told her, "Issie's bane."

The whores were pretty and the devil's bane. They covered their hair, if they had hair. Maybe their hair was fire and the black veils like a cool cloth to calm the fever of it. Maybe at night their heads burned on the pillow. Maybe their eyes became like coals. Maybe their faces were the only human thing about them, and under their long black dresses was a river of fire flowing down the street, and at night their faces melted and they went to hell.

When the devil put on his disguise he came up from hell wearing the face of a beautiful woman to snatch away children and good men like Suzanne's daddy. The devil was tricky; you could never be sure.

Suzanne watched the nuns from the safety of her father's arms and thought these things until the black ink of them flowed into a swirl of color somewhere in the next block and disappeared.

Nuns seldom came to Pelican Lake, and it was four years before Suzanne saw another one. She drew pictures of their fiery faces and stared into their smoldering eyes until she didn't fear them anymore. She hid the pictures under the wrapping-paper lining of her dresser drawers and took them out on Saturdays to see how the whores of Babylon had changed. By the time Suzanne was nine the eyes of the veiled figures looked back at her without the fire but with, instead, a clean and wistful love. And then it seemed that love was what she had really seen right from the beginning.

"I want to be a nun," she announced at the dinner table on her tenth birthday. "I just wished it and I blew out all my candles."

"Don't be saying such things," her father warned. "Only heretic Catholics have nuns."

"Then I'll be Catholic."

"You will not! Not and stay a daughter of mine. Heretic Catholics. Pagans. No difference."

"I'm surrounded by crazy people here." Isabelle forced a laugh.

"Incense. Mumbo jumbo. Nothing to laugh at, Issie. Didn't you hear what your daughter just said? She wants to be a nun. I'll be damned if I let her go off to one of those convents, where priests come sneaking through tunnels and their bastard babies are killed at birth and buried in a common grave."

"I'm surprised at you, Henry, talking like that. Tearing down the girl's dreams like that. She's only ten years old; she'll change her mind a hundred times before she graduates from high school."

"Whores of Babylon," he muttered, and left the table without eating his cake.

"Don't you be upset, now, Suzie. Daddy's never been able to abide the Catholics, never since I've known him. It's a knot in his mind he can't untangle. It just gets tighter and tighter and it pulls at him. But you don't have to be knotted that way, darling. If you want to meet some of those Catholic nuns, you just tell me. I'll see to it."

"Really?"

"Really, honey."

SUZANNE knelt in the eggshell-colored mud on the point that jutted into Pelican Lake and scooped it out by handfuls. She piled it on a flat rock and began to shape it into the image of a woman, tall and dressed in flowing robes and a veil that draped over her shoulders and fell smoothly down her back. The woman's face she fashioned calm as the lake at sunset when it reflected the trees perfectly.

After she was finished she remembered that in the beginning God had done the same. Preacher Isaac told the story often, how God found the statue he made was good. Then God leaned down from heaven and breathed life into the clay and it became a living being.

Suzanne leaned over her creation and thought it didn't look one bit like any whore of Babylon. She drew into her lungs the fresh damp air that had collected in mists over Pelican Lake and held it inside her until she could feel it mix with the blood of her heart and lungs and brain. Then slowly, evenly, with all the care that she possessed, she poised herself above the woman made of mud and breathed.

XVII

Music is given never simply for our pleasure;
we are its servants.
Music is our daily bread, our life.

SISTER MARY'S MUSIC NOTEBOOKS, 1958

Mother Thomas Ann's eyes, leveled on Elise, shone with the luster of chipped flint on Black Rock Beach. She might as well have never known her before, for all the good it did. The nun treated her like a stranger, a situation not to be commented upon because one was not to notice such things. Things are most real as God sees them and not as they exist in this fallen world.

The five new postulants sat at desks in the first and second rows of the novitiate classroom. Their hands were folded on the tops of their desks like the hands of first graders. Mother Thomas Ann faced them, as she would face them for the almost three years of their training, with perfect composure.

"It wouldn't matter if every holy rule were burned, if an earthquake swallowed each one, if a devastating wind scattered the pages like crisp leaves to the four corners of the world." The novice mistress talked like Tennyson or the apostle Paul. "We could reconstruct every word of it from observing the life of a faithful nun."

Her body, trained by forty-two years of religious austerity, rose like a ramrod from her straight-backed chair. To Elise she resembled a puppet hanging from strings manipulated by some gigantic hand. Perfectly straight. Perfectly rigid. Perfectly perfect.

"You are no longer who you were, Sisters. Before, when you went into the world, people saw you as Elise or Suzanne or Imelda or Amy or Sarah. Now they will see you as a Sister of Our Lady of Peace. Take care not to dishonor that identity. Elise must die. Sarah must die. We all must die to our past, to our individual selves, to our families and friends, and live only as members of this humble community."

The top of Elise's head spun like a gyro. All the energy in her body rushed upward and collected there. She couldn't feel her legs or arms. Except for her heart and head she might as well have disappeared. Her heart pumped madly against her ribs and fueled the cerebral whirling. Any minute this pressure might become pain, the same sort of pain she had felt with a new piece of music when her fingers wouldn't produce the sound her mind played.

"Why do you do that to yourself?" Sister Mary had wanted to know. "Enjoy the learning itself. Enjoy the note as it moves toward perfection, toward the fullness of its mystic potential. Hear it change. Delight in its development."

Elise felt herself to be a note played over and over by Mother Thomas Ann, an imperfect note. Maybe the potential wasn't there. The instrument might be inferior. Mother Thomas Ann expected a Steinway sort of soul.

The other postulants appeared calm. They continued to sit like primary school children, eyes alert, little smiles adorning their faces. Amy was shaking her foot, though, like fidgety Timmy Johnson in the barbershop. Such a long time ago that was. Three weeks! Elise ought to have waited for Sam to cut her hair. This long hair, braided and wrapped around her head under the white day cap and the waist-length black wool veil, smelled of perspiration and oil and produced an itchy scalp. Back home she washed it every other day. Here it could be washed only on Saturday afternoon.

Everything had its time. A bell began and ended each activity. The bell, instructed Mother Thomas Ann, is the voice of God. When the bell rings at five in the morning, rise and pray, *"Benedicámus Dómino!"* giving thanks for another day of serving the bridegroom. There was a bell for prayer, for meals, for study, for recreation. Bells regulated even the novitiate bathroom breaks, a practice that Elise found to be constipating. In the second week, on the brink of toxicity, she began sneaking into the bathroom during the sacred silence while all the others were asleep. A poor instrument indeed.

On Saturday afternoons, after baths and shoe polishing, after spot removing and clothes brushing and ironing, after dorm cleaning and bed making, Mother Thomas Ann gave the postulants permission to visit the trunk room.

"Two by two, Sisters," she reminded. What did she imagine one of them might do if she were allowed to climb the stairs into the large attic room and explore the contents of her steamer trunk alone?

"Why can't we go up there alone?" Elise asked Suzanne the second Saturday. A few strands of Suzanne's clean red hair had escaped the day cap and shone like coppery spider weavings in the sun's rays that filtered through the dust on the octagonal attic window high over the stairs. Elise kept her hand from reaching to touch those strands. She hadn't touched another human being since the sisters hugged her after the entrance ceremony.

"Sisters always go everywhere in twos."

"But why?"

"Search me. Maybe for protection."

"Protection from what?"

"Maybe to keep from breaking the rule?"

"Maybe."

Elise opened her trunk. Home floated out. A picture album. She opened it; there were her mother and father, Michael's face turned as usual, showing the good side, Kate squinting into the sunshine. There was Gramma Meghan standing by the hollyhocks. Elise's stomach did a somersault.

"Homesickness really is a sickness," Mother Thomas Ann told the postulants on the second day of Elise's convent life. "Don't invite it."

Elise closed the album.

"What did you come to get?" Suzanne rummaged through her unworn T-shirts and bloomers.

"I need another apron," Elise lied, but lifted one out from under her collection of music. She would bring it back next week and trade it for a pair of cotton stockings. Then, as if by accident, she opened the score of Mozart's Rondo in A Minor. She could hear the delicate tones in her mind, she could feel the vibrations of the music as if they issued from the printer's ink that scored the page.

She laid the music down and touched her fingertips together. The delicate nerve endings shivered and sent to her brain a desire for the piano that was more than emotional or artistic. The yearning was physical.

Elise hadn't touched a piano since her first night at Our Lady of Peace. During the prescribed recreation that followed dinner, Mother Thomas Ann had asked each postulant to stand and tell her vocation story. They sat in hierarchical order at school desks arranged to face one another in a long rectangle. The youngest postulant sat closest to Mother Thomas Ann and the oldest novice sat farthest away.

The stories began with Imelda. When she was twenty-one and still filing medical records at the doctor's office in Willow Lake, Father Weisenberg told her she likely wasn't listening closely enough to hear the call of the divine Lord. The young men of Willow Lake hadn't the maturity or depth to see what lay under Imelda's shy surface. But God doesn't miss that sort of thing. So the priest brought her to Bemidji and the sisters saw what all the young men missed.

This story needed to be culled in fits and starts. Imelda's face looked feverish. Her tongue stuck. Mother Thomas Ann assisted her with the story about Father Weisenberg filling up the parlor, that day in April, with his booming voice and his praise of her.

Suzanne said the convent had been her destiny from the moment of her birth. And the desire to be the bride of Christ rose up in her before she even knew she was Catholic. Until she was ten years old she thought she belonged to the Church of Holy Jesus and the Freedom of God. Imagine her surprise when her mother told her she'd been Catholic all along, baptized by a priest on the day she was born.

Sarah said she had every intention of beginning her sophomore year on the reservation and had never considered being a nun. Then she lost control of her car on the dirt road while taking lunch to her dad, who was mending nets on the banks of Red Lake. She nearly hit a jack pine. From that moment she couldn't get being a nun out of her head, so Sister Josephine at the mission called Mother Thomas Ann, and here she was.

Amy said she loved Sister Carol, who taught English, and she wanted nothing more than to be just like her.

Later, in the more keen vision of middle age, Elise would see the postulants in her memory as if they were not veiled. Her sight would pierce the caves of their skulls and perceive what had been hidden from her on the day they told their stories: their patterns of reason or imagination, those intricate paths each had followed to arrive at Our Lady of Peace. She would understand that the stories they told by way of explanation were feeble attempts to affix words to the inexplicable. What they had called reasons were hardly reasons at all, but some mysterious attraction from the core of each of them that would develop, as they lived, into labyrinths on which they were set to travel. Each would make her journey toward that center she could see but not reach directly, because such paths turned again and again back and away.

On that day of stories Elise didn't know what to say. It was inconceivable that she would talk about her vision.

"I can't remember when I didn't want to come here."

She was about to be seated again when Mother Thomas Ann smiled at her and motioned for her to remain standing.

"Elise plays the piano expertly. She has been a student of our own Sister Mary for several years." She turned her head from the group to Elise. "Will you play for us, Sister?"

"I don't have my music . . ."

"Excuses are prideful. Just play something simple that you have committed to memory."

The nun rested against her straight-backed wooden chair and waited. Elise walked to the novitiate piano, an upright with checkered varnish. Her mind flooded with melody. Something simple. That must mean don't show off. Something anyone would recognize. Her mind played the opening measures of the first movement of Beethoven's "Moonlight Sonata." Perfect. But the C-sharp key stuck when she depressed it and rendered no sound, leaving a void in more than half the measures.

"Beautiful," Mother Thomas Ann breathed when Elise completed the movement and returned to her seat. "Wasn't that lovely, Sisters?" A cue for the novices and postulants to applaud. "At Christmas you will accompany the novitiate in the singing of carols." She nodded her head with sharp decision, and Elise with her music was, for the time being, dismissed.

So FAR Elise's schedule included no time for piano practice. She saw Sister Mary only in the chapel and the refectory, and even then the nun kept her eyes lowered. Elise felt strangely invisible, disembodied. Even a direct hello elicited no reply. Finally on the third day Mother Thomas Ann took Elise aside just after Sister Mary had brushed past her in the hallway on her way into the professed sisters' community room.

"You are making life difficult for Sister Mary, Elise."

"I am?"

"Yes, you are. You must curb your desire for attention."

A kind of paralysis crept up Elise's body. She said nothing.

"Except for special occasions there is to be no conversation between the professed sisters and those still in the novitiate. Your teachers here, such as Sister Mary William, are dispensed from this rule. All of the other sisters must render it a strict observance. Please don't make it difficult for them. I understand that you and Sister Mary have known one another for a long time, and after your first vows you will have ample time to continue as members of the same community. For now, however, I must ask you to observe the novitiate cloister and keep silence and custody of the eyes in her presence. Now come along. You shouldn't be standing here by the community room."

And what about playing the piano? Elise wanted to ask. What about my lessons with Sister Mary, and practice time, and this God-given talent? Respect your God-given talent. How often had she heard those words? From Sister Mary herself those words had come.

On Saturdays in the attic she turned the pages of Beethoven's Sonata no. 30 and Chopin's Barcarolle in F-sharp Major and wondered how much her fingers would forget. She tucked the Rondo in A Minor under a new set of blue towels on the very bottom of the trunk, where, if Sister Mary William were to inspect for neatness, it would not be seen.

"You're Snow White and I'm Rose Red." Suzanne and Elise walked together through crisp October leaves by Lake Bemidji. It was Gem Day, a Thursday afternoon of recreation. Mother Thomas Ann lifted the rule of silence and the novices and postulants played like the children they so recently had been.

"The fairy tale?" Elise responded. She could feel Suzanne next to her, not physically so much as like something that resembled a current of air or a musical tone beyond the range of hearing.

"Yes. They were sisters. Inseparable. Named after the rose-bushes in their mother's yard. Their love and courage retrieved a great bear's treasures from a wicked dwarf, and the bear became a man in gold, the king's son."

"And we're like them because we're—"

"Inseparable."

Elise couldn't deny it and didn't want to anyway. The friend-ship began with the trips to the attic, with secrets shared quickly while they sat together on Elise's trunk in the soft light filtered through a dusty window. They shared one treasure of memory each Saturday, no more than one, because Mother Thomas Ann cautioned them against frivolity. Trips to the attic are utilitarian, not to be abused with idle talk. But nothing of their conversations could be called idle. They spoke only those secrets of the heart. They spoke of music and poetry. Elise told of the war and of her father's two faces. Suzanne showed her a clay figure of a woman only six inches tall.

"She's beautiful."

"I made her years ago."

"She looks like the Blessed Virgin."

"She's everything I wanted to be."

Elise looked at the other girl's face. The light caught a few strands of her coppery red hair. "It's what you are."

Neither girl had analyzed their friendship until that moment of comparison. Snow White and Rose Red. Inseparable.

On Thursday afternoons they laid out bits of themselves like brightly colored stones, marveling at the similarities. Even their dif-ferences proved the truth of the metaphor that was in itself a para-dox. One Thursday they went together to the convent library, and finding the book of *Grimm's Tales*, they read the story aloud. After that they spoke in its codes and images of the feelings that were growing in their hearts.

"We will not leave each other."

"Never so long as we live."

XVIII

Music engages life.
It is life
Lived directly.

Sister Mary's Music Notebooks, 1950

"What kind of abomination is this?"

Suzanne cowered on her bed as her father pulled the drawers from her dresser and turned them upside down. Panties, undershirts, and ankle socks tumbled onto the floor along with the paper liner and her collection of pictures. He waved the drawings in her face.

"What are these?"

"My pictures."

"Idols. Thou shalt not make any graven image."

"They're just pictures."

"They are receptacles of power, child. They are the work of the devil."

He calmed his voice a bit, but it still shook in a way perhaps all the more frightening because of his efforts at restraint.

"Suzanne, Suzanne. I know you didn't mean to do evil. But I must protect you, child. They must be destroyed."

"No, Daddy!"

"I'm sorry, Suzanne. You must burn them."

"I can't."

She was crying.

"You can and you will."

"Please, Daddy."

He leafed through the childish drawings. Later she would wonder what he could have seen in them that caused such fear, but they would no longer be there for her to study. The peacock hair. The eyes of the nuns.

"You won't even miss them, child. It will be a relief, you'll see. The devil will let go of you. He'll let go of all of us." His voice, now, was low, almost soft. "Come with me."

He took her hand and she went with him. He built a fire in the burn barrel. She noticed how rusty it was, trashy. She thought of all that had been burned there. Junk. Garbage. Once the rotting carcass of a dog. When the fire roared he handed her the pictures, one by one. She watched the edges curl, the paper turn brown, and the images become vivid just before they fell to ash.

Then he spanked her.

"Never forget," he kept saying as his hand came down on her bare flesh, "there is one God, one alone. Thou shalt put no other god before him."

The stinging stopped her tears. She thought she might never cry again.

Afterward, making sure she was alone, she went into her closet. She crept behind her clothes into the far corner and sat, staring at the thin beam of light that entered under the closed door. Something must be done. Something must be saved from this, this . . . no words existed for what had been done to her. Her eyes adjusted to the dimness and she reached up onto a shelf for what her father had missed when he burst into her room and found the pictures. It was a wooden cigar box containing the clay statue. She held the clay woman in her hands, caressing the clay as she had when she first formed that flowing body. Of everything she had, this must be saved, idol or no idol. She wrapped the statue in a purple scarf and put it back into the box.

THE PRIEST answered the doorbell of the rectory. He wore a long black coat with a sash around his waist.

"Well, well, what have we here?"

His eyes looked kind, though his overall expression conveyed solemnity.

"And who might you be, young lady?"

"Suzanne Behr, Reverend, sir."

"You aren't Catholic, I take it."

"Not exactly, Reverend. I'm from the Church of Holy Jesus out by the lake."

"Ah yes. Holy Jesus and the Freedom of God."

"Yes, Reverend."

"And what might you be wanting from a Catholic priest, young Suzanne?"

She held the box with the clay statue tightly in her hands. How much could she tell this man in the black coat?

"I was wondering, Reverend, could you protect something for me? You see, sir, I want to be a nun, and—"

"Aha, a nun, is it?" He shook his head slowly. "This is most serious, Suzanne Behr. I suppose you are aware that a young woman like yourself must be a Catholic in order to become a nun."

"Yes sir, Reverend, I know that. And in a way I am Catholic."

Inside the rectory, sitting at the kitchen table with the robin's-egg blue tablecloth and drinking a glass of lemonade, Suzanne told the priest her story except for the part about the spanking. She took the clay woman from her wooden box and set her on the blue cloth.

"She needs a place to stay until I can leave home and take her to the convent with me."

"And you want me to give her sanctuary?"

"Sanctuary?"

"It's something the church has done for hundreds of years. When someone's life was in danger, she could come to the church, and once inside the walls, no one could touch her. Not even civil governments had greater power or authority. Not even a person's father could defy the sanctuary of the church."

This was exactly what she wanted.

"I'll come for her."

"I know you will, Suzanne Behr. And in the meantime, your lady will be safe here."

"Thank you, Reverend."

"Call me 'Father.' "

"Okay, Father. Thank you."

"You are very welcome, child."

His name was Father Sloan, and that September, when her fifth-grade class was released on Wednesdays for religious instruction,

Suzanne began to accompany the Catholic children to his church for classes on the sacraments and the Sacred Heart of Jesus. He told stories of the beautiful Virgin Mary, who was without sin from the moment of her conception in the womb of her holy mother, Anne. He said that keeping statues of the Virgin in the house and even talking to them as though they were alive was not a sin and certainly not idol worship. He said that the nuns were not, nor ever had been, the whores of Babylon and that they were, instead, the holy brides of Christ.

If only her father could know all this. But instinct told her he could not. He could not even be told that she set foot inside the Catholic church, or he might burn her the way he burned the pictures! No, she would learn what she could, and when the time was right, when she was old enough, she would herself seek the walls of this church for sanctuary.

Suzanne started finding words for the clay in her hands and for the sunset that turned the water of Pelican Lake into a shell pink veil. Her words felt shaped by the spirit of these things. She flung those words out from her like a thread, like the sticky thread a spider makes that waves almost invisible in the air until it catches a branch and holds. And then she spun. She actually imagined herself a spider. In a bush once she had seen a golden spider, sunlight splashing all around her, small legs reaching out to join the fragile tendrils of her silk into her intricate architecture. The creature defied her. She could not have drawn what she saw. No picture could communicate such ethereal quality.

A thought began to form in her mind that she could *be* what she had seen or held in her hands, and that her words could be a web so nearly invisible that God himself might wander into them and be captured there.

"I do believe you are becoming a poet, Suzanne." Father Sloan held her sheet of lined notebook paper in his hands. He sat in the black leather wing-backed chair in his rectory living room. She sat across from him in the other chair of the set, the one that had no wings. Despite that, it dwarfed her. She ran her fingers up and down the cracks in the leather of the overstuffed arms where its real color showed through. The living room smelled of pipe tobacco and dust, a warm smell, a safe smell. The priest sat on an island in a sea of books. He had stacked them in piles all around his chair, on his desk, in the corners, under every window, on the dining room table, everywhere. A floor-to-ceiling bookcase covered one whole wall, but it was filled. Books leaned against one another. He'd stacked them and stuffed them into every possible space. He'd ordered books that still occupied their shipping boxes, unopened. She saw religious books—a thing one would expect—but also novels and history and poetry and politics. He owned a great dusty set of the Great Books bound in leather. The poetry of T. S. Eliot and Archibald MacLeish lay open beside his chair.

At noon hour almost every day Suzanne left the school yard and walked the three blocks to the Catholic church. She told no one, and the priest would keep her confidence. She couldn't tell how old he was, maybe older than her father. His hair was not yet gray, though. He wore glasses with wire rims, and behind them his eyes asked questions that he rarely put into words. He listened to her.

"This is really very good." He had read her poem again. "Very, very good."

"It doesn't rhyme."

"It doesn't need to rhyme. It makes a picture. It appeals to the senses. It is delicious on the tongue. It has such fine rhythm—just listen."

He read it to her. Her heart thumped in her chest when she heard her own words spinning out from the priest's mouth.

A week later he gave her a box wrapped in white butcher paper and tied with twine.

"Just a little gift."

"For me?"

"Just something for the writing."

It was a diary.

"It's for the poetry." His eyes smiled. "It's for collecting poems from all those separate pieces of paper, so they won't get lost."

It was red leather with gold printing. *My Diary.*

"I've never had a diary."

"Now you do. Words are holy, Suzanne. Never forget."

Words are not idols. God is himself a Word. Words are from the beginning. "In the beginning was the Word." No matter how strict her father might be, he could not argue with that.

It had a lock.

"I can keep it locked and hide the key."

"You sure can."

"No one will be able to read my poems except the ones I choose."

"Exactly."

She wished she could throw her arms around his neck and kiss him, but he was a priest.

"Thank you, Father."

"You are most welcome, child." And he smiled that kindness once again.

SHE HID the diary anyway because you couldn't be too careful when it came to her father. She'd learned her lesson, though, about hiding precious things, and this time she didn't put it in the bottom of a drawer or behind the boxes in her closet. He searched those places regularly and found nothing. She put that diary, and the ones that followed that one each year until she graduated from high school, on the shelf of the bookcase in the living room. Her father never looked there.

Then she was eighteen and she would do what she would do. Father Sloan helped her with the papers the nuns required. Her mother took her to Minneapolis, where they bought a black steamer trunk, gramma shoes with Cuban heels, and two dozen men's white handkerchiefs. At home again she packed the trunk. Her father didn't speak to her. He took the boat out on the lake or sat outside the shed whittling on a birch branch. She packed her pillows and her blanket and six red-leather books of poetry. The day before her mother drove her to Bemidji, she visited Father Sloan.

"I came to say good-bye."

"So the big day has come."

"Thanks to you, Father."

"If God had not used me, he would have used some other instrument."

"You were what I needed."

"Perhaps, child. Perhaps."

"And thank you for everything, for the years, for the poetry. Thank you for believing in me."

"It wasn't hard."

"You are my true father, you know."

He took her hands in his and squeezed them. Then he went to his desk and took from the bottom drawer the clay statue wrapped in a purple cloth.

"You can protect her now."

"I'll take her with me."

"The convent is where she belonged from the beginning."

Suzanne took her clay statue and then put her arms around the neck of the priest and kissed him good-bye.

XIX

Nothing of the music you hear
survives
outside the chambers of your own mind
and heart.

Sister Mary's Music Notebooks, 1958

The days shortened and the nuns rose in the predawn, shaken out of sleep by Sister Mary William's voice, nasal above the clanging of her brass bell.

"*Benedicámus Dómino.*" Let us rise and bless the Lord.

"*Deo Grátias.*"

"Come, let us bow down in worship; let us acclaim the Rock of our salvation. Let us greet him with thanksgiving; let us joyfully sing psalms to him."

ELISE's feet hit the cold wooden floor of the postulants' dorm. She splashed her face with icy water to dispel the nausea that dizzied her when she popped out of bed so fast, standing, still teetering with sleep. Suzanne, who slept by the light switch, flipped it on as she began the prayers, to which the other postulants responded. "I offer you my prayers, works, joys, and sufferings of this day . . ."

They prayed aloud with the memorized words as they dressed, made their beds, kissed the floor, and hurried off to the chapel, all in fifteen minutes. Rush and skid to a halt. Once in the chapel they entered the cocoon of prayer—matins, lauds, and an hour of meditation. God wrapped himself around them in the words of the psalms, chanted as they bowed, as they knelt, as they stood tall. "O that today you would hear his voice: 'Harden not your hearts.' "

Don't be like stone, the psalmist sang. Or if you are like stone, let it be the stone in the desert, in Meribah, where the people knew thirst. Let God touch you. You will bring forth sweet water. You will flow with life.

Suzanne prayed beside Elise, her voice a soft, breathy alto. A violin kind of voice. Elise was a flute, clear, a sound like rain. The chant rose and fell, waves breaking gently on a shore. Sister Josepha lisped and lagged behind by half a word. Mother Thomas Ann took the solo parts, moving into the aisle, turning first to the altar, then to the community, bowing, singing, "To you I pray, O Lord; at dawn you hear my voice."

Elise's heart felt large, her spirit safely contained within the song. Then silence. The sisters sat, opened their meditation books, read for a moment, and gazed at the tabernacle.

Elise sat down and promptly fell asleep. Outside it was still dark, and in the chapel the silence, the warmth of women's bodies, the indistinct sounds of pages turning, of breathing, of an occasional cough, became a lullaby. Her head bobbed. Suzanne reached over and tapped her on the knee. Elise pinched her own arm. If only she could move about, but tradition required her to be still. She measured the hour in breaths, in the bobbing of her head, in a hundred brief dreams. Afternoon meditation would be different; Suzanne would nod off and Elise would waken her.

"Live Jesus!" Mother Thomas Ann rang her bell and broke open the cocoon. The postulants emerged and climbed the stairs to the choir loft, where they and the novices chanted the mass.

Inside the cocoon her dreams differed every day. The tone she felt from Suzanne's presence changed, as did the tone of the feast days that circled around the year marking the seasons, remembering the saints.

The last evening of the month Mother Thomas Ann called each of the novices and postulants to approach her chair in the community room. A fan of blue leaflets emerged from her right hand as though she were a magician with a deck of cards.

"Sisters, let us kneel to receive our saints of the month."

As she approached her novice mistress to receive her October saint, Elise prayed to get the card on which was printed *Saint Thérèse of Lisieux*. She kept a picture of the young Carmelite by her bed and talked to her in whispers about the offering she had made to God's merciful love.

"Let me be like you. I, too, want to be the victim of God's love."

Thérèse in heaven listened as a friend; she listened even more closely than Suzanne, and the secrets she could be told were more deeply hidden. Maybe talking to her like that was a childish thing, but Elise's heart felt lighter every time she looked at the picture. Thérèse's tone, her core note, almost could be heard.

Every day had its saint to commemorate, which made each day a bit like a birthday.

Elise knelt at Mother Thomas Ann's knees and selected one of the blue cards. Saint Hedwig. Saint Hedwig? What could she have in common with a woman married to a duke in Silesia who got her pregnant seven times? After he died she entered a convent. The leaflet didn't say what happened to the seven children. The Saint Thérèse card went to Suzanne.

On Halloween Mother Thomas Ann laughed at Elise when she asked when they could carve their jack-o'-lanterns.

"Don't be ridiculous, Sister. This is no pagan place. We celebrate All Hallows' Eve in silence. It's the eve of All Saints, not some fantasy of witches and goblins. We remember those who died. We reach out to them in our minds and hearts. It's time to grow up, Sister. Let go of your childhood."

"I always liked the candle flame inside." It was recreation hour and the voices of the postulants and novices wove in and out of one another just like the colorful threads they plied as they learned embroidery.

"We never celebrated Halloween," Suzanne said, "so I guess I don't have anything to miss."

"No Halloween?" Elise had never heard of such a thing.

"My dad's church didn't permit it. He would have had a fit!"

"So you didn't get to smell the pumpkin as the flame blackened it?"

"What's so great about burned pumpkin?"

"Nothing, I guess. I just get lonesome for stuff like that."

Mother Thomas Ann snapped the lid of her sewing box shut. "It is time, Sisters, for the sacred silence. We will pray now and then retire. You will want to rest up for tomorrow's feast."

IN THE middle of the night Elise awoke to see Suzanne standing over her. The long white gown and red-gold hair gave a ghostly impression, so that Elise almost laughed about it being Halloween and a ghost coming to her bed, but the other girl's face looked stricken, and besides that, it was sacred silence. Suzanne motioned to her to follow.

They climbed the attic stairs. The moon shone through the octagonal window, casting an eerie beam on Suzanne's trunk. The two white-gowned girls sat down in the milky light.

"I need to talk," Suzanne began.

"We can't."

"I have to."

"It's sacred silence."

"I have to anyway."

What could be done? Maybe it would be a sin, but that couldn't be helped.

"I'm remembering something that's scaring me."

Elise took Suzanne's hand and it felt clammy and cold. Sometimes being silent and remembering maybe wasn't such a good idea.

"It's my father."

"What do you mean?"

"Well, he was very strict, you know? He had strong, strong beliefs about God and how God had made him head of the house and everything. He hated Catholics and I didn't know why until after I started talking about being a nun. It was because my mother was Catholic."

"She was?"

"Before they were married."

"Usually in mixed marriages the non-Catholic has to make promises to raise the children Catholic. My dad had to do that."

"Well, my dad wouldn't. He made my mom swear she'd never go to a Catholic church again."

"And she did that?"

"She loved him, and anyway, she was pregnant with me."

"Did she turn Protestant?"

"She tried, but he was always afraid the Catholics would steal her back from him like they stole me."

"When you came to the convent?"

"No, before that. When I was born. It was the last time my mother saw my grandmother—her mother. She told me about it when I started talking about being a nun. She said the night I was born my grandmother wrapped me in a blanket and took me from the house while my dad was out celebrating. She put me in her car and drove me over to the Catholic church, to the rectory, and had me baptized. What's done can't be undone. That's what my grandmother told my dad the next morning.

"Afterward he thought he'd beat Catholicism out of me. He used to tell me that he was the hand of God. When he'd spank me for not being how he wanted me to be, he'd say, 'Feel the hand of God, child, and know his chastisement.' "

"That sounds awful."

"It wasn't so bad, actually. Afterward I felt relieved, like all my sins were burned up in the fiery sting of his hand on my bare skin."

"Well, it still sounds awful to me."

"It did get awful."

Suzanne gagged. "Oh, Elise, it got so awful." She began to cry in a strange manner, her mouth open but silent, her breath coming in little gasps, and tears running down her cheeks.

Elise reached for her.

"No." The other girl gasped. "Don't touch me. I'm sorry. I can't be touched."

"What's wrong?" Elise wanted to call her Rose Red. She wanted to hold her, to kiss her face, to wipe away her tears.

"I thought he stopped spanking me after I was ten and started going to the Catholic church for release classes. He kind of faded from my life then. At least I thought so, but tonight . . ."

She sobbed once and was silent for what seemed a long time. She had pulled her hand away from Elise when she first began to cry, and now Elise felt disconnected from her, teetering on the edge of her silence.

"You remembered something else?"

"Yes. Yes I did. I was lying there like Mother Thomas Ann taught us, remembering the people in my life. The saints, you know? Father Sloan. My mother. My father. And I saw him . . ."

"What was he doing?"

"Spanking me."

"Yes?"

"And I was twelve and I was thirteen and I was fourteen. I was a woman, and I was lying over his knees and the hand of God was coming down on my naked bottom and the fire of God wasn't any longer in my heart, it was between my legs, and he was calling me a whore."

Elise's stomach twisted into a knot.

"How could your father do that?"

"I don't know."

"How could you forget it?"

"I don't know that either. I guess it was just too awful to remember."

Elise opened her arms and Suzanne fell against her. Elise's heart pounded, her throat constricted. It was too awful to think about. She began to sob. Together they sobbed until they were exhausted.

"Do you think I have to tell Mother Thomas Ann? Do you think they'll let me stay here if they know?"

"Jesus loved Mary Magdalene more than any of the other women. Maybe that's all you need to remember. I mean, you didn't do anything wrong, Suzanne. It was your dad. It was what he did that was wrong."

"Still . . . maybe this means I'm not a virgin."

"A spanking can't take away virginity."

"I feel like it did, though. I feel like what he called me—whore." She didn't sob. Tears stained her cheeks. "My father called me whore."

Snow White and Rose Red sat in the moonlight mourning something stolen they could not retrieve.

"We will not leave each other," Elise whispered. "Never, so long as we live."

⌒

"It's wrong," Kate said right away to Michael. They were on their way home from that first visiting Sunday afternoon in November. Bare birch trees etched the gray sky.

"We can't know that," he replied in an ironic twist of roles.

"Yes, we can. She's not herself. Surely you saw that she's just not herself."

He had. His daughter felt cold in his arms, cold and stiff. She turned her face when he tried to kiss her lips. He'd always kissed her lightly on the lips since she was a child and had given him the gift that Beauty gave the Beast.

"And did you see how her face is breaking out? Her skin always has been clear, right through adolescence. Why should it be breaking out now if this is right for her?"

"She can come home if she wants. She knows she can come home."

But maybe Elise didn't remember home. What could do that? What could bring on such forgetfulness in one so young? Irritation climbed like red ants up the back of Kate's neck. She told herself to ignore it. She looked out the window at a stark landscape rendered in shades of brown. Once past Blackduck it was mostly scrub trees and bog. Blackened trunks littered the horizon north of Waskish from the fire that had burned unchecked some years before. If only it would snow.

CHRISTMAS came and went without a visit. Michael sat by the Christmas tree and listened to the recording of Elise's last recital. At 11 P.M. on Christmas Eve they stopped by Hollyhock Cottage to look at Meghan's tree with all the decorations that marked the years since the fire. Then they walked through the snow to Corpus Christi to attend Midnight Mass. Kate prayed for Elise. She stretched her mind out over the miles to join it to her daughter's in that convent chapel in Bemidji where another priest was reciting the same words and another choir was singing the same antiphon, *"Dóminus dixit ad me: Fílius meus es tu, ego hódie génui te."* That other child's mother didn't let go for thirty years. Mary kept Jesus home, or he stayed. Whichever it was, it couldn't have been this wrenching. And even when he did leave, she followed him. Kate's mind did a little twist. Maybe she should enter that convent, too. At least there she could keep an eye on her daughter, protect her. Maybe she ought to have been more attentive earlier. If she could have been warmer, Elise might not have left.

On Christmas afternoon her mind stopped. All the thoughts melted, evaporated, left her empty. She drifted, felt nothing. Felt like blank paper crumbled and blowing across the snow. She was shards from a glass vase that could not be reassembled. She was water standing thick under six feet of ice.

Michael watched her. At night he tried to hold her, but she pulled away and curled up tight at the edge of the bed as far away from him as she could get.

VISITING Sunday arrived just after the twelfth day of Christmas.

Kate and Michael waited twenty minutes in the convent parlor before Elise came down the stairs. Again her face was full of red splotches, getting worse. Kate's hand reached out. Elise turned from her. The veil swished across her shoulder.

"I'm sorry to be late, but Mother required that I carry her sewing box to her room before leaving the cloister." Elise sat on a straight-backed wooden chair. Kate and Michael sat on a firm couch facing her.

No one saw it coming. An hour went by. Two hours. Elise told her parents about her classes and all that Mother Thomas Ann was teaching her. Mother Thomas Ann said she had a talent for tailoring. Mother Thomas Ann inspected the delicate rolled hem Elise was forming with tiny stitches and silk thread on the long, almost transparent veil that would replace her postulant's veil on reception day. That day she would wear the traditional habit of a Sister of Our Lady of Peace for the first time. Elise held her hand up before Kate's eyes as if it were an object not connected to her body. Mother Thomas Ann, she informed her parents, said her fingers still were good for something.

Kate screamed.

"Mother, Mother, Mother. Stop it! Stop calling her Mother! She's not your mother! I'm your mother!"

She stumbled from the room into the vestibule, past the Christmas tree, which crashed, scattering bright slivers of fine glass and green needles across the waxed oak floor.

She pushed open the heavy door of the guest lavatory and locked it behind her. She leaned over the toilet and vomited her breakfast, and after that her stomach turned again and again, heaving out the pain that had begun to sour long before her daughter left her, even before Michael's desperate return from war, when his pain had inexplicably eased her own. The core of it remained. Something had turned to poison in her and she was no longer thick enough to hold it in.

"PARENTS have their own sacrifices to make, Sister," Mother Thomas Ann explained to Elise later that day after Michael led Kate to the car and settled her into the front seat. Elise watched from the parlor window. He started the car. Exhaust enveloped it in a cold cloud. The tires slid on ice in the convent drive. Then they were gone. Elise stared at the place they had been.

"God asks a gift of them, Elise, and that gift is the best they have to give. It is you, my dear. Take care that you do not interfere with God's work in the lives of your parents. Your mother will rise to this. Kate is a good woman. She will respond to God with love. That is not your concern. Your concern is your own response; your concern is to be the best postulant possible."

Elise knelt in her assigned place in chapel. Light through the stained glass cast a purple glow across her face. Golden light slanted over the sanctuary and fell on the Christmas crèche, where delicate wooden parents bent over their child with an awe that never changed. Sister Mary began to play the organ. Bach. "Jesu Joy of Man's Desiring." Elise took a deep breath. Into the gateway of her heart a heavy stone rolled and settled into place.

⌒

Could she love God alone? She posed this question to herself on the convent path at the spot where she had, as a child, witnessed the appearance of the sacred beings. It was January, just a week after the visiting Sunday when Elise's mother had behaved so strangely. The sisters were observing their retreat of the month. The holy rule advised each nun to retire into the silent chamber of her heart and there meet the divine bridegroom alone. Elise welcomed the opportunity simply to be by herself.

The lake stretched out, a flat white plain, toward barely observable trees lining the other shore. This lake, farther south than her own Black Sturgeon Lake, lacked the drama created by the Canadian tectonic plate that thrust ancient granite up from the earth's jaws, leaving islands like dinosaur teeth. On Black Sturgeon's slate-colored rock the tamarack clung, and birch trees died from lack of nutrients or were toppled by lightning or simply froze in winters colder than forty degrees below zero. On jutting cliffs prehistoric tribes had drawn their history in ocher-colored petroglyphs. During winter powerful currents broke the ice and piled it in blue-white mountainous crags. Black Sturgeon Lake reminded Elise of Beethoven.

Lake Bemidji's music, even in winter, had more the properties of Bach. Pines and cedars, their branches weighted with snow, lined the shores. She saw no islands. Clean. Simple. Pure. Maybe not like Bach at all. Like Gregorian chant, perhaps, or at its most dramatic, Palestrina.

She caught herself. Did she have to compare everything to music? Even her experience of God came as a musical theme, more refined and rare than any other. Couldn't she love God purely and without comparisons? God alone?

As IT turned out, Elise hadn't been asked to play Christmas carols for the novitiate. Sister Mary came down to the recreation room instead, and Elise sang along with all the others.

"It's a sacrifice you can make to the infant Jesus," Mother Thomas Ann had explained to her in spiritual direction during Advent. "Perhaps you might think of it as a gift you are bringing to the manger, a gift truly from the heart, like the shepherds who had little but gave everything they had."

"THESE are your golden years, Sisters; treasure them," Mother Thomas Ann had told the postulants just that morning as she prepared them for this day of retreat. "If you give yourself, heart and soul, to God alone, I promise you that God will not be outdone in generosity. Never again will you have this opportunity to live completely without distractions. After the novitiate your mission to the church will, of necessity, occupy your mind. Then you will long for these days when your whole heart and mind were free for God alone. God alone, Sisters. Let everything else go: your families, your friends, your likes and dislikes. Ask God for the grace to love and serve him alone."

Certainly this must be a test. Three years of novitiate—as postulant, canonical novice, senior novice—focused on God alone, was not too much to ask. The piano would be waiting when the time was completed. She would remember. Her fingers could be retrained; with practice they would be strengthened again. Sister Mary must have encountered all the same rules, and her technique was flawless, her interpretation inspired.

Elise opened her small black notebook. Mother Thomas Ann had given one to each postulant and told her to write down retreat resolutions. During the coming month each sister would examine her behavior and measure her progress. Each day at noon they would meet in the chapel to record the number of times they succeeded and failed to accomplish their resolves.

"Keep it simple, Sisters. Posture is a good place for most of us to begin. Control the body first; the mind and soul will follow."

Not posture. Not for Elise. Years of piano practice had sculpted her body as surely as if she had been a dancer. It was the constant flow of music in her mind she needed to control. It was the yearning in her heart to play. Her hands and fingers ached from lack of use. If her life were to be lived for God alone, then controlling her need for the piano must be the place to begin. She set her black Shaeffer fountain pen on the lined page. "Whenever the thought or desire for music comes to my mind or my heart or even into my fingers, I will turn from it to the thought of God and I will repeat the words 'To you alone, O God, I surrender my soul.'"

It will work, she thought. It has to. God will not be outdone in generosity.

SUZANNE was coming down the path. Her rosary dangled from her right hand and her eyes were swollen from crying. In front of Elise she stopped. They stared at each other. Elise felt her throat contract. Should she speak? Retreat silence equaled the sacred silence in its severity. She kept the secret of their attic meeting, sin though it was. There could be no telling, and both girls knew it. Telling would separate them. Even the priest in the confessional could not be told because he would insist they tell Mother Thomas Ann and refusal would make absolution invalid.

Snow White would speak, would ask if she could help, or just say, "There, there," like Gramma Meghan would have said. "There, there, sweet honey, you just go ahead and cry if that's what you need to do. The world won't melt from tears." But then again it might. Strange how that world had changed in so short a time. Elise no longer knew what the world might do. She no longer seemed able to judge whether or not to speak. The rule said no. No, don't speak. Don't speak on retreat days. Don't speak on the stairs or in the hall or in the classroom before or after class or in the lavatory or the refectory or the dorm; don't speak at all after night prayers and speak only when necessary at other times of the day. Don't say anything frivolous except at recreation, which will be for half an hour every evening and for two hours every Thursday and Sunday afternoon. Don't say anything of a personal nature except to your superiors, in case you might disturb the recollection of your sisters.

"At first silence is a discipline, Sisters, but as you practice it you will eventually become the silence. Then, in your heart of hearts, you will hear the Word of God." Such was Mother Thomas Ann's promise.

Suzanne and Elise looked at each other in a strangled sort of way. It might be another horror like the secrets told in the attic. Or it could be small. Funny how small things could be made to seem large, how even small hurts could assume tragic proportions here.

"Oh God!" Suzanne whispered and then put her head in her hands and sobbed.

"There, there," Elise murmured, and embraced the other girl. "There, there."

The path, open and within view of the convent windows, clearly was not the place to continue this interaction. Elise took Suzanne's hand and guided her to a sheltered spot down the bank where a willow tree hung over the water in summer. She had discovered this nest when she was thirteen and waiting, after her piano lesson, for Meghan and Kate to finish visiting Mother Thomas Ann. Now the snow had been flattened by deer on the lake side of the bank. The girls crouched down where they could not be seen.

"What's wrong?" Elise asked when they were settled and facing each other in the small space.

"Mother says I mustn't write poetry anymore."

"Not write poetry?"

"She says it's not the time for worldly things. But my poetry . . . Elise, it's how I meet God." Suzanne produced a red leather diary from under her shawl.

"When she gave us our retreat notebooks I thought it would be okay to show Mother Thomas Ann that I'd been writing all along, ever since I was a child."

"And?"

"And she said to burn them."

"Burn them?"

"She said all must be left behind. She said the retreat notebook isn't for flights of fancy. She called my poetry flights of fancy! She said the time has come for being practical. The retreat notebook is for resolutions, not for imagination."

"But this diary isn't your retreat notebook."

"I know. I guess it doesn't matter, though. She said to burn it."

"You can't burn your poetry."

"And I have five other books like this in my trunk."

"You can't burn them."

"What am I going to do, Elise?"

The postulants looked at each other.

"Those years with my father, Elise, during those years it was poetry that kept me sane. I'm afraid I'll go crazy if I can't write." She reached out and took Elise's hands in hers. Hers were cold. "I feel something and I never know what it is until I write it down. I move my pencil on the page and what I feel just sort of appears in words. If it gets lost inside me, I begin to feel like I'm drowning." She looked out over the lake. "I never should have showed it to her."

"She won't let me play the piano, either."

"Really?"

"God alone. That's what she told me."

"What are we going to do?"

"Well, I'm not about to burn my music. She can stop me from playing the piano, but she can't make me burn my music."

"She told me the devil sneaks in where our desires are strongest."

"You really think it's the devil, Suzanne?"

"That's what she said. And it's what my dad would say. It really scares me, that it's what my dad would say."

"I don't think it's true. Not with music. Not with poetry."

"Then why do we have to choose?"

"Maybe we don't. Not forever, anyhow. Maybe just for a while. We could think of it as an engagement gift. We'll get it back when we make our vows."

Elise took another look at the red diary and then handed it back to Suzanne.

"No. You protect it for me. I'll hide the others, but she'll ask me about this one. I'll have to say that I disposed of it. So you keep it, okay?"

Elise nodded. She slipped the diary through the placket of her postulant's dress into the deep pocket of her petticoat, where it bulged. Fortunately, no one would ask about bulging pockets, the only place the postulants had in which to carry odds and ends. She would sneak up to the attic before supper and hide the diary in the bottom of her trunk along with her sheet music.

You had to be like a lawyer, measuring the words spoken by your superiors, protecting your secret life in the rare spaces between them.

The girls held each other's hands in silence until the bell in the convent tower rang, calling them to vespers.

ELISE knelt with her sisters. She breathed slowly. Mother Thomas Ann intoned the Magnificat antiphon.

"*Respéxit Dóminus humilitátem meam, et fecit in me magna qui potens est.*"

As the novice mistress turned and bowed, her veil floated gauze-like over her face. Watching her, Elise realized that a nun could be delivered from the cloister only with a caul over her face that would prevent her from seeing clearly either past or present. Elise's own caul, woven by spiders in threads fine and transparent, was already being formed. Who would suspect it could one day be opaque, that it could render her blind?

Already the rules were creating for Elise a new skeleton, this one outside her flesh. She might become an armadillo, a turtle, a chambered nautilus. Her inner bones had softened. She felt the weight of Suzanne's diary in her pocket. Without the holy rule she could barely stand. She bowed. She reminded God that she was new to convent life and didn't understand all that it required. She told God she felt caught between the rules and what seemed right. Suzanne's poetry was like a child, she argued, a child yet unborn that must be saved. But even at that, she wasn't sure. Mother Thomas Ann taught that the holy rule made it possible for the nuns to know God's will in every second of the day. A nun could be assured that in the voice of her superiors God revealed his plan.

That winter afternoon, sitting with Suzanne, looking out across a white expanse, she felt on the verge of some great undoing. It was as Mother Thomas Ann had said: Everything Elise had been, God would wipe away. He would replace that girl from Black Sturgeon Lake with someone else. Mother Thomas Ann thought it would be someone holy, someone worthy of divine love. But what if she was wrong? Elise felt the weight of Suzanne's diary and she imagined herself as one of God's poems. Why would he erase her? And if he did, how could she be sure he would have any words left for her at all?

XX

Raise your hand gracefully from the keys.
Let your arm be like the wing of a bird
in flight.

SISTER MARY'S MUSIC NOTEBOOKS, 1959

Meghan removed the decorations from her Christmas tree, a task
performed always on January 7, after the feast of the Epiphany,
because it wasn't proper to end the celebrations before the three
kings reached Bethlehem. If Christmas trees could last until February 2, she would keep hers up until then. She observed this feast of
lights as if it were her own drama. The purification of Mary became
each year a cleansing of her own soul, the presentation of Jesus in
the temple her own sacrifice.

The little doves flying. She wondered if the high priest let them
fly or if he killed them like the Passover lamb. Fly, little doves, she
prayed. Fly. The good Lord wouldn't want the killing, no matter
what the Bible said. Fly.

Each year the box for storing ornaments got bigger. The first
glass balls, those she and Willie collected, were gone, of course.
Burned. Lost with Willie. Lost with baby Michael and with the
piano and the house and with all but Kate and a few old photographs. She smiled, remembering a little village of wooden houses
made and hand painted in Germany. How Kate loved those houses,
set carefully on the branches from top to bottom of the tree, surrounded on Christmas Eve by candles. The whole Christmas tree a
village. Kate sat for hours mesmerized, mumbling to herself. Who
could know what she imagined, what kind of stories she made up

about that village? Ah well. Gone from the ornament box but not from Meghan's memory. That village existed in her memory as clear as yesterday.

This year was the first that she had received no ornament from Brian. Poor Brian, in Saint Vincent's Home in Crookston, he didn't recognize a soul. It happened suddenly. A hemorrhage in the brain. Now he walked up and down the halls smiling, nodding at everybody, hugging the women, talking gibberish. Didn't have a clue who he was. Probably didn't know he wasn't talking English. Probably wondered what was wrong with everybody else. Last time Kate took her to visit, the old priest grabbed her up in his arms and whirled her through the hall in a ballroom waltz step like they were twenty years old. Then he kissed her full on the lips. Old man. Tasted of stale ashes. Let her go. Dashed off to waltz with some other woman. Amazing he could walk. Those brain things had strange results. Attacked parts of your brain and you lost those parts and that was that. Though Brian seemed to have been left with the best of it.

She wrapped a small glass bird with amber eyes and put it carefully into its individual box. It was his first gift to her. "Such a little bird," he had said, and she knew he wasn't talking about the gift. He had touched her hand and the thrills traveled through her. She was too old for thrills now, but every ornament from him triggered such memories. Funny that his forgetfulness of her caused no sadness. But then, she'd been saying good-bye to him most of her life.

Elise's little handmade ornaments had a separate box that fit inside the larger one. Her tiny handprints in plaster, painted gold, too heavy for the tree but always placed prominently beside the scene of the nativity. The child's hands beside the divine child. From paper cutouts of snowmen to cross-stitched carolers, treasures every one.

The porcelain angel with the red velvet dress that adorned the top of the tree had come from Kate. Meghan smoothed the velvet. Poor Kate. She missed Elise and couldn't express it. Couldn't express much of anything. What happened to that girl, that beautiful firstborn? Kate. There was a time that Meghan thought Kate's pain must have come from her, or through her somehow. She thought there must have been something she could have done but hadn't. Never could she figure out what that something was. Now it occurred to her as she stroked the red velvet that nothing could have been done. A mother is simply a safe space.

The thought comforted her. She kissed the angel before she packed her in the box from Daytons. Dear Kate. She couldn't afford such expensive gifts.

Meghan made sure that each object fit snugly in the large cardboard box. No sense courting disaster. Then she taped it closed. The tree stood dark and tattered except for the long string of cranberries she would leave for the birds. Michael could take it outside when he and Kate returned from their visit with Elise.

Meghan took up the question of her own visits to Elise with Mother Thomas Ann, but it seemed there was some rule or other that allowed only parents to visit during the first two years. Silly rule. Actually, downright cruel. Not to be able to give Elise her Christmas hug! More than that! Two years! Why, she'd be old by then. Eighty. Clara Monroe was old enough herself to make some exceptions in that all holy rule of theirs! Friends all these years, and what good was it?

She pushed the box into the hallway and pulled the cord to release the attic stairway that slid down, unfolding on hinges. She secured it and began to climb, resting the Christmas ornament box on each step in front of her as she went. When she reached the top she would slide the box along the floor to the place against the west wall where she had kept it all these years since coming to Hollyhock Cottage. But when she lifted the box onto the second-to-the-top stair, Meghan felt an explosion in her chest, a lightning shock. Her field of vision flooded with crimson light, then white. She fell backward, propelled, almost flying over all the stairs, and lit with a thud on the hallway floor. The Christmas ornaments tumbled after her, bouncing off each stair, ripping open the box, scattering like jewels to decorate her dead body.

⌒

Mother Thomas Ann summoned Elise to her office in the novitiate cloister. As she made her way down the hallway to the room just this side of the heavy novitiate doors, Elise's mind pounded a staccato of fears. "Mama must be dead, or Daddy, or the house burned down."

Her lips were white and her hands shook once she stood in front of the nun who was her godmother.

"Sit down, dear." Mother Thomas Ann busied herself with papers on her desk. "Well," she looked up, "how are you liking your life in the novitiate?"

What? This couldn't be why she had been called. Small talk? A novice mistress couldn't engage in small talk, at least not with the likes of a mere postulant.

"It's fine, Mother."

"You are happy then?"

"Yes, Mother."

What was this about?

"Good. I admit that I've had some concern about you. It must be difficult not to be playing the piano."

"Yes, but it is good to have something to sacrifice."

"Yes." Mother Thomas Ann looked away, out the window at the frozen lake. There was silence for a moment. Then, "You know that I've been away for a few days?"

"Yes, Mother."

"Ordinarily I wouldn't leave here during the Christmas season, but I needed to spend some time in Eagle Inlet. Your mother and father send greetings."

"Thank you, Mother."

Good. Then they were okay.

"But I'm afraid I have some sorrowful news."

Elise's heart contracted.

"I went to Eagle Inlet to attend your grandmother Meghan's funeral, dear."

"Funeral?"

There had been a funeral? That meant that her grandmother was dead. But no one had told her. She ought to have been at the funeral. What about her mother? She ought to have been with her mother. How could there be a funeral without her?

"Yes, dear. Your grandmother died suddenly the day after Epiphany. It seems she was putting the Christmas ornaments away and suffered a massive coronary attack. You can be comforted that her soul was taken up immediately to be with our Lord. It is a great blessing that she experienced no suffering at all."

"But . . ." Elise stammered. "But why didn't anybody tell me?"

"I considered it, but felt that it would be best for you not to be distracted."

What? Gramma Meghan's death a distraction? Elise's head spun. "Distracted?"

"Yes, dear. You have your postulancy duties. You probably would have wanted to return to Eagle Inlet."

"But I should have been there."

"You see? And it is against the rule. Only for the death of a mother or father can the novitiate cloister be broken. I could not have allowed you to attend your grandmother's funeral. Don't you see? I wanted to spare you this dilemma. Grief could have led you to an immoderate choice. I attended in your place."

Gramma Meghan. All alone. The day after Epiphany—that meant that her mother and father were here for visiting day. They must have come home to the news. Or maybe they walked into Hollyhock Cottage and found her there. They must have called the convent immediately; they must have wanted Elise to know, to pray, to come home. And she hadn't been told. Not even told! The moment could never be retrieved. Gramma Meghan gone.

Elise felt a sudden need for a sweater. She held her body stiff against a trembling that was spreading out from her heart. Even her teeth wanted to chatter; she clamped down on her jaw.

"Thank you, Mother."

"I'm pleased with you, Elise. It's a big sacrifice. Be assured, dear; the Lord will not be outdone in generosity."

Elise stood and backed out of the room in the customary act of respect for her superior.

Once she was in the hallway the ice dam in her heart exploded like a rifle shot. Fire melted it. Fire licked out toward her extremities. Head on fire, feet on fire, fire shooting down her arms and into her fingers. She ran from the novitiate through the heavy doors into the main part of the convent. Her footsteps echoed off the tiled walls.

Behind her studio door Sister Mary was playing Mozart. Elise knocked. The music stopped and the nun's footsteps could be heard approaching. Then Elise was in her arms. The heavy woolen sleeves smelled of incense.

"There, there," the nun murmured, as Gramma Meghan would have done. "There, there."

Kate handed Mother Thomas Ann a blue porcelain dish. They sat together in the convent parlor three weeks after Meghan's death.

"It was your mother's."

"Oh?"

"Yes. I thought you might remember it."

"I don't think so. Our kitchen, though—it was blue. It might have been hers."

"It was."

"And it came to you through . . ." Mother Thomas Ann kept her voice as cool as the porcelain.

"My mother."

"Did she get it at a rummage sale or something?"

"No, a gift from your mother. From Helga."

"Oh? When?"

"I only remember stories. It was after you entered."

The nun turned the dish around in her hands. How delicate it was; she hadn't remembered that it was delicate. Her memory made it garish. The bright orange flower, a rose or maybe a lotus, it was hard to tell, adorned the bottom. Around it, in lighter colors of blue, were painted shadows of the same flower. She turned the dish upside down. Yes. Her mother's dish. She touched the strange insignia, the artist's signature probably. As a girl she'd wondered where it came from. China, maybe? But the characters seemed more fluid than Chinese. Maybe the Middle East. Persia. What was that country called these days?

"I see." The nun's tone remained vague.

"I was so small then," Kate went on. "Just a child. My mother served ice cream in it as a treat."

"It seems more like a display piece."

"I think so, too."

Clara Monroe had eaten oatmeal from the blue dish. Helga would dig a great spoonful of the sticky gruel from the cast iron pot and let it drop on top of the orange flower. These were the mornings during that summer before she entered Our Lady of Peace, when Clara's eyes were still red and puffy from crying over Tom Lenz. Her mother sprinkled brown sugar on the gruel and slathered it with thick cream newly separated from the milk.

"Anyway, Mother, I was going through my mother's things and there it was."

The nun said nothing.

"Maybe you could use it for holy water or something."

"Yes. Perhaps."

"On the other hand, if you don't want it, if you'd prefer—"

"No. No, really, it's quite thoughtful of you, Kate. Thank you."

Mother Thomas Ann placed the dish on the table in the convent parlor and tried to ignore it. Strange how things come back to haunt you. The blue dish. After all these years.

"I wonder if I could see Elise."

The nun felt a flicker of annoyance.

"It would be highly irregular."

"I know it isn't Visiting Sunday, but I thought that since I was here . . ."

"It's a critical time for our Elise."

"But her grandmother just died."

"Yes. Yes, I know that."

"I should see her, hold her."

"Like I said, Kate. It's critical."

"She needs me."

"No. She needs only God."

Mother Thomas Ann turned away from Kate. She picked up the blue dish and crossed the parlor to place it on a rosewood shelf that hung on the wall.

"Perfect."

Kate opened her purse, took out a hanky, and blew her nose.

"I'd best be going."

"It won't be long, Kate. Two weeks. You can see her then at the regular time."

"I suppose."

"This way the other sisters can enjoy it."

"Pardon me?"

"The blue dish."

"Oh."

"It's really for display."

"Yes. Yes, I suppose it is."

XXI

When your fingers refuse to strike the melodic note
and cacophony results,
begin gently to empty the mind.

SISTER MARY'S MUSIC NOTEBOOKS, 1959

Small bits of Elise begin to flake off. Little scraps of herself, like
Kleenex or the soft down of baby birds. Wind blows the scraps away.
Ah, ah, my God, please, she prays. Ah.

Please. Please what? How can she know? To say please make me
a saint is to be proud, vain. How can she be a saint? Scrap of dust—
that's what she is. Not even nothing. There is some honor in being
nothing. All the saints prayed to be nothing. I am as nothing before
you, Lord, prayed the saints. Dust. Blown away by the wind. Dirt.
Filled with sin and shame. Not even a Magdalene. Much was forgiven Mary Magdalene because of her great love. Elise's love blows
away with the rest of it. Lost.

Cleo's cry. She hears it in her mind at night. She feels the spray
of waves from Black Sturgeon Lake against her face. She is five years
old. She wants her mother and her mother doesn't come.

Please, God! Please!

She prays. She puts her pillow over her head. Her head throbs.
Something screams outside in the snow. Something is attacked, dying.
A rabbit. It sounds like a child. She holds her ears. Her heart goes wild.
Scream. Scream! It is sacred silence. It is against the rule to scream.

Mother Thomas Ann warned there would be things, things held
on to, things of the devil that could damn you to hell for all eternity,
things of the world holding the soul down. Attachments. All must be
given. All sacrificed.

Elise walks the halls like a ghost at midnight. Bare feet. White gown. Black hair flat against her back. The sisters in the adoration chapel don't see. She smiles. She must be invisible. Please, God.

Yes. She will please God.

God is not outdone in generosity.

Frost on the attic window. Moonlight beckoning into Candlemas. Night passage between Brigid's feast and Mary's feast. February cold. Stone hidden in a velvet pouch. Musical score of Rondo.

Now her bare feet on the cold stairs going down, past the praying nuns, past the window of angels. One door opens to snow and moonlight.

Bare feet on snow. A stone from home sinking into snow on a frozen lake. Her heart a stone. Hard. Deliberate.

Where did she get the candle? The match? Still night, under the moon. She cannot see how blue the cover of the Rondo score is in the darkness.

She lights the candle and consigns the music to the flame.

⟅⟆

Sister Mary William draped the statues in violet, and Father Austin reminded the sisters of their beginning and their end. Up from dust, return to dust. They knelt on the cold refectory floor and, kneeling, ate their cereal without sugar, their soft-boiled eggs without salt, and their toast dry. Sleet pelted the windows. Elise shivered. She glanced at Suzanne, whose cheeks were scarlet and who didn't return the look.

"Lent is preparation," Mother Thomas Ann had instructed just the day before. Elise sat on the little chair at the novice mistress's feet. "You must prepare not only for Easter but for your reception of the holy habit. Sister Mary William tells me you have finished hemming your veil."

"Yes, Mother."

"As you work, Sister, remember that the habit is only a symbol. As you sew, let your mind and heart realize that you are preparing to clothe yourself in Christ."

Each stitch, minute, careful, perfect, a prayer. She felt what it meant. The needle in and out. The thread following. Binding her to her sisters and their bridegroom. In. Out. The needle piercing cloth, piercing her heart and mind. Thread woven through cloth, the holy rule through her mind, and the spirit of the Sisters of Our Lady of Peace through her heart. This weaving made her one fabric with them. Soon nothing of Elise would remain. Her heart, her mind, her soul, would take on a religious habit. It wasn't enough simply to wear the habit; she must internalize that habit. Afterward, for the rest of her life, she would appear in her dreams clothed like a nun. Once woven together with the sisters, she never would be able to separate the weave.

"I am pleased with you, Elise," Mother Thomas Ann continued. "I can see that you are faithful in both little things and great things. Even the smallest sacrifice made for love is great. Are you willing to make a small sacrifice this Lent?"

"Anything, Mother."

"Good. It would be a shame, don't you think, if after having left your mother and father for the love of God, you were to dilute your commitment by holding back some lesser love?"

Already she had burned the music. What else could there be?

"I don't want to hold anything back, Mother."

"Of course you don't. This is why I want to talk to you about Suzanne."

"Suzanne?"

"Yes. The two of you are good friends. Am I right?"

"We have a lot in common."

"Yes, you do. Both of you have an artistic temperament. Both bright. You must have a lot you can talk about."

"When it is permitted."

"Of course. But there is a bit of a problem here, Elise. Sister Mary William has told me that the two of you aren't sharing yourselves enough with the others. The scriptures warn us that if we love those who love us, what grace is there in that? The greater love is toward those with whom we are not so compatible."

"Suzanne and I help each other."

"God alone is to be your help, Sister. Now I'm asking you to make this sacrifice for the love of your divine bridegroom. You will, of course, continue to love Suzanne and to pray for her, but I want you to seek out different postulants and novices at recreation time.

These affinities between sisters who are much alike in temperament can grow dangerous. They can take us from our fundamental commitment to God. And to be honest, Elise, you are prone to these kinds of passions. Your piano. Sister Mary. Now Suzanne. It's important to nip this in the bud."

"But I can't just stop talking to her, Mother. What would she think? I have to talk with her about not talking with her, don't I?" Something was flaking off in her mind. Something falling. So disorienting.

"You needn't worry about that, Sister. I will be speaking with Suzanne as I have spoken to you. The divided heart, Elise, is the devil's playground."

Trials of mind and heart are the fire of God, the refiner's fire in which the chosen are purified. Elise wrote of this fever in small script along the margins of her daily missal and on the blank pages in the back of her formulary of prayers. Mother Thomas Ann had said the retreat notebook was to be used only for recording resolutions, but she said nothing about the margins of books. Strict obedience stretched a lifeline across the chasm of hell. The one who could be faithful in small things would be faithful in great. Such maxims held her taut when the fever climbed the back of her neck to the top of her head, where it buzzed like electricity in a high wire.

AFTER ASH Wednesday breakfast Elise consulted the work roster. Sister Mary William had changed it. The day before, Elise had been washing dishes with Suzanne; now she was assigned to clean dorms with Imelda. Because Imelda was least like her of all the postulants, Elise also joined her for afternoon walks. Imelda lowered her head into the wind and ignored the burned tufts of sumac under their weight of snow.

The novices walked two by two along the convent pathways and into the woods skirting the lake, where they hid behind bushes, their black shawls like mounded earth above the snow. They tracked a herd of white-tailed deer that grazed on young birch along the lakeshore. A lone doe appeared first from the thicket, stood against the white expanse of lake, and lifted her head.

Without Suzanne, one companion was like another. Later, Elise would look back on those outings. She would be unable to retrieve any extended conversation between herself and her sisters. The fragments of their lives collected like scraps of cloth in a sewing box with nothing to hold them together. Elise would try, and fail, to make a pattern of it. Flakes of life, she thought. We were nothing but dust. But she would also remember the way red berries clung to thornbushes and how the black shawls flapped in the wind like ravens' wings.

THE SUN through the little rectangular panes of glass patched the wooden floor of Saint Helen's dorm with a crazy quilt of light. Elise knelt on all fours, her postulant's veil pinned behind her back, a scrub brush in her hands. She gasped. Her mind split. Fear seized her.

"Imelda!" The word gagged her.

The older postulant left her scrub bucket at the other side of the room. Stood above. Looked down. Elise pointed to the floor.

"What is this?"

"What do you mean?"

"This white stuff. What is it?"

"Dust, I guess."

"You don't think it could be fragments of the host?"

"What?"

"The host! The Blessed Sacrament. You don't think somebody could have dragged it up here from the chapel, do you?"

Imelda didn't say anything for several minutes. She just put her hand on Elise's shoulder. "How could it be," she said finally. "How could the host get from the altar way over here to the dormitory? It would be impossible."

"Maybe on our clothes?" Her mind was flaking away like hoarfrost off tree branches as the day warms. One voice in her mind laughed. You're crazy, and now everyone will know. Another voice hammered away about her responsibility. If she was the only one who could see these blessed fragments, then she was the one who needed to remedy the situation. The Lord must not be trampled upon. If the others thought her crazy, so be it. Such trials must be endured in the service of God. The fragments must be gathered. But who would do it? Only a priest could touch the Blessed Sacrament. She tasted bitterness. Her stomach churned. The dormitory walls began to spin. Imelda's face liquefied.

The two nuns sat facing each other without a desk between them in order to demonstrate their equality. Mother Thomas Ann, the mistress of novices, and Reverend Mother Esther, the major superior of the entire convent. Their equality was, to be more accurate, a balancing of powers. The mistress of novices did hold the upper hand when it came to the young women in her charge, but the reverend mother remained, technically, her religious superior. This actual discrepancy in power was not admitted openly by either of the women despite the fact that Clara Monroe, while still in training, had been the other nun's student, back in the years when Reverend Mother Esther was, herself, the mistress of novices.

Reverend Mother Esther looked on her protégée with pride. The circumstances of Clara Monroe's admittance had been questionable, to say the least, but the girl possessed a strong will and had risen above her shame. Her present position in the community of nuns proved that God's grace, combined with a woman's fortitude, worked miracles.

So young Sister Esther had been then, only twenty-six and just graduated with a master of arts degree, the first Sister of Our Lady of Peace to achieve that. The General Council appointed her mistress of novices, saying, "The novices deserve the best we have." What a swelled head that remark created. Well, the years had brought her down a peg or two, the Lord be praised, and here she had stayed. The Lord used ordinary instruments to achieve his purposes. Few of the professed sisters could say they had not felt the touch of her mind on their thoughts and the grip of her will upon their desires.

Clara Monroe. What promise in that girl. Poor, dear Clara. Esther had held her when she cried; there was no sense denying the memory. For some situations there is no rule. Late at night and the girl was kneeling in the chapel, her arms spread out, sobbing. What took Esther to the chapel she never questioned. God, of course. The grace of God. The tenderness of God toward his beloved. There are times that sacred silence does not apply.

Beautiful Clara Monroe. Still beautiful Mother Thomas Ann.

There are secrets between women, never spoken, secrets among brides of Christ. God brings his brides together and fulfills their sacrifice to him in their love for one another.

During Mother Esther's years as mistress of novices she had recognized the potential of many girls and she had loved them for that raw material given her to place in the good Lord's hands. But Clara was her first.

Now Mother Thomas Ann had a protégée of her own in Elise Pearson. Elegant. Talented. Much would be required of her. Much given.

"I am concerned," she was saying to Mother Thomas Ann, "that you may be hurrying Elise along too rapidly."

"The sacrifices asked of her have not been ours to determine, Reverend Mother. Her grandmother's death, her religious studies, which preclude her musical development—these are our Lord's doing."

"Perhaps we ought to temper the harsh realities of life just a bit by easing her through them, softening the rule just a bit. She has a delicate spirit."

"I differ with you, Reverend Mother. This girl has a difficult path, but she's strong and will benefit from strict observance. I wouldn't want to weaken her with coddling."

Some things did worry Mother Thomas Ann, though. Not that she intended to tell Reverend Mother Esther. These were things she would take upon herself, and by so doing, she would attach Elise to her by cords of gratitude. This wasn't the first time the novice mistress had encountered a case of the scruples.

"But, Mother," continued the reverend mother, "she's losing quite a lot of weight. She's looking downright haggard. I believe you have a responsibility to her, even to her family."

"I must be careful when it comes to her family."

"Because of your connections with them?"

"Yes, Reverend Mother. My sense of responsibility toward them could become exaggerated because of those connections."

Reverend Mother Esther reached out to Mother Thomas Ann and took her hand.

"Of course you are concerned about your attachment to them. But surely—"

"Please, Reverend Mother, trust me about this girl. You wouldn't want my attachment to her family to be responsible for turning her from the will of God. Remember what you taught me long ago. Of God's beloved much is asked."

As a matter of fact, Elise's desire for holiness had begun to exceed the bounds of rationality. On the other hand, what was a postulant to think? The book of the saints was replete with every penitential practice the girl wanted to perform, and more besides. Still, she was the only one among this new group of girls who asked permission—regularly asked permission—to perform additional penance. And as her superior and spiritual guide, Mother Thomas Ann always denied her that permission. Obedience was the greatest penance of all.

Mother Thomas Ann had put the dilemma before the child. "How can I permit you to increase your penances while you are haunted by inadequacy in the performance of your daily tasks? Do the ordinary well. It is all that is required. Live each moment fully. Love. Nothing else matters."

But the girl came to her with such outrageous stories! Guilty of this, guilty of that. The blood of the Lord. She claimed to have seen it flooding the sanctuary. She was guilty of the Lord's body. She claimed to be able to detect the smallest fragments of the Blessed Sacrament scattered on the floor before the altar. She feared she had cancer, or epilepsy, or tuberculosis, and had not made that condition known in time. All imaginary. But she sat on the small chair at Mother Thomas Ann's feet and wept as if her poor heart were crushed under her sins. Then she begged to perform the discipline on her bare back until she drew blood, to fast on bread and water, to wear a hair shirt, to spend an hour during the middle of the night lying prostrate on the dormitory floor.

"Absolutely not!"

"But I will be condemned!"

"That's ridiculous."

"It is the will of God that I love him in this way."

"*I* will tell you the will of God for you."

"God will not be pleased with me."

"If God is displeased, I will take his displeasure upon myself. I will take responsibility for this. You have only to obey. The responsibility and any guilt is mine."

"But, Mother, God can't do that, can he? I mean, God knows. God knows, and even then God may not be able to fix it."

"Fix it?"

Elise began to sob. "How can anyone be sure of God, Mother? How can they? How can you know what to do? And if you don't know, anything could go wrong. You can lose what you love; someone can die, even, when you ought to have been there and weren't, and it would be your fault and God couldn't do a thing about it."

The novice mistress took the girl in her arms. "Hush now, child. God can't be like that. We're told that God is love, everything we desire. God is abundant mercy. Even if you condemn yourself, God will not condemn you."

It would pass. Scruples had been known to plague many fervent aspirants to the religious life. The condition, most often, was temporary.

Of cause or cure Mother Thomas Ann knew nothing.

⁓

Elise sat on the little chair at Mother Thomas Ann's feet. She was crying into the third huge white linen hanky and the nun reached into her drawer for a fourth.

"You must stop this nonsense, Sister." Chest voice. Crisp consonants. Eyes of chipped flint. Mercy hadn't succeeded. "A delicate conscience is a good thing, but a scrupulous conscience is an insult upon God's mercy. I have told you that I will take this responsibility upon myself."

Elise hiccuped like a child, gasping for breath between her sobs, unable to speak.

Mother Thomas Ann sent her to the chaplain's quarters.

OLD Father Austin needed more in life than a good stroll with his rosary along Lake Sagatagan at Saint John's Abbey and had come to live out his retirement as chaplain to the Sisters of Our Lady of Peace. Naturally tonsured, round as the legendary Friar Tuck, he possessed a charm and emitted a kindness the nuns found irresistible. Priests for convent work were scarce and most nuns would have had to make do with a part-time chaplain who drove out each day just to celebrate mass. It had taken Reverend Mother Esther three years to complete the negotiations with the abbot. Now Sister Agatha, the cook, pampered the old man with steak or southern fried chicken, and Sister Hildegard kept his rooms both spotless and cozy, the combination of which was no easy task.

He took Elise's hands and called her "my child." He led her to an overstuffed chair, the first her body had felt since her entrance day. She sank into the soft brown leather. He brought tea in china cups with flower decorations. On an ornate end table he set a plate of Sister Agatha's butter cookies. He sat across from her and lifted his cup. His hand trembled from early stages of Parkinson's disease and the china wobbled and clicked like false teeth.

"I was so sorry," he began, "to hear of your grandmother's death. I knew her well, you know, and poor Father Murphy. She took fine care of him all those years. A saintly housekeeper is a gift of God."

He smiled like a grandpa. "Take some tea, child," he urged. "It will help."

"But I'm not crying about Gramma Meghan," she blurted.

"Oh?"

"Mother Thomas Ann sent me here because I'm scrupulous."

"Ah, is that right? And what am I to do about it?"

"I don't know."

"Well then, child, we'll just let it be and enjoy ourselves. Not often I get such lovely company. Tell me about your grandma."

She ate Father Austin's cookies and told stories of Hollyhock Cottage, of the many nights spent with Meghan. Her words activated her senses. She saw the trunk filled with pictures, touched the ivory satin and lace wedding dress. It seemed to her she opened Gramma Meghan's music box that stood on fragile brass feet and heard again a melody played nowhere else.

He told her of visiting Father Murphy in years before she was born. He painted word pictures of delicious meals and crisp bed linens and intelligent conversation. "Nothing like a bright and articulate woman to liven up conversation." He laughed. "And your grandma could hold her own with any priest and with the bishop, too. That didn't happen often, though." Father Austin chuckled. "That rascal, Murphy, kept his treasure out of the bishop's field of vision."

This was a part of her gramma's life she hadn't known.

"Do you know what *epikeia* is?" he asked just as she was finishing her third cup of tea and the last of the cookies.

"No, Father."

"It's my reminder to enjoy life. Every moment's a gift, child. Who am I to say it's not? I'm just a bag of bones. So I practice the virtue of *epikeia*."

"What does it mean?"

"Noticing the gift that's hidden and sometimes all but buried alive by our rules and laws. Celebrating that gift. Relaxing and letting God take care of things, which is something God's going to do anyway."

Suzanne was a gift. Gramma Meghan, too.

"But the Bible says we're supposed to be perfect." Despite God, her mind went on spinning. In spite of God. She must be perfect for spite. No, she must stop thinking like this. It must be sinful to think this way. Blasphemy.

"Yes. And a long time ago I came to the conclusion that I was making a gigantic mess of it. Every time I tried to be perfect I ended up with a whole bunch of bits and pieces. Nothing connected. Nothing worked. I finally realized that making me perfect is God's business. My business is to thank him for the job he's done. Chances are he doesn't want me perfect anyhow. Maybe even God appreciates a bit of surprise and a good laugh now and then."

Father Austin leaned back and took a deep breath. "That's the secret, Sister. We trust the mercy and accept the freedom. Without that we're all of us just dry bones."

He put down his cup and stood up.

The interview must be over. Elise slipped to her knees in front of the priest. "Thank you, Father. May I have your blessing?"

He placed his hand on her head and muttered for a moment in Latin. Then instead of sending her back to the novitiate cloister he took her hand and pulled her to her feet.

"Come with me, Elise; I want to show you something else."

They climbed the back stairs that led directly to the sacristy of the nuns' chapel. She breathed the combined scent of incense and beeswax. He motioned for her to follow him into the sanctuary, to the altar, where the sanctuary lamp cast a red flickering light on the white linen altar cloth.

Father Austin folded back the linen.

"Give me your hand, child."

"Why?" These were the sacred places, not to be touched by those unconsecrated.

"Put your hand alongside mine on the altar stone."

"Is it allowed?" The holy chalice rested on this stone. The altar of sacrifice. The sacred place of meeting between heaven and earth.

"Not just allowed, dear. Necessary."

Elise placed her right hand, palm down, between the four crosses, one at each corner of the marble stone.

"Can you feel it?"

The stone felt cool. It also felt like satin. But what Elise felt more than the texture of stone was a rush of fever traveling from her hand directly to her heart.

"I feel warm."

"It's the bones, the relics of saints contained in the altar stone." The old priest chuckled. "I know they call me superstitious, and they might be right. Doesn't matter. I think of these fiery women's bones, feverish inside the stone. These wild saints. All that passion. It could issue forth like lightning at any moment, like the shining sword of God."

She ran her hand lightly over the altar stone and it felt alive. She could almost feel their hearts, the throbbing of their desire, their spirits—subtle enough to pass through stone. She almost heard their whispers of release and the freedom of their songs.

"Like *epikeia*."

"Exactly." The priest's eyes twinkled. He unfolded the altar cloth again and let it drape over the edge.

Still and all, it was a troubling thought. All that passion locked in stone.

As if he read her mind, the priest turned to her and smiled. "What will it be then, child? Dry bones, or the shining *epikeia* of the saints?"

THE next morning when Elise picked up her toothbrush a voice inside her head suggested that perhaps she ought not brush her teeth before mass because she couldn't tell whether or not she might have swallowed a bit of toothpaste without realizing it. It would break her fast. It would be a sin. She wouldn't know whether or not to receive communion, for which an absolute abstinence was required. Then she remembered *epikeia*.

She squeezed toothpaste on her brush. Afterward she licked her lips, her tongue collecting droplets of water. She licked her teeth. Certainly God wouldn't send her to hell because of toothpaste. God would have to be crazy.

She slipped her postulant's dress over her head and tied her veil in place. Then she caught up with Suzanne. "Praised be our Lord Jesus Christ," she whispered. Suzanne smiled and the two of them walked together down the hallway, in silence, toward the chapel for the morning mass.

XXII

With each repetition
the theme becomes a more haunting refrain,
an aching that can barely be endured.

SISTER MARY'S MUSIC NOTEBOOKS, 1959

Kate dusted the piano. She lifted the blue alabaster bird, its throat rounded with song, and cupped it in her hand. Her fingers closed over it. Its coolness reminded her of night, of that moment before sleep when a breeze moves through the room, or of waking to the cry of her child and rising to go to her, lying beside her, holding her firm body in the cup of her own. The resistant surface of that child, her skin cool to the touch. This singing bird that Kate gave her on her twelfth birthday and set on the piano as music, as the fullness of a mother's dream, Elise left here just like everything else. The piano silenced. Song stuck in the alabaster throat.

Kate replaced the bird and sat down on the piano bench. She lifted the cover from the keys and placed her fourth finger on E. Slowly, her heart pounding, she began to play "Für Elise."

There is no end to what God can take away. Now even the name was lost. *Elise.* Gone.

The baby Elise, her head round as a world, hair of black silk, of night over the ocean. She lay in her crib, a miracle to be touched only with reverence. Kate's fingers moved with grace, producing tones that rang, that ached, that shone like light. Thank God for such simplicity, the music in her fingers, something she could play for memory's sake to make the piano sing again now that her daughter was gone.

The woman Kate, middle aged now, wandered daily through her house dusting what remained of Meghan and Elise. She felt like a land eroded by God and death. She felt like a river flooded with sorrow and lying still and stagnant over fields no longer fit for life.

"There never was enough time," she told Michael the night after Elise received the habit and the new name. What she meant was she hadn't found her way into the girl while she still had a chance. At first she felt a shyness she couldn't explain even to herself. Michael talked the language of the child, took her to the dock, introduced her to the gulls. She watched from the dining room window. The father lifting the child above his head, making her fly. Kate couldn't go to them. She said work kept her inside, the books, the dishes, the meals, the tourists. But the truth was that once she refused herself permission to join them on the dock, she'd set her fate. Their morning communion belonged to them alone.

Kate circled her child like a planet around a star, never too close. They were winged creatures, this child and her father. She should have named her Angela. Shivers of light across her heart, both of them. They took her, used her up, pinned themselves to earth with her weight. She became their gravity or they might have turned together into music, into air or fire.

It happened despite her. Elise, who had been music, now was air, and Michael, his flesh consumed, was fire.

She finished "Für Elise" and closed the piano. She rose from the bench, opened it, and took out an ornate brass key. She inserted the key into the lock and turned it until she heard it click. It was finished; all of it was finished. Elise gone. The piano silenced. She dropped the key into its black velvet pouch and drew the cord tight.

Upstairs, Meghan's steamer trunk rested against the far wall of the attic. In it lay the other silent things, pictures without voice now that Meghan was dead. Kate lifted the cover and tucked the piano key among the photographs, beside a picture of herself as a child sitting at a Stark player piano, her feet dangling from the bench because her legs were too short to reach the pedals. Her fingers depressed the keys, and her face, transformed by the music, seemed that of the eternal muse. She closed the cover of the trunk, turned out the light, and went back down into her silent house.

~~~~~

"Elise is now dead to the world."

The bishop traced a cross on her forehead with holy chrism and conferred upon her the name Sister Michelle. Kate wept into Michael's handkerchief.

Afterward the novice carried her gifts in a cardboard box and set them on Mother Thomas Ann's desk. Her heart was a tough cord wrapped around each gift, attaching it to herself. One by one the novice mistress lifted the gifts and turned them before her eyes like jewels.

Kate's hand-carved statue of the Sacred Heart. Kate's eyes had shone when Elise unwrapped the delicate object that for as many years as Elise could remember stood on a little corner shelf in the living room.

"This was your grandmother's, and her mother's, and on back as far as anyone remembers."

Its wood glowed with the patina of age. As a child she imagined that generations of prayer had buffed it smooth. The statue embodied her family's soul.

Mother Thomas Ann held it up. "Sister Agatha's devotion to the Sacred Heart would be enhanced by this lovely statue, don't you think, Sister Michelle?"

"It's been in our family for a long time, Mother. I think my mother intended it for me."

"Of course she did, Sister. But whoever loves family more than the Lord is not worthy of him. We own nothing individually. When your mother made a gift of this statue, she gave it not to you but to the community. You have died, Sister, and your life is buried with Christ in God. If, despite this, your heart remains attached to a statue, it is not free to love the Lord whom the statue represents."

"But she would be hurt if I gave it away."

"It is not yours to give, Sister, and besides, your mother need never know. This statue has achieved its ultimate meaning for your family. Sacrifice. It is not for you to keep what belongs to God alone."

She was allowed to use the New Testament, a gift from Gramma

and Grampa Pearson, and the stainless steel wristwatch from her
father. Each new novice had received one, a gift recommended to
the families by the novice mistress herself. Everything else—a black
sweater hand knit by Mrs. Osborn, a leather-bound book of psalms,
a porcelain statue of the Blessed Virgin from her old friend Margaret, an onyx rosary from Father Quinn—she left on Mother
Thomas Ann's desk for redistribution.

DURING the month that followed, Sister Michelle noticed a peculiar
pressure at a point between her breasts where an indentation the size
of her thumb was imprinted on her sternum. The pressure increased
until her breath, passing over the point, burned her. Her thoughts, it
seemed, were dropping one by one into her heart, catching fire,
turning to ash that was blown away by her own breath. That heart
ticked like the metronome in Sister Mary's studio. As the novice
made her way through the cloistered days and nights, through the
convent's world of rituals and rules, she felt played like a musical
instrument. Nothing of her own mind or will remained to obscure
the music. Round and round went the musical theme, a song of
"yes" and "Jesus," and the music filled her cells and became her
heart, until everything in her sang this song.

Summer came to the lake. The gulls returned from wherever
they had flown to escape Bemidji's subzero cold. Fishermen trolled
past the convent in launches that bore the names of nearby resorts.
They waved to the nuns who walked the paths along the shore.
Veiled, draped with layers of black wool, bound in linen, Sister
Michelle's skin crawled with prickly heat. What did it matter? Heat
was a descant, a note impossibly high, in the song she constantly
sang to the beloved. Her religious habit was her wedding dress.
Each morning as she pinned the veil to the white linen, as she
looped the cords of her cincture around her waist, as she hid her
small breasts beneath the linen wimple, her heart swelled under the
indentation in her sternum. "My beloved is mine as I am his," she
prayed. "Let him seek me among the lilies."

"AND how's my little worry wart?" Mother Thomas Ann reached
down to take Sister Michelle's hands. The novice was seated on the
child's chair where each young sister sat during her spiritual direc-

tion as a reminder that she was a beginner in this ancient way of life. When she was a postulant the chair had embarrassed her. Now she felt comforted to look up into the older nun's eyes, to feel the warmth of the older nun's knees at a level with her breasts so that if there were sorrow in the novice's heart she could easily lay her head in Mother Thomas Ann's lap and cry.

"The worry is gone, Mother. God lifted it. You and Father Austin, you were angels."

"Hardly!" The novice mistress laughed. "And your piano, Sister; do you miss playing your piano?"

"The piano is merely an instrument, Mother. God is teaching me that I'm his music."

"Perhaps we'll make a nun of you yet, Sister." Mother Thomas Ann stroked the novice's hand.

ELISE had been mopping the hallway in front of the novice mistress's office when she was summoned in and told to close the door.

"I see the desire in you, the yearning for the beloved." Mother Thomas Ann took Sister Michelle's hands and brought them up to her breast, placing them on the silver profession cross that hung by a black cord around her neck. The novice felt the softness and the rise and fall of the older nun's breath beneath the linen and the wool.

"Are you afraid of me?" asked Mother Thomas Ann.

"No, Mother." But she was breathing heavily and her heart pounded.

"There's nothing to fear, dear one. I'm your godmother. I've loved you since you were born. You are twice my daughter, once in baptism and now in religious life."

"Yes, Mother; thank you, Mother."

Clara Monroe laughed lightly, a caress. "You are afraid, aren't you, dear?"

"Maybe a little."

"When you were a postulant, my dear, I needed to be strict with you. Even hard. Because I have chosen you, Sister Michelle. Much will be asked of you; much is always asked of those to whom much is given. But you needn't be afraid. Our Lord will prepare and protect you, and I will do all in my power to make you ready."

"Ready for what?"

"For the transformation, my dear. For love."

"What do you mean?"

"Here, child, feel my heart." She pressed the novice's hands into the hollow between her breasts. Then she moved her own hand to the hollow spot, the indentation in Sister Michelle's sternum. With the heel of her hand resting on Michelle's breast, she pressed with her fingers into the hollow. Michelle felt her heart rise to meet the touch, felt it pound against bone. She became hot and broken and breathless all at once.

"Yes," the older nun murmured, "yes, you feel it, don't you? The fire?"

Michelle's head buzzed. The little hairs stood out under her veil at the nape of her neck. Her stomach churned.

"Yes, Sister. Yes, I do."

"We are mother and daughter, my child. We are spiritual sisters. You are chosen to complete the work I was chosen to begin. We share one soul."

"I don't understand."

"Understanding is not necessary. Simply do as I tell you. God will do the rest."

"Are you sure?"

Mother Thomas Ann didn't answer her. Instead she placed her hands on Sister Michelle's face and tilted it up. Her breath smelled of mint. Her tongue flicked against Michelle's closed lips.

"Open," she whispered.

Michelle obeyed.

Mother Thomas Ann sighed, she blew slowly and long into Michelle's mouth, and the novice received her breath.

"My breath, your breath," the nun chanted. "My life to your life."

The two women breathed in and out of one another, slowly, rhythmically. They pressed their fingers into the hollow of each other's hearts, where the fire throbbed. Sister Michelle felt something open in her, and within that opening the presence of what could only be divine.

After that she remembered nothing until she heard Mother Thomas Ann say, "Let this be a secret between us, Sister. Let this be our secret of divine love."

Sister Celina couldn't sleep. She slipped her black robe over her nightgown and tied her night veil on her head. In the chapel she was alone. Page after page of the sacred text read, pondered. She dug like a miner in the dark. The sanctuary lamp flickered.

She buried things. The little clay statue under a birch tree. She did it on a summer night while all the nuns slept. "May the angels lead you into Paradise," she prayed, "and with Lazarus, who once was poor, may you have everlasting rest." The five remaining red-leather diaries she buried deep in the sand by the lake's edge. Water filled the hole and the poetry dissolved. She covered the grave with rocks as large as she could carry. The moonlight covered everything without discrimination. She stood barefooted in the water that soaked the hem of her seersucker gown. She didn't notice. Nor did she notice the tracks made by her wet feet on the marble floor of the convent chapel, where she went afterward to kneel with her arms spread in the form of a cross.

In the daytime she moved like a dancer from one moment to the next. She sat at the library table with three different translations of the Holy Bible open before her. She searched the scriptures. No longer would she be Suzanne. The promises were clear. For the wedding feast of the Lamb she had prepared herself as a bride. Her heart was a white stone inscribed with a new name. Now her tears should be wiped away. The secrets were unearthed and she couldn't put them back. Elise said nothing. Suzanne understood. They were no longer themselves. Their hair had been shaved from their heads, their names obliterated.

The past is gone. It is as though it never were.

Do not be afraid, the bridegroom whispered in her ear, and she could feel his wet breath. If your eye should cause you to sin, pluck it out. If your hand reaches out to evil, cut it off. It is better to go through life maimed than to burn in hell. Do not be afraid. I am with you always.

No one else. He is a refiner's fire. He burns away impurities. He is the babe of Bethlehem; the virgins nurse him at their breasts.

Each night she lay flat on her face in the sanctuary, arms out-stretched, a human cross. I am yours. I can belong to no one else.

My heart yearns to compose a canticle of love. When shall I enter and see the face of God? She awaited the piercing of the lance, the sound of a hammer on nails.

Pastor Isaac's voice rang, a bell in her head. Mountains fall. The oceans turn to blood. The virgins sing; their robes are washed in the blood of the Lamb.

ONCE she was her father's favorite person in the world. She believed him when he told her that the spankings that he gave were good. Spare the rod and spoil the child, he had said and hugged her. She still can feel his arms around her, his lap under her, still can hear him reading Bible stories and asking her to scratch his head. How he loved her fingers in his hair. He gave her quarters if she just would scratch his head. Then, when she was finished, he laughed and said she could have another if she scratched for just ten minutes more.

Once they fixed the roof together. That was when she was eight years old. He lifted her to places he couldn't fit and then said how clever she was, how small and clever, and he kissed her and tickled her belly.

It had started with her bath when she was ten. He wanted to give her baths. Her breasts were coming out early, little hard circles budding around the nipples. He touched them with his fingers full of soap and he said how lovely. You are my little woman, he said. She asked him please to stop because she was too old now for her father to be giving her a bath, and he said of course, that he would stop. And stop he did for several weeks, but it didn't last. She locked the door to the bathroom, but he stood outside and said please very low on his breath and he said he loved her and she was his buddy.

She knew he was the hand of God.

He came to her room. She was eleven. She'd gotten her period by then. Her breasts were big for her age—always too big. Still too big. Too soft. She bound them in rags but her mother said that it was bad for her and she could hurt herself. He came at night when her mother was asleep and everyone was asleep, even though her brother and sister wouldn't have known the difference, being so much younger. Please scratch my head, Suzanne, he said to her, and he gave her a quarter. She put the coin under her pillow and did it. She scratched his head and his hair was soft, just washed and smelling like Prell. She sat on her bed in the middle of the night and scratched her father's head and he took the covers off her and laid his head in her lap. He nuzzled in, his nose and mouth in her crotch. She had her nightgown on but she could feel his breath there and it was warm.

She didn't know anything. She knew where babies came from, but how they were made she just didn't know. She had never asked. So when he put his hand on her and his fingers came up into her, she cried and said why, why? And she said please, Daddy, stop. And he told her she was his lovely girl and his buddy and he loved her more than anyone and he would touch her gently and make her body feel good because that's what fathers were for when their little girls grew up. This was his God-given duty and his privilege, he told her, to make her ready for a husband who would come someday in the future. She couldn't believe him, though, because her heart was turning over in her chest and she knew in a deep place in her mind that after this she could never be buddies with her father again.

He took off her nightgown and put his mouth on her breasts and sucked them like a baby might. Spread your legs, Suzanne, he said, and his voice sounded like when he used to say pick up your toys. Then he said more gently, it's okay, honey, spread your legs. And when she didn't, he took his hands and spread them. He licked her. She said to stop because she had to pee. And he lifted his head and looked at her and smiled. How odd, that he would smile. He said it wasn't pee. He said God made women this way. Just let it go, he said, and you'll see what women are. He said he'd show her.

Then he fumbled with his pajamas and got naked. His penis stood straight out. She'd only seen her little brother's penis and had no idea one could get so big. He crouched on top of her with his mouth in her crotch and his tongue licking and licking and his penis hanging in her face and he lifted his head and said, suck me, honey, suck. But she gagged and couldn't.

Scared as she was she still could feel the thing he told her she would. Her whole body swelled up, throbbing and aching. He knew it even though she was crying pretty hard by then, because that was when he turned himself around and laid his whole body on top of her and his penis was like a mouse trying to get into its hole. And finally it did.

XXIII

Some musical phrases require a focus so intense
and a concentration so complete,
you will seem to have dissolved into the sound
that you have sacrificed yourself to produce.

SISTER MARY'S MUSIC NOTEBOOKS, 1961

"There is no right or wrong for us, Sister," the novice mistress told Sister Michelle as they walked together by the lake at the beginning of Elise's third springtime at Our Lady of Peace. "There is only love. Saint Augustine said it well. 'Love God and do what you will.' "

What of their love could be called sin? It expressed itself in breath, in a worship of the cross, in reverent touch. Its gifts were wild roses, stones from the beach, a perfect feather from a gull's wing. It was love calling for sacrifice. Over and over it broke open the heart.

LATER the same day Sister Michelle watched from her window as her novice mistress walked the lake path with Sister Celina.

"Our little sister is delicate as a hummingbird wing," the novice mistress explained to Sister Michelle. "Your heart must be large enough to hold all those who come to me since our two hearts are one. Can you do that, beloved one?"

What were they saying to each other? The older nun stopped and turned to the younger one. Their veils lifted slightly in the breeze. The novice mistress put her hand under Sister Celina's chin and lifted her face so that their eyes met. Sister Michelle strained to open her heart to include the other novice. Perhaps Snow White and Rose Red, forbidden now to each other, could meet in their love for Mother Thomas Ann.

After more than a year of meeting several times a week alone in the novice mistress's office, Sister Michelle and the older woman had developed a practice of meditation that dropped the young sister into ecstatic trance. Their right hands touching each other's hearts, their breathing synchronized, they gazed into one another's eyes. Heat shot from Sister Michelle's heart upward toward the top of her head, where it swirled into a white-hot point of light. Instantly she became that light and joined a soft golden glow that surrounded the eyes of Mother Thomas Ann, obliterating or dissolving every other part of her body. Light and the gaze of her eyes. Light in which the women were no longer two but one.

"Do you see the light?" Sister Michelle asked afterward when she knelt at the novice mistress's knees and received her blessing, a cross traced upon her forehead.

"It is the light of Christ and you are his chosen one."

She drank light; it dizzied her. She went alone into the woods.

"I give it all to you, all of it," she told the beloved. "I give you my love for Mother Thomas Ann. Purify it." She felt a love pour out of her that left her weak. She fell on her knees. Her long dress spread in a circle over the brown pine needles. Light was everywhere. A thornbush with red berries shimmered gold. She drew in breath and prostrated herself on the altar of earth, crying, "My God, my God!"

"I gave you up," she told the novice mistress. "I want the others to have you, to have everything you have given me. I want to be nothing to you. I want only God."

Mother Thomas Ann's eyes. Her hands. Her lips on the lips of the novice. Tears. Her breasts under the silver cross. Her breath on eyes, on lips. Her hands moving across breasts, seeking the place of fire. Light then, golden, around her. Her voice, gentle, compelling. "The beloved comes to you through me. Love me, little one. Love is God."

SISTER Celina's face grew pale. In the refectory, dishes slipped from her hands and crashed to the floor. Each night at supper she wore broken glass or china on a cord around her neck and went from table to table with her veil lowered over her eyes to ask forgiveness. Mother Thomas Ann exclaimed if this were to continue the sisters soon would be eating from cupped hands. Sister Celina blushed and bowed her head. The mistress of novices called her to her office.

Who could know what happened to her there?

She cried at night, muffling her gasps and sobs with her pillow.

She seemed unable to get her veil on straight. Her linens were damp with sweat even on a cold day, and she smelled like dirty feet. As if she knew this, she knelt at the door to the chapel every Wednesday afternoon and requested permission to kiss the feet of the sisters as they passed on their way to vespers. One by one the sisters stopped and Sister Celina bent low to place her lips on each nun's polished black shoe.

In the middle of the night she rose and took the discipline. Sister Michelle awoke to the thud of the little chains on soft flesh. She saw Sister Celina's bare torso in the moonlight and the flick of silver as the chains etched red paths on the skin of her back and breasts.

"Mercy!" Sister Celina whispered over and over into the sacred silence.

Sister Michelle listened. She turned her head away and the cotton pillowcase felt cool against her cheek. Maybe madness was a thread in the weave of holiness. Perhaps ecstasy required the faithful bride of Christ to drop the mooring lines that held to a common reality.

SISTER Michelle and Sister Celina met in the cove by the lake on the last day of the ten-day retreat preparing them for their vows. It was an afternoon of solitude during which there would be no conferences and each sister could go off by herself to complete the examination of her life and to formulate those promises she would make to her beloved at the moment of nuptials, when she pronounced her vows. The meeting between the novices wasn't planned. Sister Michelle had been coming to this place each retreat of the month since she was a postulant. On this day, when she arrived, Sister Celina was already there, seated on a log, staring out at the lake. Sister Michelle sat beside her.

Silence was an absolute requirement. Sister Michelle took the other novice's hands. They were clammy. She breathed in synchrony with Sister Celina, who soon began to cry. Sister Michelle tightened her grip on the novice's hands.

"I can't do this," Sister Celina sobbed.

"Shhh, we mustn't talk."

"We must!"

"The rule . . ."

"Please, I have to talk to someone."

The lake, except for the gulls, was empty. Fishing season hadn't begun. Oak and birch leaves, delicate as flower buds, reflected on its glassy surface. A hawk screamed. Sister Michelle lifted her hand to Sister Celina's face and wiped away tears. "Talk, then," she said.

"Don't ever tell anyone. Do you promise?"

"Yes, of course."

"Because I was never to speak of this. I took a vow. I could be damned for all eternity. But if I don't tell someone . . . I don't know what I'll do. I've thought of killing myself."

"Nothing can be that bad."

"Yes it can. Really, it can."

"Wouldn't it be better to tell Reverend Mother Esther, then, or Mother Thomas Ann?"

"That's the problem. Mother Thomas Ann is what it's all about."

Sister Michelle's heart contracted. She held her breath. For two years she had watched Celina and the novice mistress from her window, disappearing into the woods. For two years she had prayed to be generous, to let go of any jealousy. She had given the two women to each other over and over in her prayers.

"I don't think this is something I ought to know about," she told the other novice as gently as she could.

"You are the only one I can tell because I know that you love her as much as I do, or think I do. Please listen."

Sister Michelle listened. The story took over an hour to tell and then the novices held each other, breathing in and out together, hearts pounding, having no more words and no answers at all.

⌒

The next day, May 1, 1961—the feast of Saint Joseph, who protected their religious order as he once protected Mary, their patroness—the novices at Our Lady of Peace Convent pronounced their vows. Both Sister Michelle and Sister Celina walked in procession with their classmates to the front of the chapel. They wore their finest veils. They carried tall beeswax tapers in their gloved hands.

They knelt at the feet of Reverend Mother Esther and promised to live lives of poverty, chastity, and obedience. And they did this because each of them knew that it was too late to do anything else.

Sister Celina's father held her mother's arm. He bent his head and smiled when Sister Josepha took his hand. He looked to be the kindest and gentlest of men. Sister Celina watched as the novice mistress greeted him with a cool detachment. Her hand tightened around her new profession cross. Her lips were pale.

The sisters and their guests ate roast turkey with cranberry sauce at tables draped in white linen and laid with stainless flatware and crockery plates. Afterward they walked by the lake and on the paths at the edge of the woods. Kate lost her earring somewhere on the path and didn't notice it until they were at the car saying good-bye. She started to cry.

"It's so silly. Just an earring." She sniffled and kissed her daughter on the cheek.

"I'll find it. I walk there often."

"They were cheap, honey, just costume jewelry." She cried harder. "I don't know what's the matter with me."

"I'll look, though."

"You take care." Michael's voice was gruff. "You come home if you aren't happy, you hear?"

"Yes, Daddy, I hear." But vows were vows.

Sister Michelle heard the rustle of Sister Celina's sheets and then the faint swish of her robe. It had to be past midnight.

"Celina?" she whispered.

"Shh."

"Are you all right?"

"I'm fine. Go back to sleep."

"Please, Celina."

"Don't worry."

Her slippers made a noise like the wings of moths against a screen door.

Sister Michelle lay awake for more than an hour, and when she finally went back to sleep, Sister Celina's bed still was empty.

• • •

SHE was the one to find her the next morning just after the rising bell, when she went into the bathroom. The door to the tub room was closed. It was never closed unless a sister was taking a bath, and no sister took a bath at five o'clock in the morning. She knocked but there was no response. She opened the door.

Sister Celina's robe was folded neatly and placed on the chair at the side of the tub. Her slippers were under the chair. Sister Celina herself lay covered with water, her white seersucker nightgown billowing around her, reddened now with her blood. Around her neck she wore her silver profession cross on its black cord. Her open eyes stared at nothing.

SISTER Josepha brought buttered brandy water. Sister Michelle couldn't stop trembling. She sat against the pillows in the infirmary bed and reached to take the cup. Her hands shook. A splash of the hot liquid burned her hand.

"Ah, sweetheart," clucked Sister Josepha, "I've gone and made it too full. Let me hold it, then, dear. Poor sweet little sister. We'll just use a spoon. Like the good Saint Paul says, we're just babies anyhow, fed on the sweet milk and honey of the Word of God."

"It's my fault." Michelle choked and the tears came again. The crying wouldn't stop. Even when she wasn't crying tears ran down her cheeks. There was no end to them.

"Nonsense, Sister, how could it be your fault?"

But she couldn't say. She was like a priest in the confessional. A promise sealed her lips. Sister Celina had deposited her secrets in Michelle's soul and there was no getting rid of them. How did priests do it? How could they bear to keep everyone's secrets?

"It just is."

"Now you stop that kind of talk!" Sister Josepha's round face made an attempt at severity. "You're distraught, is all."

Michelle swallowed the secret with the hot brandy.

"You sleep now, Sister. And don't you worry about our Sister Celina. The good Lord loves her more than we do. He came to take her to himself, you can be sure."

"But, Sister, suicide . . ."

"There's plenty of time between the act and the coming of the Lord. Our blessed Jesus caught the soul of our little bird. It's the poor ones, the weak ones, he loves the most. It's our faith that's being tested; Sister Celina's singing with the angels. Her robe's been washed in the blood of the Lamb."

THE bishop himself came to Our Lady of Peace for the funeral. It was determined that Sister Celina was not in possession of her senses when she ran the blade down the long vein of her arm. The bishop held with Sister Josepha's merciful interpretation. Regardless what might have been on the young sister's mind when she folded her robe and left it on the chair and when she stepped into the tepid water and when she held the blade, no one could judge the moment of her death. It was the night of her profession of vows. Certainly she would have called upon the beloved Christ.

The sisters buried her in their cemetery with its simple white crosses.

Sister Celina
Born 1940
Baptized on the Day of her Birth
Professed 1961
Called to the Lord on Her Profession Day

After everyone had scattered a bit of earth on the lowered wooden coffin, Sister Celina's father fell on his knees by the grave. Sobbing, he cried out her name, Suzanne, Suzanne. Finally Reverend Mother Esther took him by the arm and led him to the convent chapel, where he sat, bent and shuddering, in the back pew.

SISTER MARY'S studio was silent. Michelle knocked. Her vows had released her from the novitiate cloister and placed her in the community of professed nuns, to whom she now could relate more freely.

"Come . . ."

It was almost a week following Sister Celina's funeral, and Michelle's stomach continued to knot whenever Mother Thomas Ann glanced her way. The novice mistress had tucked a holy card into Michelle's prayer book, where she would be sure to see it.

Stronger than death is love.

Behind the calligraphy, the image of a cross entwined with lilies. On the back, in the novice mistress's careful hand, was written, "Nothing can separate us from the love of Christ."

Michelle crumpled the card in her hand and threw it into the incinerator.

"Ah, Sister Michelle. Good." Sister Mary motioned for her to sit in the antique chair where she had sat as a child to listen to interpretations of Mozart. "Sit. Sit. We will talk of old times, yes? Or perhaps you want to play?"

"It's been three years, Sister."

"It comes back. It comes back quickly; you'll see."

"Sister Mary, what am I going to do?"

The nun sat with her as she cried. She didn't touch her. She didn't say, "There, there." She didn't urge her to stop. She simply was present like an angel of strength. She didn't ask why or what. Michelle felt her presence like the presence of earth under bare feet, like the presence of an oak tree or of the lake. No lights appeared around Sister Mary. There was no talk of love. No talk of God's will. Just the sobbing, and something ancient that received it like the earth receives the rain.

She cried herself into silence.

"I think I would like to play, to try playing."

She placed her fingers on the keys. The Rondo in A Minor came from them, through them. Round and round, the grief, the guilt, the fear, seeping through fingers onto keys into music.

In Sister Michelle's mind Sister Celina smiled and said good-bye.

XXIV

Some music you will play for years
but do not presume to have fathomed its mystery,
for to the extent that you believe you understand,
to that extent it will elude you.

SISTER MARY'S MUSIC NOTEBOOKS, 1961

Two weeks after Sister Celina's funeral, Sister Michelle sat on a low stool in front of the dead nun's closet.

"Sort her things, Sister," the novice mistress had ordered.

"But—"

"There are no buts."

"Yes, Mother." Why should she argue? These were precious things, Celina's things.

Sunlight delineated patterns of dust particles whirling in the disturbed air. Sister Michelle removed the stack of white undershirts, of long-legged cotton pants and cotton stockings no longer black but turned gray or slightly purple from frequent washings.

"It's the devil, Sister."

She heard Celina's voice clearly. But it was memory. It must be memory from that first night in the convent, when all of them had taken their new black stockings to the sinks. The stockings in her hand brought the image back. The sound of running water, the feel of hard soap in her hand, the postulants lined up beside her at the sinks, Suzanne one of them. Later, in the darkness, Suzanne's voice. "It's the devil."

A devil more crafty than she knew.

Than any of them knew.

Sister Michelle threw the purple socks into a bag she would take to the incinerator. Poor Celina must have developed blisters on her feet from wearing them. Great lumps of tangled darning cotton adorned the heels and toes. How they'd laughed at this while Celina was alive. How often Sister Mary William had taken Celina's darning from her hands.

"It's just weaving, Sister. Just in and out."

Nothing could be easier.

It was sad, really. So awfully sad.

Michelle placed the piles of wearable clothes in a box to be redistributed. She'd remove Celina's number tags during afternoon prayers.

What would be left of her when all of them were done?

Something in the shadow, back in the corner of the bottom shelf, made a clinking sound as Sister Michelle pulled out Celina's winter shawl. She crouched down and reached for it.

Gramma Meghan's blue porcelain bowl. It had to be. How could two bowls like this one exist? Michelle sat on the floor with the bowl in her hands. Its midnight blue edges brought back those nights at Hollyhock Cottage when her gramma handed her the bowl filled with ice cream.

"The surprise bowl!" Elise always laughed and clapped her hands.

"Maybe." Gramma always pretended to be serious. "Things aren't always what they seem."

But it always was. They made a game of it, slowly eating the ice cream, lingering over the last bit before scooping it up to reveal at the bottom of the bowl a brilliant orange flower outlined in gold.

"Surprise!" Gramma always laughed.

Now it was filled with tiny stones and bits of broken glass. Each bit of glass Celina once had worn on a cord around her neck, the glass of her shame. Stones from the cove, washed upon the sand, smoothed by centuries of waves.

How odd that she saved these things.

But then, what do any of us have? What remains? Sister Michelle's mind slowed to a cadence like the measured chant of "Dies irae." Only stones and broken glass. That's all. Fragments of a dream.

Oro supplex et acclínis,
cor contrítum quasi cinis.

Our sorrow turns us to ash scattered on the ground. Our hearts break. Forgive us. Forgive.

What was it but a blue dish filled with stones and broken glass? It meant nothing. It meant everything. How could it hold so little and so much? She didn't know. She did know the dish belonged to her now. She wouldn't ask Mother Thomas Ann's permission. She'd left the novitiate and didn't need it anymore. Besides, Mother Thomas Ann's yes or no couldn't change what Sister Michelle knew.

Celina left the dish for her.

Bits of glass and stones. She would treasure them. Treasures. Of course. The treasures rescued by Snow White and Rose Red.

She stood up, walked over to her side of the dorm, and placed the blue dish underneath her crucifix on the stand beside her bed.

You said you'd never leave.

The broken bits of glass glinted in the sun.

⁓

Mother Thomas Ann blotted the ink of her signature, applying an exact pressure to prevent smearing. Once this document was filed in the archives of the Sacred Congregation of Religious in Rome, Sister Celina's life and death would be redeemed, all blot of suicide wiped out. A hundred years from now, a mere breath in the life of a church that the good Lord promised would endure until the end of time, not even the nuns at Our Lady of Peace would possess a record of what had happened to her. Of what she did. What Celina herself did.

A shame. The girl possessed such potential. If only she had been able to let go, able to believe that love would redeem her. When she had whimpered and cried that she had come to Our Lady of Peace for sanctuary and that now she wanted only to die, Mother Thomas Ann interpreted her words—finally she could admit it—wrongly. Poetically. She thought it a drama into which the novice had fallen, one her artistic nature concocted to enhance the experience. What could a girl Celina's age know of death?

More, it seemed now, than the novice mistress had supposed. Well, it simply couldn't stand as suicide. Mother Thomas Ann folded the official document and inserted it into the white envelope. She passed the edge over the sponge that sat in a bowl of water on her desk and sealed the lie. The important thing was not to lie to herself. Of course, she couldn't know what Sister Celina thought the moment of her death, whether in fact she did draw back from her decision and call upon the mercy of the Lord. But she had her suspicions, and they were not in accord with the sworn document soon to be on its way to Rome.

HADN'T Tom Lenz squirmed on top of Clara Monroe, trying to get his soft little thing between her legs? Hadn't he ripped her white lace gown and called her bitch and whore? And hadn't he, crazed as he was, bit and punched and finally thrown her on the floor and used the cold marble towel rod on her until she screamed and lost her senses? He had. After all of that, for years, she believed she would be broken forever. For years she detested what she was. Even as a novice who looked serene in her white linens and veil, she knew herself in all truth to be as Jesus described: a whitened sepulcher filled with dead men's bones.

No. Sister Celina never once had fooled her.

The nun who by the grace of God and with her gentle hands redeemed Clara Monroe no longer lived at Our Lady of Peace. Sister Lydia was thirty-seven when she died of consumption in 1932, a saint. Sister Lydia, the only person Clara ever told willingly of Tom's abuse of her, cried when she heard the story. Mother Thomas Ann, for her part, had never cried and still had not. But Lydia cried for her.

They were in the woods. It was long ago, before she had been appointed mistress of novices. They went to a secret spot at Our Lady of Peace, where the lake sparkled just beyond a circle of trees. "Show me, my poor darling sister; let me take the pain away."

It must have been the Clara in Sister Thomas Ann who agreed. She had, after all, lived many years in pain and in disgust. In Lydia's eyes she saw clarity and a love she couldn't fear. The religious habit is cumbersome but will yield itself if one is patient. Lydia's tears fell on Clara's body. She laid her hands on the small of her back over the kidneys so injured when the marble rod was used against them. Lydia laid hands on every injury and kissed it. She held Clara Monroe and rocked her back and forth until she was redeemed.

•   •   •

THUS she concluded that women redeem women, and in this work Sister Thomas Ann became a missionary. Every woman suffered something. Each was marked with wounds, wounds that must be touched, must be loved by another woman whose own wounds had been healed, whose own life had been redeemed. Now, as novice mistress at Our Lady of Peace, Mother Thomas Ann believed herself to be that one. She became an adept at touch. Each touch matched and countered perfectly the injurious blow.

So SHE had followed Sister Celina into the woods, knowing the young nun's need. She had seen the way the child's father looked at her. Only one thing produced such a look. She caught up with her where the path turned, by the thorn tree.

"Wait, Sister."

And when the novice turned, her face was stained with tears.

"You're crying."

"Yes."

Celina had stood there, waiting, so innocent, beautiful. Nothing could stop what must happen, the healing that must happen. Mother Thomas Ann felt Clara rise in her. The heart of Clara quickened. Clara's breathing deepened in her until she felt it flow up from her feet, spiral around in her belly, settling in a pool where her ruined womb once was. She felt ready to give birth.

"Come with me."

She led the novice to the place in the woods where birch trees formed a circle, white, slender as angels. Clara within her was similarly white, slender, a cool flame. Clara held the sobbing Celina. Clara kissed the tears. Clara smoothed Celina's hot face with her hands, touching the novice's eyelids, whispering prayers. "You are beautiful as a young doe, as a tree that grows beside the waters. You are the chosen of God, the bride of Christ. You are myself. We are the same. One bride."

Clara knew what to do. She brought Celina to the circle of trees again and again to heal her. She sang lullabies. She called upon the Holy Mother as she touched the novice's body through the thick woolen dress. "*Ave, ave, María.* House of Gold. Comfort of the Afflicted. Morning Star. Mystical Rose."

Celina cried each time but she always followed.

Clara woke Celina in the middle of the night just by thinking of her. It was summer. She stood at midnight under a full moon wearing only her long white gown and a white night-veil. Celina came to her, barefooted, over the grass.

Mother Thomas Ann remembered it as a dream but it was not a dream.

Clara took Celina to the lake and she undressed her there. The moon made a path over the water. "You are beautiful," Clara told the shining girl who stood on the beach. "You are completely without sin. You are the virgin most pure."

"I once made a statue of a woman who was pure."

Clara removed her own gown and veil. Gently, so gently, the women touched each other everywhere.

IN THE end even Sister Michelle would come back to her. No one could resist forever. She would weep for having lost trust. Clara Monroe would kiss the tears from the young sister's face; she would taste their salt. Tears were the blessing women brought in payment for the redemption of her touch. Of her own tears Mother Thomas Ann knew nothing. Sometimes she felt they were contained in glass and stored deep within her. And this is why Clara let the others cry instead, because if Mother Thomas Ann were to let one tear fall, even one, the glass would shatter and she would drown in the flood.

Yes, Clara Monroe always knew exactly what to do. Mother Thomas Ann reflected on this fact as she rose from her desk and walked down the long hallway to the portress's room, where she would place the document regarding Sister Celina's death in the outgoing mail.

Sister Michelle's face, reflected back to her by the lake's uneven surface, pulled to one side. Daddy's face. Strange to call him that as though she were still a little girl. For as long as he lived his face would be etched by a death he didn't die. And her face? Her distortion turned inward. Only the lake gave back a true image.

I have forever to learn to live with this, she thought as she leaned back, hidden in the alcove on the beach where Celina had shared her secrets only one month before. Every day, the same. She was buried,

Celina was; the nuns had made her disappear as Amy once had disappeared, and others, long ago. Suddenly a novice would be gone, all trace of her wiped out. Her trunk gone from its place in the attic. Her voice absent from communal prayer. And no one ever said a thing. It was as if she never had been with them at all.

At least Celina's name couldn't be wiped away. It was chiseled into stone.

Once when she was Elise, Sister Michelle had asked Mother Thomas Ann if she would be the next whom the nun would make disappear, as though the woman were a magician with a vanishing act. Now, witnessing her own face change with the movement of the lake, Michelle understood that her disappearance could be accomplished only by a magic of her own.

Since Celina's death, one day fit upon the next like a telescope folding into itself. The scratch of wool upon skin. Linen soaked with perspiration. The sticky sweet odor of menstrual blood mingled with incense. Sister Michelle lay in bed before dawn and listened to her heart beating, and to the occasional absence of its pulse, a space in her, a tunnel through which she might slip into nothing at all. She whispered the name of God into the thick darkness. Whom else could she address? Only Celina, who did not answer, and God. Silent conspirators, the three of them, breathing death in and out like the sticky air.

Mother Thomas Ann said grow up.

"Grow up, Sister. You are not the dead one, after all."

"Yes, Mother."

"You must stop your moping. It is not pleasing to our Lord."

"No, Mother."

"You may talk about this with me anytime. My door is open. You know that, Sister, don't you?"

"Thank you, Mother."

And that was all. She wouldn't go to her. Not again. Never.

Sister Michelle knelt in the sandy lakeside soil and picked peas, dropping them one by one into her blue-and-white calico apron, which she had gathered up and fastened with a large safety pin to make a cloth basket. Sister Kateri, the former Sarah Beauchamp, worked the next row.

"Something terrible must have happened to her, right?"

"What?" The moment stretched itself out like still water under a morning mist. She imagined the gulls, their cries like those of lost souls.

"Celina. She must have gone crazy. Something caused it; people don't just kill themselves, do they?"

The question floated like a drop of oil on the taut surface of Michelle's secret, Celina's secret.

"I don't know."

"She didn't tell you? I thought she might have told you. You were such good friends."

"Well, she didn't."

It was the first lie. She argued with herself that it was necessary, a protective lie, a lie such as a priest might tell to keep a promise. What right did Sarah Beauchamp have to know the truth? None. No one had a right except those to whom Celina had entrusted her secret. Celina's father knew some of it, of course, because he shared the shame. He caused it, to begin with. He helped murder her, along with the novice mistress. That was the truth, if truth be told. But no law punished that kind of murder. Such punishments are left to God.

It was the first lie, a stone laid in uncertain soil that became a cornerstone. Upon it Sister Michelle began to construct something without a name, something almost alive, something heavy that weighed upon her heart.

"I worry about you, Elise." Kate covered Sister Michelle's hand with her own. "You look so pale. Are you eating well?"

Now that Sister Michelle was a professed nun her parents were not restricted to designated Sundays and could visit when it was convenient, so long as this privilege was not abused. The family sat alone in the parlor.

"Maybe you're working too hard. Or is it that friend of yours, that girl who died?

"Sister Celina?"

"Wasn't that the strangest thing? It must have been horrible for you, dear, to have found her and all."

"It was a shock."

"Of course it was. Thank God you have Mother Thomas Ann

here to keep you on an even keel. It's a blessing for me to know there's someone we trust who is right here watching out for you."

The irony of it struck Sister Michelle dumb.

"You aren't all right. Are you sure you don't have the flu?" Kate reached over the table to test the temperature of Sister Michelle's forehead and cheeks with the palm of her hand. "You are warm, dear."

"It's just the heat. It's summer, Mama, and all this wool!"

"Well, all right, then. But you just have to put this Sister Celia out of your mind."

"Celina."

"Yes. Just put her out of your mind. You have your whole life ahead of you, honey, so just pick yourself up now and get on with it."

Sister Michelle focused on that life ahead of her like a camera recording every detail to be studied later, pondered, wondered over. A flashbulb in a dark room, illuminating every corner, emphasizing faces, fixing with exactitude each image.

"You're right, Mama." And that was the second lie.

SHE SORTED herself like grain into containers. Upon the most precious, the secret seed, she set a seal. The task at first felt arduous because her mind insisted on mixing everything up: Mother Thomas Ann with the mother tree and Black Sturgeon Lake with Celina's blood. But in those silent hours provided by the holy rule, Sister Michelle sifted through the pile in her mind. In the chapel during meditation she sifted. Walking the path by the lake, she sorted out what she could say to this person or to that, even what she could reveal to herself. And by summer's end the floor of her mind was cleared and around the edges of her soul stood marked jars, like Greek amphorae, sealed, their contents ready for use or storage, according to her will.

AUGUST came and went. Dog days with suffocating humidity. New postulants led the procession of nuns out of chapel. New novices kept their eyes cast down. Sister Michelle walked by the lake alone. She avoided the cove as she avoided her thoughts.

Father Austin's vestments changed from green to violet to white to red and back to green again. A year passed and Sister Celina stayed dead. Sister Michelle stood before the Blessed Sacrament with her hand in that of Reverend Mother Esther and renewed her profession of vows.

"Is it your will to bind yourself by the vows of poverty, chastity, and obedience according to the rule of the Sisters of Our Lady of Peace?"

"It is my will."

And she believed that she told the truth.

❧

Sister Mary of the Holy Cross waited until the other nuns left the council room, and then she closed the door. Mother Thomas Ann, still in her place at the table, was blotting her signature on one of the documents the sisters had just finished discussing.

The other nuns seemed, to Sister Mary, bewitched. Blinded by some kind of spell, they couldn't see the novice mistress as she was. Dangerous. The woman deflected such suspicions like a mirror.

One would think that Sister Celina's death might have changed that. But no. The girl herself was blamed. And now even Sister Michelle had stepped into line, acquiescing without argument to an irresponsible council decision, one that could cripple her for life. The council had deprived Sister Michelle of her future as a pianist. What could she do, though, young as she was and without power in the religious community?

The novice mistress looked up from the papers she was arranging in a manila folder. Arranging the lives of the young sisters. Sister Kateri a nurse. Sister Angela an accountant. Sister Michelle not what she should be.

"Yes, Sister Mary?" Her face betrayed nothing of her feelings. Maybe by this time in her life she had no feelings.

"What you have done is wrong, Mother."

"What I have done? And what is it that you think I have done?"

"I think you have satisfied your vanity by depriving our Sister Michelle of pursuing her God-given talent."

Mother Thomas Ann lifted an eyebrow. "Naturally you would think so, Sister, since you yourself have always sought to control Sister Michelle according to your own will for her. It is God's will she must embrace."

"God's will, or your own?"

"The will of God is shown us through our council's decision."

"A council you control."

"Ah! And do I control you, Sister? You vote as you will, do you not? You live as you will. Have you ever been deprived of your music? Do you not have your piano, your Steinway, and are you not granted permission to keep that instrument month after month and year after year?"

"This discussion is not about me."

"It is. From the time that girl was a child you have attempted to make her into another Imogene von Bingen, to send her out into the world to live the life you sacrificed. Or perhaps you didn't sacrifice anything. Perhaps you feared the concert stage, feared failure, feared that after your Carnegie performance you would rise no further. But she could do it for you. Elise Pearson could do what you feared. And in the will of God for her you see the frustration of your plans."

"I see only that you understand well the psychology of control. Is this because you have become adept through practice? I did not give Sister Michelle her talent. God did that. I did not create in her a desire to play. Her own heart did that. I have simply been her teacher, a guide in the development of an art which she has in greater abundance than I ever did. And now it is my responsibility to be her advocate."

"All responsibility for Sister Michelle is out of your hands, Sister. It is not your business."

"It will always be my business. Sister Michelle herself made it my business when she played for me her first note. And I will not abandon her to your destructive plans."

Mother Thomas Ann picked up her pen and the manila folder and rose from the table.

"In this matter, Sister, you have no choice. It is Sister Michelle's to decide what creates or what destroys. Now, you must excuse me. Important matters require my attention."

XXV

Between episodes
for the space of an instant
lift your fingers from the keys.

SISTER MARY'S MUSIC NOTEBOOKS, 1962

"Let me talk with her." Kate called her daughter on the phone after receiving the letter announcing the council's decision regarding college. "She's a family friend; she's your godmother! I've known her forever. I can make her listen."

"Please, Mama, don't."

"What are you talking about, don't?"

"That's right, don't."

"But you mustn't abandon your piano. You can't."

"Yes, I can. Anyway, I'm not abandoning the piano. It's not like that."

"Not like that? Just what is it like if it's not like that? The piano is your life, Elise. I know. I'm your mother."

So irrational. What did being her mother have to do with it? Elise felt impatience like a thin stream of bile seeping out of her heart.

"I don't want to talk about it."

"Listen here, young lady, Sister Michelle or not, you are still my daughter and you will not dismiss me so easily. It's inconceivable that you would give up your music. A sin. Do you understand me? A sin."

"How can it be a sin? I don't even want to play the piano."

The other end of the line was finally silent. Then her mother hung up.

• • •

ACTUALLY, Sister Michelle had discovered, it was the truth. She no longer desired to play the piano. What a relief. Even Celina's secret didn't feel heavy anymore. Maybe following the holy rule, even if it happened to be imposed on you, really could channel your emotions like a river. If you didn't look at it, you almost could forget that it was flowing there. For the first time since entering the convent, Sister Michelle felt nearly normal.

Kate's voice on the phone.

"Elise? Darling?" A pause.

"Mama?" It was March 7, 1963, the day following Sister Michelle's twenty-third birthday.

"Darling, your father . . . he was shoveling snow and his heart . . ."

"Is he . . . ?"

"He's alive. He's in the hospital."

"I'll come."

"Mother Thomas Ann said no. In fact I'm not supposed to be calling you. She said your work there prevented . . ." Her voice broke.

Not like when Gramma Meghan died. Not again.

"She can't tell me what to do; I'm not a novice anymore. I'll come."

"Gus will come for you. He'll be there in about three hours."

"Courage, Mama."

"We're so young."

"I'll be there by this afternoon."

THE rule would take care of itself. Her mind whirled. Daddy.

Sister Kateri helped her load her suitcase into the station wagon, hugged her, said, "I'll pray."

"God will do what God will do."

Daddy.

Peat bog, swamp, spruce islands extended to the horizon of a flat landscape that once had been the bed of prehistoric Lake Agassiz. It drained at the end of the glacial age, leaving a chain of lakes on the ancient granite of the Canadian plate. Black Sturgeon Lake, Lake of the Woods, Lake Winnipeg.

Michelle ate a sandwich and a cookie from the bag Sister Kateri had given her as she got into the car.

Gus kept his foot hard on the gas.

"He made it through the war, he can make it through this."

His voice congealed like candle wax.

They arrived at Eagle Inlet just before dark. A crescent moon curved on the horizon like a wing.

Kate stood outside the hospital.

"Thank God you're here."

"I love you, Mama." Her voice came out in a whisper. "How's Daddy?"

"Not good. I told him you were coming."

IN THE cardiac care room of the thirty-two-bed Eagle Inlet Community Hospital, Michael Pearson lay connected to a heart monitor on one side of the bed and to plastic bags of saline fluids on the other. He looked dead. In one swift glance Michelle took in his sunken cheeks, his cavernous mouth, his gray skin, his dull hair oily with perspiration. The image imprinted itself on her mind. She would never, after that, be able to rid herself of it. Then he breathed, an agonizing rattle. The monitor jumped. Michelle focused on the little beeps that meant he was alive. In the days to follow she would count those beeps. She would watch the screen, each line tracing the pulse of his life, as though her concentration would keep him in existence.

"Daddy?" Her voice broke.

"Elise." He sounded like an old radio. "Good." A breath between each word. "You're . . . here."

"Don't talk, dear," Kate murmured. She stroked his clammy forehead. "Save your strength."

FOR TEN days Michelle watched with him while Kate went back and forth from Reel 'Em Inn, where they were already getting things in shape for the coming season. It was best, Kate said, because the activity kept her from going crazy. She always came in time to kiss Michael good night.

Short visits from old school friends punctuated Sister Michelle's vigil, as did quick meals at Gen's Cafe downtown, and sleep. She breathed with him, in, out, willing him to keep on. "God," she repeated with each breath, and hoped she might be praying. The divine name pulsed through her, the sound her heart made as it beat.

Now and then her father spoke. He told her he loved her. He told her the convent was a hurdle he couldn't jump. He asked her to hug him. He said he wished her veil were gone so he could see his little Elise once more. He said she was the finest gift life had given him.

Every time he spoke she cried.

"There, there," he croaked. "There, there."

MARGARET Henderson visited her in the hospital waiting room. She'd married Jeremy Walker right after high school and moved into a mobile home beside the big house on his parents' farm. Two years and two babies later Jeremy began construction on a two-bedroom house up against a wooded area kept for a windbreak. As it turned out, his parents moved into the new house and Margaret and Jeremy took over the big house because they now had another baby on the way.

"Mother Walker's taking care of the babies. Gee, but it's good to see you." She held Michelle out from her and hugged her and held her out again. "I'm really sorry about your dad; how's he doing?"

Margaret pattered on about the farm and the children while Sister Michelle watched her, listening but disconnected. A wide gulf spread between her and this childhood friend. An abyss. She couldn't cross it and didn't try. Margaret's eyes gleamed. Her hormone-rich hair waved down her back in the popular style.

"You seem happy, Margaret."

"Oh, I can't complain. We sure have come a ways, though, haven't we?"

"And Jeremy? Is he a good husband?"

"The best." Margaret passed her hand over her pregnant belly. "How about you? Are you studying piano? You sure could play nice."

"I don't play anymore."

"How come?"

"Our religious order doesn't need another pianist."

"But, Elise—you were so good at it. Don't you miss it?"

"I really don't have a lot of time to think about it."

"Well, I just think it's terrible, Elise. You act like it doesn't matter."

The face of the nun smiled despite a roaring deep in her mind.

"Of course it matters, Margaret, just not in the way you imagine."

But the roaring wouldn't stop.

Two days later Michael Pearson died. Sister Michelle held one hand and Kate held the other.

"Elise," he rasped. "My Kate."

"Go with God, Daddy," she said over and over, and then he did. Kate wept. The one he called Elise just stared at the still body, the ravaged face now in repose, both sides the same.

⟋

Michelle wanted to play the Rondo in A Minor, but the piano was locked. Time—three days between her father's death and the funeral at Corpus Christi—pressed in on her like stale air in a small room. She and her mother remained at the house in town, where Gramma and Grampa Pearson joined them each day to sit in the small living room and receive guests.

It was Gramma Pearson who decided to get the piano open.

"I'll call Grand Forks or Minneapolis if I have to," she growled as she attempted to jimmy the lock. "I'll get a locksmith out here."

"What are you doing?" Kate came in from the bedroom.

"We didn't want to wake you. It's locked."

"Yes."

"Well, where's the key?"

"I thought no one ever would play it again."

"That's silly. You play, don't you?"

"Not well."

"Not well?" Her mother-in-law laughed. "You don't have to be Horowitz to play your own piano! Besides, there's Elise. What's she supposed to play when she's home?"

Kate's eyes filled with tears. "It seemed she wouldn't come home. It seemed she was gone for good."

Dorothy and Sister Michelle put their arms around Kate and the three women stood huddled like that for several minutes, Dorothy and Kate both crying and Sister Michelle saying as Gramma Meghan would have, "There, there; it will be all right. There, there."

Kate led them to the attic and opened the trunk.

"Is that you?" Dorothy picked up the picture of Kate at the player piano.

"I was only about eight years old. I could have been really good, I think, if the piano hadn't been destroyed."

"Well, life's not over." Dorothy slipped the key out of its velvet pouch.

Sister Michelle played from memory. Her technique was rusty and the piano out of tune, but the music broke her heart anyway.

A CARLOAD of nuns arrived the morning of the funeral. Mother Thomas Ann enveloped Sister Michelle.

"I had to come," Sister Michelle said as she felt her body stiffen.

"Of course you did, Sister. I was wrong. I'm sorry. I had no idea that God would take him so soon."

Sister Josepha, Sister Mary William, Reverend Mother Esther, Sister Mary of the Holy Cross. They brought the convent schola, the novices and new postulants, to join the tiny choir of Corpus Christi. Sister Mary played Bach on the new electric organ. Sister Michelle held her tears until the delicate *"In paradísum,"* when she visualized her father, his face whole and shining, led by Gramma Meghan, Grampa Willie, baby Michael, Sister Celina, and all the other saints and angels into Paradise.

THERE was no burial. Sister Michelle would return after the ground thawed to bury Michael Pearson on a brilliant May morning in the cemetery above Eagle Inlet.

⁓

Kate put down her pen. Her signature on the thank-you notes betrayed a shaky hand. Thank you for the flowers. Thank you for the mass stipend; a high mass will be said. Thank you for the contribution to the heart association in his name. You are a good friend.

Nausea covered every other feeling. It surged each time she picked up the pen and opened one of the little cards with the picture of the Good Shepherd on the cover. She chose them from the various designs Elmer Lundgrin laid out in front of her over at the funeral home. The Lutherans liked that psalm. "I shall not want." But every time she saw that picture and those words her stomach turned.

You have to eat, Dorothy urged. Soup gagged her. Even corn flakes felt too heavy. She forgot to drink water. Young Margaret Walker brought roast chicken, a whole dinner with mashed potatoes and dressing. The smell of it drove her into her bedroom, where she lay with her face in a pillow, and when that didn't work she climbed behind Michael's clothes, still hanging in the closet as though he might wake up anytime now and put them on. The flannel robe held his scent. She never would wash it, she decided, she never would move from this spot. His robe would cover her like a burial shroud and she would follow Michael's scent into a different world.

The morning he'd been dead a week Kate staggered out of the bedroom. Morning sickness. It felt just like morning sickness. Her head gyred. Crackers. Crackers might work just like in those early days of pregnancy. She reached to the top shelf of the pantry. Saltines. Dry. They stuck in her mouth. She needed something wet. She turned to open the refrigerator door and it was the last she knew.

Dorothy found her on the floor behind the open door of the refrigerator, unconscious, lying in a pool of orange juice and soggy crackers. Kate struggled up from a swamp, thick water, tangled vines, muffled sound.

"You fainted."

"I almost never faint."

Dehydration. Low blood pressure.

"Well, it's no wonder," Dorothy sputtered later over the phone. "You've been starving yourself to death. I'll bring you some bananas; they're easy to stomach and high in potassium. And drink water!"

A widow can die of grief during the first six months. It's touch-and-go. Widows get cancer; their bodies close down. Dorothy read about it in *McCall's*.

"It's a sin what those nuns are doing. They'll be sorry, that much I can say; they'll be sorry when you're dead and gone."

The bananas saved her life, and her nausea gave way to lust.

"Sometimes I think I didn't give Michael the love he deserved."

Kate and Dorothy walked on Black Rock Beach. The honeycombed ice looked about ready to break up. It was the first week of April.

"I never heard him complain."

"No, he wouldn't. But I know I held back. I didn't want to, I just didn't know how not to."

"He must have understood, don't you think?"

"I don't know. He was patient."

"He loved you."

If she could have had him back she'd give him anything. She'd touch him in all the ways she'd always known he wanted to be touched. Now she could let her inhibitions go, she knew she could. She dreamed of it. He came to her in dreams, he touched her, kissed her, loved her, until she awoke dissolved in orgasm and in tears.

Why didn't they tell you widows must endure such things?

Men looked delicious. They came into church behind their wives and Kate undressed them with her eyes. She fantasized a charitable organization of women who would loan their husbands to widows to comfort them. A kind of sexual lend-lease plan. Just to be held, just to be caressed, kissed, entered. It didn't matter who did it. She hadn't known how rich she was when Michael was alive. If only women could know what she now knew, they'd be generous. That's how she'd have been, knowing then what she knew now. Why, she would have sent Michael out to Sandra Locke when Ben was killed in that boating accident last summer. Go to her, Kate would have said. Comfort her. Fill up some of her emptiness. It would have been a gift, made her feel queenly. But even as she fantasized these things she knew she wouldn't have done it, really. She would have kept him to herself. They all did that, all women.

What could she do but imagine meeting a stranger and running off with him to Hawaii, where they would lie on a secluded beach and make love night and day for a week? She wouldn't even ask his name.

No wonder widows kept their secrets to themselves.

THE ice melted. Robins appeared one morning, testing the still sleeping lawn for worms, cocking their heads, listening. Elise returned for

Michael's burial. All three women stood with Charles beside that gaping hole and listened to the priest tell them, "Your brother will rise again." They held hands as Michael's body was planted in the wet, sandy soil by the lake's edge.

AFTERWARD Sister Michelle and her mother went down to the dock at Reel 'Em Inn, where her mother stood watching the gulls. Michelle slipped her arm around Kate's waist.

"Remember how dad once brought me a chick from Gull Rock?"

"Cleo. What ever happened to that bird?"

"I don't know."

"I used to watch from the window, you and that bird and your father."

"You did?"

"And I felt so alone."

"I didn't know that."

"You were a child."

"I wish I'd known."

"You were just a child."

THEY all left and Kate sat alone in her living room in town. Michael seemed to be all around her. She heard herself telling him she was too old to play the piano he had bought for her. For the first time she felt how those words had hurt him. She hadn't meant them as a rejection, but they were. A rejection, first of all, of herself. She gasped as the thought came to her. Why, all along, all these years, it had been herself she had rejected. Poor Michael, all the times he had reached out to her, to touch her, and there was nothing there. And now, dead as he was, he was somehow here in this room, actually touching her, giving her back to herself.

Dorothy was right. She didn't need to be Horowitz.

Kate sat down at her piano and lifted the cover from the keys.

A tunnel constructed of lake rock led from the convent proper to the three-story academy for young women run by the Sisters of Our

Lady of Peace. Copper-colored roaches as large as the Texas variety tucked themselves into the warm crevices alongside the heating pipes and sometimes scurried across the concrete floor, from which they could easily be swept up into the folds of a long black woolen skirt.

"What are those beetles?" Michelle blurted out the day after returning from Eagle Inlet, when she and Sister Kateri were assigned to clean the place. Outside, a spring windstorm gusted over the expanse of lake.

"Roaches, I think, except I've never seen them that big. Emma Sweetbreath had roaches, and when we were kids we taunted her about them, called them her pets. We huddled in her kitchen after dark and listened to them scurry over the floor and across the walls like spirits."

"Do you think they can get out of here?"

"Like into your bed, you mean?"

"Well?"

"I don't think they eat human flesh, Michelle."

"Reverend Mother ought to hire an exterminator. These things are disgusting." Michelle lifted her skirt higher and scanned the rocks above her head.

"They probably do, but these creatures could survive the bomb. I read that even if everything on earth were wiped out by a nuclear winter, the roaches would survive. I guess they eat dust."

"I'd be eating dust myself if I had to come through this place every day on my way to teach. I'd rather brave the storm."

"That's pretty silly, you know."

For some reason the roaches reminded her of the frogs at Reel 'Em Inn, except she'd wanted the frogs to live. Strange. Of the roaches she would become the murderer if she could. Disgusting, how they scurried, how they hid. The frogs were delicate, their bones fashioned of blown glass, hollow, shining. The roaches lived forever, covering the earth like a gleaming copper swarm in the sun's glare, a whispering spirit in the dark.

Such thoughts troubled her more often these days. One must take care, though, not to let such troubles show, except, perhaps, in the relative safety of the confessional. Every time she passed Mother Thomas Ann in the hallway something in her wanted to point a finger. There she is, a voice in her announced. Don't you see what she is?

While in her mind something with a different voice whispered "Ssshhhhh" as it scurried into the dark.

SHE DIPPED her scrub brush into the pail of soapy water and rubbed it back and forth over concrete, so smooth after all these years of washings that it resembled marble. A musty smell came from the walls and ceiling of the tunnel and pressed in on her. She gagged and thought of canaries, how miners take them into the shaft as warnings. They die of gases the men can't smell. Get out, the canaries are dying! Too bad they have to die, that they can't show when they're sick and get out beforehand. They can't, though. She'd read that even in aviaries you never know that a canary is sick. They just sit there on the perch looking perfectly fine. Why, they don't even close their little eyes. They sit there singing while inside their tiny bodies everything is going wrong. It's instinct. If they show they're sick, the other birds will eat them.

Sister Michelle pushed her scrub brush back and forth in silence and in rhythm with Sister Kateri's brush. What a shame. You come in one morning and your canary's lying still and dead on the floor of its cage.

⌒

Sister Michelle saw the world from inside. Now she awoke in the morning with a cacophony of voices, Celina's and her father's, whispering from the center of things, and she turned inside out like a glove that's removed quickly. Nothing is as it seems, she told herself as she made her way down the sidewalk in Bemidji on a summer afternoon in 1963. She passed a café. An old man wearing a fisherman's cap sat at the small round table by the window. He held his cup with both hands and lowered his face toward it to drink. Who was he? Who was he, really? Some part of her that felt mercurial moved toward and into him, took his shape. She felt how old hands tremble, felt the fineness of the china cup. He raised his head and looked out the window at her, smiled, lifted his hand, and tipped his head in greeting. She felt the softness of her black veil brush against her cheek.

Where are you now? She addressed the spirit of her father, and his answer seemed only slightly obscured by calls and laughter down at the town docks. Her father, here but hidden, as God is hidden here in everything.

Someone else would have seen the real in outer things, in the scratchy wool, in the humidity already topping ninety percent, in the afternoon heat, thick, hard to breathe as water might be. Someone else might maintain that nothing's hidden and what's seen or touched is all there is. But when she thought of her father's face and of her prayer that was answered strangely, and after years of coming to love what otherwise would have been unlovable, she knew, with a certainty no human science had the wisdom to contradict, that nothing, absolutely nothing, was as it appeared.

Back at Our Lady of Peace a cooler air, laden with incense and colored by stained glass windows, enveloped her. She genuflected and entered the pew closest to the confessional. The nuns' appointed confessor, otherwise a stranger to them, knelt at the prie-dieu in the sanctuary, waiting, she imagined, although he didn't look up from his breviary when she knelt. He laid the ribbon across the page to mark his place, folded it diagonally to keep the edges from raveling, and closed the black leather book. He didn't look at her. He looked up at the tabernacle. He left his breviary on the prie-dieu and came down the side aisle to the confessional. The nuns were gathering in the back two pews of the chapel, one of them like another, eyes cast down, veils lowered to hide their faces. The sacrament of penance is a private affair, a place of secrets, so confidential that the confessor keeps an unknowing place in his mind, a place where who you are and what you say to him is dropped and disappears.

She opened the curtains and knelt on the polished wood.

"Bless me, Father."

"*In nómine Patris, et Fílii, et Spíritus Sancti. Amen.*"

"Father, I'm afraid."

"Afraid of what, Sister?"

"I'm not sure. But ever since my father died I feel myself dying, too. My body is disappearing. I feel that I am on one side of a wall made of parchment, so old and fine that if I touch it, it will crumble. I think about doing that, touching it, passing through it. But if I do, I imagine losing myself entirely. And despite that, Father, I sometimes want to pass through."

She could hear him breathing on the other side of the grill. She could see the outline of his face, his long nose, his weak chin. She released herself as she had with the old seaman behind the café window and flowed toward the priest.

"You will not be lost, Sister. Let go. What you are experiencing is God's grace, the gift of the mystic, of the beloved of God."

"But I can't pray anymore. I try, but the words don't come to me. Instead I hear something like music and it takes me up and I float in it."

"What you are describing is prayer, Sister."

"I thought it was a distraction."

"No. It is prayer. It is a prayer of union, of the heart. You have been deeply blessed."

"I don't know."

And she didn't know. As she spoke, attempting to describe what she experienced, she couldn't pinpoint the origin of these sensations. God? That was possible. But she wasn't sure. It could be imagination. It could even be seduction. It could—and she didn't like to think this way—it could even be insanity, the path Celina took. She wanted the priest to know, to enter the hidden places, to see from within her.

"And there's something else, Father."

"Yes?"

"A secret."

"Your own, or someone else's?"

"I used to think it belonged to someone else, but now I think it has seeped out from wherever I hid it in my mind, and it's become my own."

"Someone told you this secret?"

"Yes, Father. And I swore to her I would keep it safe."

"Then you must do that, my daughter."

"But, Father, this secret—it seems to be destroying me. And not just me, Father. The whole community. It's ruining the whole community."

"Are you sure you aren't being a bit hysterical about this, Sister?"

"I don't know, Father. Maybe."

"Pray to let it go."

"I have, Father. But it's like a poison that's seeping through the whole convent."

"You're exaggerating, Sister. If you've kept the secret, how can it be a poison?"

"Because maybe some secrets need to be told."

"Promises are sacred."

"And they should never be broken?"

"Never."

"Even if you feel you'll go crazy if you hold on to it?"

"You must get hold of yourself, Sister."

"I have tried."

She felt close to tears.

What if the convent itself were wrong? If it weren't, how could Mother Thomas Ann continue as novice mistress? Why didn't anyone notice? Why didn't anyone speak up? Why didn't she herself speak up?

"Perhaps we ought to speak of this face-to-face, Sister."

"Outside of confession?"

"Yes."

"I'll pray about it, Father."

But she couldn't imagine it happening.

"As will I, Sister. Tell me a sin from your past life, now, for absolution, and then go in peace."

XXVI

A moment will arrive
when all will be understood
so that in your playing
simplicity and complexity will be the same.

SISTER MARY'S MUSIC NOTEBOOKS, 1963

Kate giggled.

"Mama, you're giggling!"

"I know, Sister; I just can't believe you're home!"

They unpacked the Christmas decorations, all those collected during the years with Michael, when they were a family, even those few miraculously unbroken in the fall from Meghan's attic. Kate hadn't planned on this. She had decided not to celebrate Christmas, not this year, not alone. It would have been the first since Michael left her to go—where, she couldn't know. And Elise, bound by those vows, might as well be dead, or so she had thought. Well, wasn't the world full of surprises? Elise home. Not forever; it was nothing like that. But for some unknown reason Reverend Mother Esther sent her home for the holiday.

A week, they had an entire week to themselves.

"Call me Elise, Mama."

"But . . . do you think it would be okay?"

"Elise is the name you gave me and I love to hear you say it; anyway, I feel silly when you call me 'Sister.' "

Like she was a little girl again, or wanted to be. She was of an age, though, that they could be friends, even sisters. That would be nice, to have a sister, especially now with Michael gone.

"All right, honey. Elise it is." She unwrapped a glass angel. "Oh, look. Your dad gave me this our first Christmas together!"

"He must have seen the fire in you. The fire in the angel."

Kate shook her head. "I don't know, honey. Whatever fire burned in me, I'd dampened it. I've been so often way too cold and distant. You know that. You've felt it. It haunts me that he might have gone through life chilled."

She hung the angel on the tree.

"Mama?" Elise's voice came out soft and just a little shaky.

"Yes, dear?"

"Mama, Dad couldn't have hurt me in any way, could he?"

"Hurt you?"

What could the girl possibly mean?

"Certainly not on purpose. You know that your father loved you more than anything—more than me, even."

Kate hadn't meant to say that last part. It just slipped out and she knew it to be true. She didn't begrudge her daughter the love, yet it felt, just now, like a fist around her heart.

Christmas afternoon Sister Michelle sat in the attic beside Gramma Meghan's steamer trunk and lifted out the contents one by one. There were the old pictures, each of them triggering in her memory the story that went with it. She arranged them in front of her on the floor. Mother Thomas Ann holding her on the day of her baptism. The fledgling gull following at her heels. Every Christmas tree since she'd been born. Father Brian Murphy smiling with a gentleness Elise hadn't noticed as a child. Kate and Michael on their wedding day.

Under the pictures lay bundles of letters tied with blue ribbon and addressed to her mother and father in her own hand. Kate had saved every letter Sister Michelle sent them. All those Sunday afternoons in the novitiate when she wrote according to Mother Thomas Ann's instructions: "Be newsy, Sisters. Say nothing that will trouble your parents." She had thought the letters insipid and heartless, omitting, as they did, the essence of her. Yet Kate had treasured them.

Under everything, including Gramma Meghan's wedding dress, she found, in the upper right-hand corner, a walnut box. It had a tiny clasp but wasn't locked. She lifted it out, ran her fingers over the dark satin grain, then opened it.

Her own treasures. Kate had saved them here. A lock of baby hair tied with a red ribbon. An arrowhead Elise had found at Split Rock Point when she was six years old. The program from her first piano recital. A letter from Sister Mary urging Kate to send Elise to study piano in New York. The convent's acceptance letter from Mother Thomas Ann.

Wrapped in tissue at the bottom of the box lay her ring of grass. Her mother must have found it in her pocket, all those many years ago, and saved it. How could she have known its significance? Elise took the ring from its tissue-paper bed and slipped it over her wrist like a bracelet, marveling that grass could survive the years. And she called out in her heart to the Elise she once had been, whoever that one might be.

WHEN the week was up Sister Michelle returned to Our Lady of Peace with nothing solved, except that a door seemed to have opened that had been shut before. One thing for certain, her mind couldn't put all this together. Whatever had happened to her, if anything actually had happened, she wouldn't find it by force of will. Trying to remember simply didn't work.

She returned to her life, to the silences and to long nights lying on her back in a small bed watching with her mind for some glint of light. She returned to her prayers, her simple work, and whatever whispers of change could be distinguished out of the Vatican Council meetings in Rome. She folded her veil at night, put it between slabs of cardboard tied with a string to hold them steady, and slipped it under her mattress to make the creases sharp. She bowed deep at the chanting of lauds, received the thin wafer of God on her tongue, caught the heavy scent of wine from the gold chalice and confused it with the scent of blood.

Sister Mary comforted her. "You will find your way, *Liebling*. Truth clears a path through the deepest night."

Spring came again. Green feathered the birch. She walked past the cove into the woods. She was solid black, a silhouette against erupting life. She was only twenty-four years old but felt ancient. Gnarled. A goddess from the beginning of time, the goddess of the oak, the loam, silent in the earth. She ought to be the maiden, green as the feathering trees, a flower springing from the rich soil—the lady slipper, the columbine.

Behind her mind she felt a fluttering of wings.

XXVII

When you believe you have performed the music perfectly,
the time has come to remember once again
that you are a beginner.

SISTER MARY'S MUSIC NOTEBOOKS, 1964

"Where did you get this?"
Mother Thomas Ann held the blue dish in her hands.
"What are you doing in here?"
The novice mistress had no business in her cell, the tiny room
Sister Michelle had been assigned after pronouncing her first vows.
"I asked how you came to have this dish."
"It's mine."
"Nothing is yours, Sister."
"It was my grandmother's."
"It was Sister Celina's."
She knew.
"How did you know that?"
"How do you think I knew that, Sister? I gave it to her."
"Well, she gave it to me."
"She wouldn't have done that."
"Believe what you want."
"I'm taking it."
The novice mistress moved to leave the cell.
"Put it down on the table and get out."
"Don't be impertinent."
"Give it to me and leave my cell."
"Really, Sister!"

"I know what you did."

"Pardon me?"

"Celina told me what you did to her."

"I don't know what you're talking about."

"She told me just before our vows, just before she killed herself."

"You're insane."

"How could you do it?"

"Do what?"

"Don't you even know? First her father, then you!"

"Be rational, Sister Michelle."

"You are incredible! You killed Sister Celina just as sure as if you'd run that blade down her arm with your own hand."

The older nun gasped. Sister Michelle reached for the blue dish. The older nun let go. It crashed, shattered, and spread bits of broken glass and stones all over the convent floor.

⟿

Nausea wakes Michelle before dawn. Her narrow bed at Our Lady of Peace stinks of sweat. If only she could return to sleep, to darkness, where even dreams might be held at bay. One night she screams herself awake. In the dream Mother Thomas Ann leads her down a road of darkness into the center of the woods. An evil wind blows. "No," she tries to cry out, but her voice is strangled. The novice mistress pulls her on and on into the darkness. Suddenly, there at the center, she sees a house made of glass, brilliantly lit by the moon. Celina dances behind the glass, her dress stained with blood. Michelle cries out and is awake.

In another dream she drives toward Eagle Inlet through green fields and forests excited by birds. Suddenly an explosion of light. Nuclear annihilation. She melts.

During the day she loses time. She loses words.

She cannot sleep. In the middle of the nights she wanders the halls of the convent. One night she finds herself outside in her nightgown, sitting under a birch tree, and she doesn't know what brought her there. Lost in a shadow, she remembers now, she was running away.

"You are ill, Sister Michelle," Mother Thomas Ann explains. She sits in a high-backed wooden chair at a long polished table. She is a spider. "You are ill. We want you to stay for a while in the infirmary. Sister Josepha will care for you."

After that she wakes up from a sleep in which there are no dreams because of the pills.

You'll want to see your mother.

No.

But your mother—

No. No one.

No Kate. No mother. No trees, even, that scream through the days and groan all night. Mother trees. No Kate. No frogs with crushed bones. No birds, especially not birds.

For people with dead eyes there is no God. God is dead. God is a swamp full of snakes. You dive into God and wish for God's large mouth to shut, wait for the bite, for the poison to put you to sleep, at last, finally, world without end. Amen.

What did you come out into the desert to find? she asks. What did you want to find?

I found nothing. Less than nothing. I found the dead eyes of God.

Round you go, round, and down, down, down into the darkness of God. Who said that? Whose voice? Who? And who is weeping so low? Who cries out? Who bleeds on the white sheets and lies in the wet slime and doesn't care? And whose hair is tangled and smells of must?

⌒

"I trusted you."

Kate closed the parlor door. The nun's rosary beads clicked against the wooden chair as she sat down.

"I did my best with her, Kate."

Mother Thomas Ann's gray eyes betrayed nothing.

"Your best?"

It was unbelievable. This woman whom Kate had known all her life, who was Elise's godmother, for heaven's sake! And this was her best?

"She had such potential. She needed to be made strong through sacrifice."

"Strong? Strong for what? You took away what meant most to her, and we can see where that led."

"I suppose you mean her piano playing."

"Of course I mean her piano playing. She's gifted. A genius. And look at her."

"It was her choice."

"Good God, Mother Thomas Ann, what is wrong with you? It was a choice she never needed to make."

Mother Thomas Ann reached up and gripped her silver profession cross.

"You don't understand."

"I understand perfectly."

Brittle words. Cold.

"You stole my daughter, Clara Monroe. You couldn't have a daughter of your own and so you took mine."

"You're being hysterical, Kate."

"Don't patronize me. You took her and you destroyed her."

"Nothing's that simple."

"It's simple enough to me. My daughter came to you and lost her mind. What's more simple than that?"

"And when she came, Kate, what seeds of madness did she bring along?"

"You bitch!"

"You're distraught, Kate. It's understandable. You never wanted her to enter the convent in the first place; I know that. I even understand it. This place holds terrible memories for you."

Kate felt caught in a spider's web.

"After all, you were here the night your house burned."

She felt caught and suddenly she couldn't breathe.

"Go to hell."

She grabbed her purse and rushed from the room, leaving the nun sitting rigid on the straight-backed wooden chair.

⁓

The convent walls rang with the strains of Mozart's Rondo. Sister Michelle drifted in and out of awareness. She cried out from time to time.

"Cleo!"

"Who is Cleo, dear?" Sister Josepha's voice turned like the tiny run of notes from E to A.

Then she sat staring by the infirmary window.

"We'll just put your veil on."

"I don't want it."

"Just the night veil, dear. The little white one."

"I want to feel the breeze in my hair."

She thought she saw Celina walking underneath the curved wing of the moon.

XXVIII

Do not listen to the sound
as if the music were outside you,
rather, feel the sound.
Be the sound.

SISTER MARY'S MUSIC NOTEBOOKS, 1965

The sisters cast their ballots in the chapel of Our Lady of Peace. Mother Thomas Ann knelt in her choir stall as though she were already a stranger to it. One by one the sisters passed through prisms of light filtered by stained glass, their black veils turning violet, red, and gold as they made their way up the aisle. *"Veni, Creátor Spíritus,"* they sang. Come, Creator Spirit. Come, light of vision. Come with sublime grace and give us wisdom.

She watched each nun bow and place her ballot on the gold plate in the center of the altar. A thurible of incense emitted a cloud of sweetness that turned her stomach.

The general chapter would close this afternoon with the counting of ballots and the reception of a new reverend mother. Five times the position had been given into Reverend Mother Esther's hands. And if it hadn't been for this meeting of bishops at the Vatican, there'd be no question about it. She'd be voted in again. But give young women the idea that things can change and they'll do it. And Mother Thomas Ann was the logical choice to replace her. The majority of nuns had been her novices. Of course, she couldn't be sure they would vote for her, but it seemed likely. They felt bound to her.

She would be the last to cast her vote. When the time came she lowered her veil and walked slowly to the altar, where she laid the folded ballot containing her name with all the others on the gold plate.

MOTHER Thomas Ann rarely used the sisters' lavatory. Ordinarily she would have been in the private bathroom reserved for the mistress of novices. But her stomach had unclenched during Benediction and she had hurried out of the chapel while the other sisters were singing "Holy God, We Praise Thy Name." What had she eaten? She was spewing up her entire insides. Afterward, exhausted, she sat on the toilet in the small green stall at the beginning of a long line of identical stalls and waited for her body to calm itself. The linens around her face were soaked from perspiration. The two sisters, when they came in, walked right past her closed door to the sinks along the far end of the room.

"Well, we're rid of her."

"I don't know why we didn't do this years ago."

"She had a strong hold on us."

"I guess so."

"On me, anyway."

"How?"

"Guilt. Secrets."

"Funny. With me it was more her rejection. I'd look out the window and see her going off to the woods with other sisters, and I'd think, I'm never going to fit here. I'm not one of the chosen."

"What did you imagine she was doing with them out in those woods?"

"I don't know. Talking about God. Getting the chosen ones ready for leadership in the community."

"I went out there with her."

"You did?"

"She kissed me."

"What?"

"She's crazy. I never told anyone, though, not till now."

"Incredible!"

"I hate her, Sister. I really do. At first I hated her because she dropped me as soon as another class of young sisters came along. And I'd watch her take somebody else on those walks. And then Sister Celina died."

"You think . . . ?"

"Don't you?"

"Well, all I can say is thank God for the winds of change blowing through Pope John's open windows!"

"Right. Her power's gone. I hear from Kateri that Thomas Ann only got one vote."

"Her own?"

"That's my guess. Even Reverend Mother Esther didn't vote for her."

"Who do you think will get it?"

"Sister Josepha. Don't you?"

"And she'll make sure that the council appoints a different novice mistress."

"That's a given. She's sweet but she's also a pretty no-nonsense woman. My guess is that she's seen through Thomas Ann from the beginning."

Mother Thomas Ann heard the hollow thud of their heels on the tile floor. She heard the hiss of the door caught by its vacuum spring as it closed behind them. A violent fist tightened around her gut and then let go. She gagged. Her hands flew to her face as if to ward off blows. She crouched in front of the toilet. A stench of vomit mixed with disinfectant enveloped her. A sob tore itself up from the empty place where her womb had been.

"But I loved them," she gasped as the tears came and mixed with the bile that spurted from her mouth.

⁓

Father Austin closed the door of the confessional behind him and picked up the narrow purple stole. He kissed the embroidered cross, placed the stole around his neck, and sat down in the ornately carved chair. This was a service he provided rarely. According to canon law the bishop must appoint a regular confessor for the nuns, someone other than their chaplain. Thus the delicacy of that relationship was maintained, as well as the freedom to be completely candid. One must not forget that. Nevertheless, from time to time, the regular confessor might be ill or out of town.

The nuns lined the back two pews of the chapel, awaiting the sacrament. He smiled to himself. The laws of the church take great care with these women. But what would he hear from them today? Peccadilloes, not sins. Sister Agatha, eating between meals again. Sister Kateri, blurting out some angry word. A lifetime of experience had brought him to conclude that most nuns could think of nothing to say and asked simply to be forgiven again for some past sin in order to receive the sacramental grace and fulfill canon law.

Sure enough, this week followed the pattern. He'd spent so many years at this convent he could match every whisper to its nun. It didn't matter, though. Outside the sacrament he never could or would let what he'd heard affect his relationships with these women. Through him their secrets passed on the way to God, simultaneously revealed and concealed.

Twenty-five, a mental tabulator clicked as Sister Josepha, the new reverend mother, rose to leave. He heard her rosary click against the confessional door. He closed the grill on her side and opened the other. He must be almost finished. His mouth began to water as he thought of supper. Sister Agatha's roast chicken, mashed potatoes, gravy . . .

"Bless me, Father, I have sinned."

It was Sister Thomas Ann. He'd heard she was ill. Must be some emotional thing following her removal from the novitiate. Difficult for her. She was novice mistress back when he came to Our Lady of Peace, and that was years ago.

"Yes, my daughter. Go on . . ."

"I engaged in inappropriate behavior with some of my sisters."

"What was the nature of this behavior?"

Encoded questions. Impersonal. Questions a priest was required to ask to ferret out the precise nature of the sin.

"I'm not sure. What do you mean?"

"Did you lack in charity? Did you fail to be truthful? Did you commit sexual indiscretions?"

Silence.

"What precisely did you do, Sister?"

"I meant only to show them a mother's love."

A hollow feeling, miniscule, began in the pit of the priest's stomach and began slowly to grow.

"And the love was inappropriate?"

"No, Father, not the love."

"The expression?"

Silence again.

"Sister, did you express your love for the sisters in a sexual way?"

"I touched them. I meant only to heal their pain."

"You sinned against your vow of chastity?"

"I touched them with love."

"What sort of touch, Sister? Was it sexual, or not?"

"I didn't intend it to be sexual."

"Did you touch sexual parts of their bodies?"

"I touched their hearts."

What was she saying?

"Did you touch their breasts?"

"In order to touch their hearts, yes."

"On top of, or under their clothes?"

"Both."

He could feel her tension like a high wire you hear humming when you stand under it. He felt riveted by that electricity.

"How many times?"

"I don't know."

"Many times?"

"Yes, Father, many."

"These were novices?"

"Yes, Father."

He'd thought he could spot the nuns with lesbian tendencies. Convent life attracted lesbian women from time to time. Mostly they remained celibate. Sometimes they formed a close relationship with another lesbian nun and the two of them struggled with the sexual part. He'd counseled some of them, struggled with them in their honest and often heroic efforts to live their vowed life. Never had he encountered anything like this! And from Sister Thomas Ann? Why, she was actually a bit of a seductress. Unconscious, no doubt, and subtle, in ways that he'd come to expect from nuns. Some nuns. They had to resolve their sexual repression on someone, and a priest is safe. He would have pegged Sister Thomas Ann for a repressed heterosexual, but lesbian? Never.

"Over several years?"

"Yes."

"How many years?"

"I think about twenty."

He wanted to get up, slam out of the confessional, pull the woman from the other side, and shake her until her teeth chattered.

"And this is the first time you have confessed this?"

"Yes, Father."

"Why?"

"I told you. I never thought of it as a sin."

Incredible! The human mind is simply diabolic in its ability to dodge the truth, to twist it, to deny. It's the Satan in us. The father of lies.

"What changed your mind?"

"I've been brought down by it. And Sister Celina died."

"Sister Celina was one of them?"

"Yes, Father."

He recalled that child's secrets, whispered to him once here in this very sacrament, in the dark of this secret room.

"I hope that you can see now, Sister, what you have done and that the wages of sin is death."

"It won't happen again, Father."

Like a child thinking all this could be unraveled by a promise to be good.

"Reparation is necessary, Sister."

"I'm not going to do it again."

"What's been broken is beyond repair. Now you are the one in need of help. Your soul is wounded. I hope you will come to me outside of the sacrament. We'll find someone to help you."

"Thank you, Father, for your advice."

She considered her confession finished. Technically, it was.

"I'm sorry for these sins and for all the sins of my past life, especially for my sins of anger."

"For your penance say fifteen decades of the rosary and seek help. Now make a good act of contrition."

As she whispered the words of contrition he made the sign of the cross.

"*Ego te absólvo a peccátis tuis, in nómine Patris, et Fílii, et Spíritus Sancti. Amen.* Go in peace, Sister, and sin no more."

She left the confessional and he knew, somehow, that he'd never hear of this again.

Tom Lenz haunted Clara Monroe's dreams. No. Not Clara. Not anymore. Sister Thomas Ann now for more than forty years. A nun, a fact that made the haunting a sacrilege. He came to her brandishing sometimes a marble towel rod, sometimes his sex, and in the dream, despite her terror, she wanted him to come. Crazy it was and sinful it would have been were dreams under her control. They were not. But her throbbing body woke her, and always for a moment she thought if she simply reached her arm over to the other side of the bed he would be there. For just a moment she thought she must be the one causing his eruptions, a thought like warm blood seeping into her mouth and behind her eyes and up into her brain.

He beat her within an inch of her life. The small of her back turned the colors of mustard and pea soup. He left bruises at her neck, on her arms, where her ribs curved around to attach to her spine, sickening bruises over her kidneys. The soft skin of her thighs stung, raw with lacerations. Bloody half-moons from his fingernails. Jagged punctures from his teeth. During all the years since that wedding night, she awakened hearing once again his yells, seeing again his flaccid penis, small and red dangling between his legs. Then the towel rod. He picked her up and threw her on her belly, and thrust cold marble up her rectum, thrusting, thrusting, until a merciful darkness claimed her.

The devil must have possessed him. Or maybe not. Maybe human beings are made that way, made to hold everything that's possible, love and the will to destroy running each inside the other like currents in a river.

At Elise Marie Pearson's baptism Sister Thomas Ann had sat in a lawn chair at Meghan's little house by Corpus Christi Church and held the baby, her daughter in God, tiny Elise Marie. Tom Lenz or no Tom Lenz, she had become a mother after all. Spiritual motherhood. In this she was like the Virgin Mary, whose motherhood extended to the entire world. The waters of baptism sealed a bond between herself and this child that could never be broken, a bond surpassing the physical. Baptism linked this child to her for eternity. The waters of Elise's physical birth evaporated. Baptism severed the connection between physical mother and child. But the bonds of the spirit last forever.

"I will teach you everything," she had whispered to Elise, whose tiny hand reached up and grabbed the finely woven wool of the nun's veil. "I will love you more than I could have loved the children of Tom Lenz. I will love you with the love of God."

The baby had cooed something unintelligible while sunlight splashed all over everything.

Now the nun knelt on the wooden floor of her small room and searched in the darkness for the face of God. It came to her that all these years, living as a bride of Christ, she had never really left the horror of the Francis Drake Hotel. She might as well be lying in her blood on that bathroom floor. What did she possess of wisdom during all these years that she might have taught her beautiful daughter in God? Every time she had strained her eyes to catch a glimpse of God, the shadow of Tom Lenz distorted what she might have seen.

I was just a child. She wept at last. A child.

It was true. Her mother told her nothing. She was sixteen. She remembered now. He was drunk from beer. Laughing. Lolling on the bed at the Francis Drake.

"Go get your nightgown on."

All lace and filmy cotton. She amazed herself in the mirror. Thick blonde hair hanging over her breasts. The suggestion of her body through the cloth. Her lips red with excitement. Now she couldn't imagine what she might have thought would happen. Why didn't she know he'd want to see her that way for a moment only? And that he'd then reach out to remove the gown.

She went to him. I look like a princess in a fairy tale is what she thought.

"God, Clara." He reached and pulled at the gown.

She flinched.

He revealed her breast and she flinched.

"What's wrong?"

He sounded angry. Why?

"What are you doing?"

"What do you think I'm doing?"

"I don't know."

"Are you nuts?"

"Nuts?"

He was drunk. He wasn't himself. Her stomach turned with fear. "Get this thing off!"

He ripped it like a rag. She screamed. She bent down to gather up the lace.

He came at her. He threw her on the bed. She lay there, naked, frightened. What was he going to do? Why hadn't she known what he'd meant to do?

Then it came to her. Of course. Like an animal. Like the horses on the farm. How stupid could she have been? Why hadn't she figured this out before?

He fell on top of her. But his penis stayed soft, a tiny organ, so childlike, so without threat.

She had laughed. It was relief. Pure relief. He wasn't going to hurt her. And she couldn't stop her laughing, hysterical laughing. Tears ran from her eyes.

"You're laughing at me." Tom stated it without emotion. His penis went even more flaccid. She couldn't answer; she couldn't stop. It was as though the devil had hold of her. Tom slapped her face. Still she couldn't stop. Again he slapped and the more he slapped, the more she laughed, until he was punching her and crying that she was a witch and a whore, and her laughter turned to screams. He shook her and tossed her off the bed. Through her own tears she saw his. His face was that of an animal, crazed now. He pulled at the towel bar with such force, then, that it came off the wall, and he came at her with it, brandishing it like a club. He hit her and she felt her ribs crack. He picked her up and tossed her on the bed, throwing her on her face. She felt the cold marble enter her from behind.

"No," she screamed. "It wasn't you! I love you." And that was the last she knew.

ALL SHE did was flinch. And the years since that moment spun out of what she thought was shame, and all along it was innocence. No one told her. She simply didn't know. Innocent she was that night, and innocent she had remained. Everything that happened afterward—it wasn't sexual at all.

XXIX

When the theme is repeated for the final time
the opposites unite
the tones flow through and around one another like water.
Lean into the music
allowing it to reconcile you to yourself.

SISTER MARY'S MUSIC NOTEBOOKS, 1965

"*Liebling!*"

Sister Mary embraced her. She felt like bones in the piano teacher's arms. Like ivory.

"I miss you so much, Sister."

"Yes."

An autumn breeze through the infirmary window ruffled the curtains.

"I hear you playing the piano."

"I play for you, *Liebling*. I play to make you well."

The nun held Sister Michelle out at arm's length and scrutinized her. "You are thin, *Liebling*."

"Yes. Food doesn't taste good."

"You are grieving, little Sister. Grief fills you up."

"My father."

"Yes. And Sister Celina. Also the piano, *Liebling*, also your music."

"I thought I didn't need that anymore."

The nun held her hands.

"Is that the truth, dear?"

She felt tears bubbling up from deep in her.

"I don't know what truth is anymore."

"Truth is wild, *Liebling*. It is a wild power in the cave of being that nothing can avenge. We go round and round it, sometimes, trying to ignore what we know. But always it will rise up, like the singing bird at the center of a whirlwind."

"So, I will know it someday?"

"Yes, *Liebling.* Soon."

"How?"

"Remember what I used to tell you about A minor?"

"When grief is overwhelming you keep your fingers on the keys closest to your body."

"And keep playing. Play through it to the end."

"You're all I have left, Sister."

"There, there, *Liebling.* It only seems so for now. A time will come when you will discover within yourself everything you imagined that you lost." The nun reached for her hand. "Remember what Rilke says?

"Dich *aber will ich nun,* Dich, *die ich kannte
wie eine Blume, von der ich den Namen nicht weiß,
noch ein Mal erinnern und ihnen zeigen, Entwandte,
schöne Gespielin des unüberwindlichen Schrei's.*

"*Tänzerin erst, die plötzlich, den Körper voll Zögern,
anhielt, als göß man ihr Jungsein in Erz;
trauernd und lauschend—. Da, von den hohen Vermögern
fiel ihr Musik in das veränderte Herz.*"

"What does it mean?"

"Let me see . . ." She closed her eyes and breathed deeply. Her hands felt warm.

"But you now, dear girl, whom I loved like a flower whose
      name
I didn't know, you who so early were taken away:
I will once more call up your image and show it to them,
beautiful companion of the unsubduable cry.

"Dancer whose body filled with your hesitant fate,
pausing, as though your young flesh had been cast in
      bronze;

grieving and listening—. Then, from the high dominions, unearthly music fell into your altered heart."

"I am that girl, that dancer, for you, Sister?"
"You have been and you are. On the day you entered the convent, I told you that every nun is alone. I was wrong, *Liebling*. Each of us echoes the unsubduable cry of the other. We cannot be separated from this cry, this voice. We listen . . ."
"And our hearts are altered."
"Then the music falls."
"And the music is . . ."
"God, *Liebling*. The music is God."

⌒

"I've felt like a canary, Mama."
Finally she could allow Kate to visit her. They sat together on the porch outside the infirmary. Sister Michelle's dark hair reached almost to her earlobes now and she couldn't bring herself to cut it. Her head felt light without the linens and veil. She couldn't bring herself to put them on. When Kate first saw her daughter that morning she had said, "Oh!" She said, "Oh," and began to cry. "My little Elise," she said, and kissed her on the top of her head. "Like when you were a baby," she murmured.
"A canary?" she responded now, several hours into the afternoon.
"Yes. They die rather than let on that they are sick."
"Is that why you wouldn't let me come?"
"I don't think so. No. It had more to do with the nuns. It was the nuns I couldn't tell."
"You couldn't tell them you were ill?"
"I wanted to do this right, Mama. I wanted to be a good nun."
"You are. I'm sure you are."
"I'm not."
Kate took her daughter in her arms. Oh my. So frail. How did the girl come to this?
"There, there, sweetheart. It will be all right."
"I go back and forth about this, Mama. I thought God called me here."

"I know, honey."

"But so many things are wrong. I tried to make things right by doing as I was told."

She stumbled over her words.

"Sometimes I think there's something deep in the convent itself that's to blame. Do you think that could be?"

"I know that nothing on this whole earth is perfect, Elise."

"And there's Sister Thomas Ann . . ."

"Yes." As if both of them understood.

"You knew her before, didn't you?"

"A little bit. I was just a child when she entered."

"What was she like?"

"Pretty. Quiet. A lovely girl, as I recall."

"But something happened to her."

"Yes. Her marriage was annulled. Her husband betrayed her, beat her mercilessly. And then she entered Our Lady of Peace."

"So she might not have had a vocation."

"That's true."

"I wonder why she stayed here."

"What else was she going to do?"

"I don't want to lie anymore, Mama."

Kate smoothed her daughter's hair. "Nor do I, darling, nor do I."

⟊

Sister Michelle sat in the cove and stared at the still water of Lake Bemidji. Her mind felt emptied of arguments. Maybe I'll never understand, she thought. Maybe a person is finally only space. No sharps. No flats. Just emptiness.

Leaves drifted from the birch trees and floated on the water. Each day she had watched them. Detaching. Falling. Drifting. Each day she drifted with them. Nothing seemed able to change what she suspected.

The convent caused her to live a lie.

She never set out to deceive anyone and ended up doing it anyway. Maybe convent walls and rules were a structure too rigid to contain her hopes. But if that were true, how could she account for Sister Mary's authenticity? How could she explain Sister Josepha's compassion?

She wanted to do the right thing.

Just then, from the open windows of the convent, she heard Sister Mary begin to play.

There is no right thing.

There is life.

A barrier broke open somewhere deep in Elise's chest and released a flood. She could think until doomsday and never arrive at an answer, because the question was the wrong one. Not what was she to do, but who was she to be? And even then the question wasn't quite right.

She stood and shook the sand and autumn leaves from her woolen dress.

Who had she always been?

I'm going home, she realized.

And even though it wasn't an answer, it left her calmer than she'd felt in years.

Outside Sister Mary's studio window the poplar and birch trees shivered gold in the sunlight. Nothing could equal the light of late summer. She played three hours without stopping. She felt no distinction anymore between the playing and the being of music. Mozart, Beethoven, Bach, all of them had done their work in her. Music had led her to its source in God.

Sister Mary lifted her fingers from the keys. The music echoed in her mind and then gave way to silence. She smiled. She closed the fall board and held the lid securely as she lowered the prop stick, then she brought down both the main and front lids to cover the soundboard and strings of the concert Steinway that had been her companion throughout life.

Sister Mary of the Holy Cross turned and walked to the chapel without looking back.

XXX

If it is to be music

you must be present to it, must offer to it

a profound self-remembering.

SISTER MARY'S MUSIC NOTEBOOKS, 1965

On a September afternoon, leaves of the ancient mother tree floated like scrolled messages from the gods on the glassy surface of Black Sturgeon Lake. Elise leaned against the familiar trunk. Down the beach, where the water was shallow and the lake bottom a terrazzo of flat black-and-white stones, gulls flocked, swooping and landing on the lake's surface in a flurry of wings and cascades of sunlit water. Then they rose and circled around her endlessly as though summer could be eternal.

Elise had left the convent still not knowing what lay in the shadow of her mind beyond Celina's death and Mother Thomas Ann's deception, in which she had felt trapped. These things come back or they don't, Father Austin told her. Sometimes dreams take care of them; like debris on the river bottom of the mind, the memories drift up in the form of nightmares and float away.

"Remember, there's no hurry," Sister Mary had said when she hugged her the afternoon before she left Bemidji. "You have your whole life."

ELISE took it slow. She let her fingers find the music again. She played short passages over and over, lingering with tones. Sometimes she played one note until its vibrations stilled to silence. Then she played it once more. She used it like the other kind of key, to open something in herself long closed. She played "Clair de Lune" and Kate wept.

"Mama?"

"I'm sorry, honey. It's just so haunting. It reminds me of Michael."

"Do you want me to stop?"

"No. No, don't stop. I haven't cried enough. The tears still feel all bottled up in me. You go ahead and play and I'll just go ahead and cry."

She played. One day she ended with "Für Elise."

" 'Für Elise.' You're named for that, you know."

"Yes."

"Little Elise. I thought I'd lost you."

"I thought so, too."

~

Elise pulled the boat onto the sand while Kate looped its rope around a scrawny tree growing by the shore of Rainbow Island.

"I wanted you to visit this place with me."

Kate spread a blanket and motioned to her daughter to sit beside her. Gulls etched the sky above the lake.

"I need to tell you something, something you ought to know."

"Okay."

Elise felt a strain in her mother's presence, a pulling against something stuck.

"Something happened here, honey."

She stopped.

"I don't know if I can say it."

Elise reached out to her and Kate let herself be held, lightly at first, keeping a distance even while being surrounded by her daughter's arms. Her breath rasped like wind forced through jagged rocks. She trembled. Elise tightened her embrace and Kate began to sob.

"Oh, Elise, honey, I'm so sorry. So, so sorry."

"There, there, Mama, it's okay. It will be okay."

Her crying reached a peak and quieted.

"Come. Walk with me."

Elise took her mother's hand.

"I still miss your dad so much."

"Me, too."

"I wonder if he knew."

"Knew what?"

"That I loved him."

"He must have."

"I'm not sure. Did you?"

"What?"

"Did you know how much I loved you? Growing up, I mean?"

"Maybe. I don't know for sure. Sometimes you were . . ."

"Cold?"

"Maybe cold. I don't think I thought of you as cold. Distant, I guess. Like this island, something that I somehow couldn't reach."

They walked until they came to a little point of land that looked back toward Reel 'Em Inn. At night from this place, the few lights from the lodge along with the beam of light from Split Rock Point were all that cut the solid dark.

"THAT'S why I brought you here to Rainbow Island, to tell you things I've never told another soul, not the priest, not even your father."

They balanced on the moment as on a child's top that spins cleanly on its tip before it wobbles and finally falls.

"You aren't my only child, Elise. Years ago, before your father and I were married, I conceived a child on this island."

"You and Daddy?" A dissonant tone rose from a deep well in Elise's mind. She attempted to quell it. It grew louder.

"Yes, honey. It happened around the time we graduated from high school. We'd come here often. I never meant it to happen, not the pregnancy, not even the sex. Father Murphy warned me." She glanced at her daughter. "You know how priests are."

"I know."

"It's just that I loved your father so much, and I felt such passion then, more than I could have imagined, despite the warnings. It didn't seem like sin until it was over. And then I ran from him. I hid. I heard him calling, 'Kate, Kate.' His voice and the darkness around me seemed like the same thing. I cried until I was exhausted, but I couldn't answer him."

"Oh, Mama. It couldn't have been a sin."

"The church says it was."

"How can love be sin?"

"Whether it was or not, I lived my whole life alongside your father knowing that when it was over I'd be condemned to hell."

"Mama!"

"It's what I was taught."

"But do you really believe it anymore?"

"Not anymore."

The mother and daughter sat for a few moments in silence. Elise listened to the gentle lap of waves against the shore. Pregnant. But that meant there was a baby. A brother or sister.

"What happened to the baby?"

"I thought I could feel it forming in me that night. I wanted it to stop but it wouldn't stop. Afterward I waited a month, then two months. My period didn't come. I thought people would notice the difference in me, but they never did. I felt like a living, breathing sin. And then I lost the baby."

"Oh, Mama!"

"It was my punishment."

"No, Mama."

"Yes, dear. I believed that."

"How did it happen, Mama?"

"Just after the third month something went wrong. Your grandmother was gone from home a week to that retreat she attended every year. The pains began while I was downtown, shopping. There I was, standing by a bolt of dark green cloth in Anderson's Department Store, when I felt a fiery knife twisted in me by some angry god. I held on to the cloth and my hands stained the green. I had to get home. But I couldn't ask anyone for help. No one could know.

"I walked seven blocks. The knife twisting. Hollyhocks heavy and pink, stems leaning. I thought sure I'd faint. I climbed the steps to the porch and opened the door. Inside, it smelled like roast beef. Even now I can't abide that smell. I stumbled to the kitchen and put my hands on the fridge. So hot. I needed ice. I felt a big lump inside me, low in my stomach; no, in my vagina. I had to get to the bathroom. The wall tipped toward me. I clung to it. Something was wrong, all wrong, and there was nothing I could do. Then it came to me: I was losing the baby. I refused to let it drop into the toilet. I needed proof it was there, that it was real. I held on to the wall. It ran down my legs. It seemed the world ended. Darkness. Spasms of labor. Sweat. My whole body shook. Everything came rushing and blubbering through me. I vomited. Blood pooled between my legs and spread out over the floor. I looked down and saw blood and flesh. Then I sank into oblivion."

Elise tried to say something but couldn't find words. She reached for her mother's hand.

"I floated on air or light. Far in the distance I could see my father and baby brother going down the road. 'Wait for me!' I called to them. 'Oh, wait!' But they didn't even turn around."

"You must have been close to death yourself."

"I think I was. But a coolness came from somewhere and woke me. When I opened my eyes it was right there on the floor beside me. A perfect baby. Four inches long. Not more than an inch and a half wide. A girl with tiny arms and legs, and buds of eyes that might have looked into my own had she not been dead. She was so perfect, Elise. Death couldn't have been her fault."

"Maybe no one's fault."

"How could I know one way or the other? I cleaned up the mess. I washed her and wrapped her in tissue. I put her delicate little body in a box and buried her under the hollyhocks.

"Oh, Mama!" Elise was crying.

"I guess I should have baptized her."

"God takes care of those things."

"I've never been sure of that."

Of course not. How could she have been?

"You can't imagine the feeling of helplessness. Like I'd buried myself right along with my tiny girl. Like I never would exist again."

"But you do exist. You are yourself."

"I felt completely wrong inside, wrong clear through, body and soul. I thought I'd be like that for the rest of my life. A helpless, helpless feeling."

"You were just a girl."

"Yes. And I was scared to death."

"But you lived."

"I put it out of my mind."

"How?"

"I hardened my heart."

Elise shivered. The sun burned red on the horizon and cast a shimmering path across the lake.

"Because . . ."

"Because I wanted you and your father safe. I wanted no more death."

⟿

She visited Gull Rock alone. Waves lapped the edges of the rock, and gulls wheeled above her. She tried to remember the soft down of the chick, the heart that beat against her fingers, her father's voice.

She examined the ruins of the haunted houseboat. It still was there, an abandoned cabin surrounded by wildflowers. The door leaned open on broken hinges. The cabin was empty but for a nest some animal had made and the pattern of light on the floor.

Life must fit together somehow, all the images and sounds, the people, the places, that make you what you are. Even the not-remembered things, the harms, whatever cannot be held because it is too sharp, so keen that it would lacerate your mind and heart. Even the mistakes, which maybe weren't mistakes at all but only plays of shadow through the light cast on the floor of an abandoned room. She didn't know. She felt she didn't know a thing.

A GULL is crying. Klee-euwwww! *And Elise is going back, back further, behind the cloister door, before the silencing of piano keys, back beyond Celina, even, and her white robe afloat, stained, washed in the blood. She hears the call from a world beyond the known, where her father smiles and holds her up, and she reaches for wings glinting in morning light. She opens her eyes to a world she has closed to memory and sees the open mouth, white teeth, the red-on-white feathers; she hears the snarls, the growls, the barks, and then a scream,* Klee-euwwww, *and a vivid flash of crimson in a spectrum of green. Then only feathers and a limp rag of flesh hanging from the dog's teeth.*

"Daddy," she cries, and lifts the fallen Cleo from the gravel, stones clinging to sticky blood. The blood is on her small hands. "Daddy." She runs

to him down at the dock, where he stands, half his face in shadow and the
other half a ferocious wound. "Daddy!"
    She hands him the limp body of the bird.
    "Fix her, Daddy."
    Then he takes Cleo in his hands, but the bird stays dead.

My God! She could see it now, his face, turned to her. The wounded
side turned to her. The eye enraged. The eye shot with blood.

What had happened next? Elise closed her eyes. Her mind
snapped open and shut like the shutter on a camera. Flickers of
memory. Pictures partly obscured as though exposed to sunlight, as
though she'd opened the camera by mistake before reaching the end
of the film. Perhaps not by mistake. Perhaps with deliberation. Pictures slashed with red, faces wiped out. Voices, too, she heard as
though underwater, under the surface of Black Sturgeon Lake. Her
stomach turned.

"Please, Daddy." She saw herself, so small, defenseless. She saw
her bloodstained hands. He still held Cleo. He was shaking Cleo.
The blood from Cleo splattered on the front of her overalls.

"God damn it, Elise, I can't. The bird's dead."

Why was he so mad?

"Please!"

"Stop it!" he had yelled. He never yelled. She had forgotten the
terror of his voice. It was a cry without words, like an animal's cry,
and it split her heart. She saw herself as the child she had been. She
watched herself crouch down close to the ground. She had wanted
to become the ground, to disappear, to keep him from seeing her.
Why hadn't she closed her eyes? It was too dangerous to close her
eyes. She watched as he swung Cleo over his head, around and
around, until he let go and the bird arced over the water.

She ran away from him. She ran because she was a child. How
could she know what he had seen? All that could not be fixed. All
the thousands dead. The boys climbing that mountain, that holy
mountain, all of them bursting open, gashed, upon the rocks. And
he had seen. Who could fix it? Nothing could fix it. Even God could
not fix it.

Cleo was dead and Michael raged at a God who could not fix
even so much as a broken wing.

She ran and hid in the crook of the mother tree. She remembered, now, the way she had thrust her fists against her eyes to make them blind and held her hands over her ears so as not to hear her own cries. She felt how he had snatched her from the tree, how he had squeezed her to himself. Her teeth came down on her tongue. Blood. She had swallowed her blood. She heard him crying out.

"Fuck! Goddamn fucking war! Fucking death. Fucking world. God damn it all to hell!"

Then he was crying. She could barely get her breath. Daddy sobbed. Her body felt like air. She couldn't move. "Daddy," she had whispered.

"Oh my God!"

He lifted her. He took her to the shore of the lake. He smoothed her hair back with cool water. He washed the blood of Cleo from her clothes.

"Don't cry, Daddy. Please don't cry."

But he couldn't seem to stop.

ELISE wept.

It was from this memory she had protected herself for all these years. Why? she wondered now. It was not Elise against whom her father fought. It was the war. It was the distortion of life. In her mind she saw again the agony of her father's face.

And then she knew. She knew. So obvious and yet so wrong. So like a child. Of course there were no words for it. She was a child. She had only her life to be spun out in a perfect spiral from that moment. God must not be blamed for his inadequacy. Nor Daddy; he must not be blamed. No one must ever know they could not fix Cleo. From that moment she would take care of them. She became Sister Michelle. She took the fixing of the world upon herself.

⌒

Anger melted her bones. It rose as liquid through her chest into her head and burned there. She woke one morning a week later in her bed, all the things of childhood around her, the same sheets, even, as cool as they had been when she was five years old and had a bird named Cleo and had a father who had been strong enough to live when every other one had died. And suddenly she could take no comfort in that fact at all. She was a pit of fire into which everything was falling, melting in dark flames she could not control.

They lied to me. A voice sighed up through the molten stuff that had been herself. God lied. It seemed absurd. How could God lie? That was her brain arguing with the voice, and then her brain melted, too. She became more than herself. She contained the betrayals of generations. What happens to all that's lost? Where are the promises we make? Where is the love? She was the house of her family, burning, and there was nothing she could do. Something cried out in her, I thought that there was something that could fix the pain. God. Daddy. Myself. If I just gave enough, I thought that all of it would be all right.

It would never be all right. Who could know where the circle of loss began? Loss. So weak a word for this betrayal. Who could know where this circle ends? Rage electrified her; anger shot out to her fingertips. She contained them all, felt the fire of them all. She felt everything women aren't supposed to feel, as though women could be protected from the truth while their fathers and their sons released every awful realization about life in the explosive futility of war. She had tried to climb the blood-slick mountain and she had been cut down. Half her face was missing. She was the cry of Cleo, cut off by dogs. She was blood in their mouths. She was their mouth, tearing at life, refusing to let go, left with the taste of death.

The sun began to rise over Eagle Inlet. Trees glowed in its reflected fire. She sat on the edge of the bed. "I have to feel this," she said aloud to a God she no longer knew, a God who either betrayed his creation or did not exist at all. This was a God who ate us with lies about all being well. Nothing was well, nor had it been for generations.

Her heart melted in the flames.

"What about my baby?" Gramma Meghan's voice cried out and it was Kate's voice and her own, Elise's, voice. "And what of Willie and the years alone?" Surging up in her from the flames Elise heard the voices of Clara, of Celina, even of Sister Mary, and each voice was a circle of flaming sound crying out for the fulfillment of promises that had been made, then melted down and turned to ash.

Where are the promises kept? she interrogated the dawn.

And then it came to her. She had spent her life bargaining with God. My life for theirs. My life to fix my father's face. My life to heal my gramma's heart, to convince my mother to hold me in her arms. My life to make things right, to bring my father home from war, to be the mother tree for the world, to protect the world from death. I went to the convent for this. I surrendered my music for this. And the world still dies a million times a day. Celina's blood pours into all the waters of creation. My mother's baby dies.

And God couldn't do a thing about it.

Who is like God? Michael the Archangel circles the world in flame. Michael lifts a shining sword against the light that fails, against all that falls away, sinks into the fire, and is lost. Michael's promise isn't comfort. It is the clash of flaming swords. The promise Elise had made and failed to achieve, that which now melted her with the anger of betrayal, never could be kept. Or rather, it could be kept only in the heart of a God she had not, so far, found.

XXXI

In the end the music will seem to others
effortless.

SISTER MARY'S MUSIC NOTEBOOKS, 1966

Elise walked slowly down the path from Our Lady of Peace, stopping at each place of memory just as she had the previous September at Black Sturgeon Lake. Each place was a shrine, a station in her own way of the cross. Celina no longer sat in the cove and gazed out over the lake. Clara Monroe remained at the convent, her mind curled around something she might never be able to release.

The presence of all she loved felt absolute. Maybe, she thought as she came to the path where Jesus and Mary once had appeared and called her to convent life, maybe what is true of memory is whatever you can empty yourself enough to receive. She knew now that her call was not to this place. Life hollows you out like the lake hollows the cove. If you listen in that hollow place, you will hear the truth like the song of God.

Elise sat cross-legged on the ground by Celina's grave and took from her shoulder bag a red leather diary.

"You knew all along," she addressed the spirit of her friend and sister. "I don't know if you saw it in your words, but you knew the truth. Listen."

During the years since Celina's death, Elise had kept the diary in the bottom of her trunk, unread, as the music alongside it remained unplayed. She sat up all night reading Celina's poetry, the last poems written before she died. When she turned the final page she felt as she had at Black Sturgeon Lake where the gulls flocked.

She opened the red leather cover. The inscription, in heavy black ink, read,

To Suzanne,
Keep writing. The Word will bring you through.

Father Sloan

Elise sat on the grass beside the grave of her friend and read the poetry, words innocent both in content and in craft but also heavy with a tart knowledge. From time to time Elise touched the ink that still held something of Celina's life, of the movement of her hand. The swirls of letters, like a fingerprint, that could belong to no one else. She read the "father poems," the one that began, "He parted the curtains while I watched the moonlight disappear." She read the "Canticles to the Bridegroom." She grew ancient as she read, and Celina became her child. She read the poem called "Wedding."

> . . . and I will sleep where mercy falls
> On the river of changing moons.

She closed the book.

I'm going to Juilliard, Elise told the spirit of Celina that hovered in this place. I'm going to play the piano, Celina. I'll play it for both of us.

A light breeze sighed in the pines.

I wanted God to fix everything, like Cleo, like you, but that isn't what God is for. God doesn't fix things; God surrenders.

Sunlight danced on the lake.

God surrenders like a woman giving birth. I thought God was in the silence between sounds. But God is in the sound itself. God is in my fingers, Celina. God is in my whole body, loving, laboring, giving birth. We looked everywhere, Celina, and all along the beloved we desired was right here, in what we are.

Then Elise took one red and one white rose from her bag and placed them on Sister Celina's grave next to the simple cross that marked her presence and absence in this world. "I will never leave you," she whispered. "Never so long as I live."

As she rose from the ground she felt a subtle movement within her, like the vibration of strings. Perhaps the whole universe is made of strings, all vibrating at once. And the world comes forth with all its joys and sorrows, births and deaths. We live and we die and that is how we learn God's song. It's like Sister Mary said at the beginning. You have to lean into the pain and move through the sorrow. Keep close to the keys. Surrender to the music.

ELISE parted the bushes and made her way to the cove. She sat alone, sifting sand through her fingers while the water lapped the shore. Her life at Our Lady of Peace was over, but Sister Michelle would always be part of her. Nothing is forever lost, fragile as it may seem. Everything is like a ring of grass that has survived the years.

Over the lake, gulls circled, calling to one another. *Klee-euw, klee-euw.* She smiled. It was her core note, a perfect A.

Perfect for a moment only. She knew that now. The note would break open, spin out in circles. Its vibrating strings would wrap around strings of other frequencies to create harmonies and dissonance. It would be a whirlpool of sound in every cell of her body, in creation's smallest particles of being. It takes life. She would live it, the music. She would set her fingers on the keys. She would play, and when the song ended she would begin again. Music cannot end. It spirals down to death. It turns. Returns. It circles on.

In her mind she heard the first notes of the Rondo in A Minor. The gulls whirled against the sun.

Klee-euw.

She lifted her arms, tossed back her head, and answered their cry. Her core note arced and echoed off the surface of the lake.

Acknowledgments

I am grateful to all those loving and patient people who listened, read, encouraged, inspired, offered little-known facts, and criticized this novel while I wrote it. To the Catholic Women Religious, who have been and are my teachers, my sisters, and my friends. To Kathleen Jesme, who first believed I could write a novel. To Jan Johnson for spurring me on. To Lisa Lanza for graciously providing me with a music lesson on the Rondo in A Minor. To Candice Fuhrman, who told me the truth about my writing and challenged me through many revisions. To Elsa Dixon for the richness of her creative mind and the keenness of her judgment. To Sarah McGrath, for her skill, wisdom, enthusiasm, and her remarkable ability to instill confidence. And most of all, I am grateful to my husband, John, who gives me constant support, love, and encouragement.

CHRISTIN LORE WEBER, a former nun, is the author of six books of nonfiction, including *Circle of Mysteries* and *Finding Stone*. This is her first novel. Having spent most of her life in Minnesota, she now lives with her husband in the Pacific Northwest.

1 <u>SD</u> 01/03